BACKWATER

A Love Story

KATE BOUDREAUX

Gilded Press

Boston, Massachusetts

www.gildedpressbooks.com

Backwater, A Love Story

ISBN: 9798986466125 (hardcover)

ISBN: 9798986466101 (paperback)

ISBN: 9798986466118 (ebook)

First Edition: October 2022

This book is dedicated to my family: Randy & Guy, Sweetie & Pop, Max, Shana, & Erik, Pawpaw Tommy & Meme, Pawpaw Billy Ray & Granny Jewel—and to anyone who has ever felt alienated, misunderstood, or villainized for daring to be a rebel.

AUTHOR'S NOTE

My family tree is full of free spirits.

Dancers, painters, musicians, naturopaths, traveling junk dealers, all using their charisma and creativity wherever they choose to wander. Like a bird captured from the wild, a cage equals death—of the soul, if nothing else.

When I first began school at our small-town Texas elementary, I knew right away that I didn't belong. But it was the early nineties and homeschooling wasn't a popular concept, so I kept going. Kept trying to fit into the narrow box known as public education. But by third grade, I'd had enough and cried every morning for the first two weeks. I can still vividly recall the way my stomach churned at the thought of being stuck in that lifeless, dreary building with a bunch of kids I had nothing in common with, yet felt compelled to mime.

Thankfully, my sweet mama recognized my distress and decided to do the unthinkable. In the span of a day, she withdrew me from school and quit her job as a registered nurse. This change fueled the decision to sell our large, two-story home and move farther out of town to a modest homestead situated on twenty acres. I was overjoyed.

There we planted herb gardens, learned to sew and crochet, made homemade soap and wine, and collected a small number of horses, cows, milk goats, chickens, and peacocks. I made friends with a neighbor boy who also homeschooled, and we spent our days roaming the woods barefoot, building playhouses out of tree branches and pine straw, swinging from a rope into the river, and swimming in ponds full of water moccasins and nutria rats. We explored abandoned farmhouses inhabited by feral hogs, rode horses bareback through fields of Bahia, and flipped giant metal hay rings on their sides to use as our own personal Ferris wheels. It's kind of a miracle we survived childhood at all. But what didn't kill us made us stronger. And what didn't make us stronger made some damn good campfire stories for years down the road.

As for my education, schoolwork was often done sitting on top of a hay bale in the barn, usually in costume. With a closet full of flea market prom dresses, dance costumes, and one exceptionally fluffy wedding dress petticoat at my disposal, there was hardly a day I didn't play dress-up. Baking cookies in the kitchen, riding four-wheelers, out feeding the chickens, it didn't matter. Think Tasha Tudor in a nine-year-old's body. Add some rhinestones and a feather boa, pink cowboy boots, and a homemade knife sheathed in a leather scabbard at my waist, and there I was, looking like some kind of Las Vegas Calamity Jane. But my parents encouraged creative play, considering it a healthier option to the video games that were becoming popular. And I used the opportunity to explore who I really was apart from outside opinion. To this day, the experience remains one of the most valuable of my life.

It's no surprise that I developed an early love of books—especially the Anne of Green Gables eight-book series. Looking back, Lucy Maud Montgomery was a distinctly kindred spirit who would influence my writing style more than any other author. But back then, all I knew was I wanted to be Anne, red hair and all.

Funny enough, years later I would lighten my own lack-luster locks to a pale blonde during my foray back into the public-school system. Yes, I went back to school. But for the record, it wasn't my idea. Mama demanded I try it out, promising I could quit at any time. As it turned out, high school was a lot more fun than I had imagined. I ended up joining the dance team, theater group, and marching band, where all the other deliciously eclectic weirdos gathered en masse. Instead of sneaking beer and partying on Saturday nights, we could be found constructing elaborate Saturday Night Live reenactments, complete with costumes and scripts to be recorded on a camcorder the size of a cocker spaniel. Nothing was off-limits. Too silly or obscure to capture on film. I had found my tribe. But despite my mostly picturesque high-school experience, I did manage to do something my senior year that shocked my friends and disappointed my parents.

I entered a beauty pageant.

And not just any beauty pageant. The kind of cutthroat hometown competition girls train for from birth. Expensive dresses, hair, and makeup. Special coaching for how to walk on stage and nail an interview. Mama begged me not to do it, pointing out the obvious. I wasn't the pageant type. But I was determined, walking into the experience with the confidence of a winner—and I did just that.

The truth is, I didn't do better than any other girl on that stage. I think the moment that separated me from the rest was during the interview. The judges asked everyone the same question: "If you were in charge of showing a stranger around your hometown, where would you bring them and why?" The other girls gave a limited variety of cookie-cutter answers, all very acceptable. When posed with the question myself, I remember trying hard to come up with something respectable to say. After a split second of extreme panic, I settled on being myself and described a little-known natural spring way back in the woods, where fresh water gurgles out of the ground to be caught in a hollow stump that's been there over a hundred years. I described the history of the spring. The one-room schoolhouse that once sat beside the well, and how the children had to eat lunch inside a pen constructed to keep them safe from the wild hogs that roamed freely. When I finished, I swallowed hard as the judges exchanged curious looks. I didn't know it then, but that was the moment I became a storyteller.

It would take me twelve more years before I first dared to put pen to paper. To start with a story inspired by the real-life rural experiences of myself and my relatives. But once I started, I knew writing would be something I'd do the rest of my life. The stories were always there, the propensity to tell them handed down from generations of oral storytellers before me. It just took me a while to realize I was the one meant to write them down.

A year later, I had a very rough first draft of *Backwater* and no clue how to get the novel published. In the years that followed, I signed with no less than three different literary agents and suffered a lot of ups and downs as I once again attempted to fit myself into a narrow box—this time known as traditional publishing.

You see, most publishers in NYC have the pesky little habit of making calls for Southern fiction while simultaneously despising everything that makes the region unique. I know because I've heard them say it. Out loud. In front of me. True to form, most publishers' tastes don't go beyond stereotypical gossips drinking sweet tea, shirtless men in cowboy hats, or the occasional memoir by some ex-Southerner who wants to blame the South for their horrible childhood or adolescence.

Backwater is none of these things.

Time and again, I rejected the call to gut the manuscript to make it more palatable for this ignorantly arrogant crowd. As a native Texan, I come from a long line of folks who are not the kind to sit down, shut up, and do as they're told. *Backwater* is authentic in a way that few will truly appreciate. But that's okay. I didn't write it to be trendy. I wanted to create something real. A love letter to the region that made me who I am.

This journey has been rocky, but God had His hand on me the whole time. At every turn, He opened doors to teach me valuable lessons about not only the kind of novels I want to write, but who I want to be as a person. I remain eternally grateful to my family for their love and support, and to *Gilded Press* for having the courage to champion unique books that don't bend to the ever-changing politics and opinions of a truly bizarre industry.

Backwater isn't just a story fabricated out of thin air. Each character and scene is inspired by the people and places I know and love. However, it's important to note I took artistic liberties with certain geographical locations—often embellishing, relocating, or renaming well-known landmarks for cohesive storytelling purposes.

In a world where gentrification has become the status quo, I hope this novel shines light on the struggle of rural communities everywhere to retain not only their cultural identity, but the environment on which it depends.

"When I find a well-drawn character in fiction or biography, I generally take a warm personal interest in him, for the reason that I have known him before—met him on the river."

—Mark Twain

BACKWATER
A LOVE STORY

CHAPTER 1

There's something about vintage vinyl. The tattered jacket worn with age, vibrant with art even after fifty years. The feel of the record. The weight in my hand as it slides out of the sleeve and onto the turntable. In a world where everything is instant, easy, just a click away, the physical act of dropping the needle is a small sort of rebellion. A cathartic release.

I close my eyes as it hums along the groove, crackling and imperfect and raw. Creedence Clearwater at their finest, three decades before I was born. No matter the age, it's my favorite album. A perfect reincarnation of time and place and feeling that seems more real, more vibrant, than anything in the here and now.

The swamp rock sound settles deep in my bones as raspy vocals layer over a sharp iconic riff, painting a picture of lyrical nostalgia – vague enough to be absolutely anywhere, clear enough to take you straight to Green River. Even here in my room, I feel the sun on my face. The cool water sweeping in around my ankles. Between my toes. It's a place of pure abandon. A place that doesn't exist. But every fiber of my being yearns to have that kind of freedom. To know what it's like to be a rebel.

My eyes snap to the window and the driveway beyond. Straight as an arrow, the limestone lane glows white in the moonlight, pointing the way to The Flame. With its secluded location and rough crowd, the high school hangout is an unsuitable place for respectable young ladies, according to Mama Pearl. But the label only serves to increase the appeal. The Flame is more than just a place to party out in the woods. It's forbidden fruit. And much like Eve, I can't wait to take a bite.

A thrill shoots through me at the idea of showing up and shocking my classmates.

Especially Eli.

I saw the challenge in his blue eyes during fifth period. "What about you, Miss Sunday?" he said, jutting his chin in my direction. "You comin' out tonight?"

I shrugged and fiddled with my paper, hating the way my face heated at the question and wishing I had the nerve to say yes. Wishing I had the nerve to say anything at all.

But who cares what Eli LeBlanc thinks. He's just like every other redneck guy at school who dips and cusses and wears threadbare jeans tucked into broke down cowboy boots. River Rats, they call themselves, with Eli at the helm. He probably wants nothing more out of life than a six pack of beer and a good time. But I do care, and that's the problem. There's something in the tilt of his head, the sparkle in his eye. Like he holds the key to a great secret. And curiosity has always been my Achilles' heel.

I plop down on my usual perch, the window seat overlooking the front lawn. Cocooned in velvet and antique glass, I sink into the soft cushion as warm night air filters through the screen, damp and heavy and familiar. Scented with jasmine and the barest hint of pine, it breathes life into the room and pulls me closer until I'm leaning in, ears pricked for the distant rumble I know is coming. Deep, growling motors growing louder by the second, vibrating across the breeze with electric anticipation. The parade of pickups headed to The Flame, roaring by in a cloud of dust all big tires and blaring stereos and metal truck nuts. For Eli's crowd, it's the ultimate power flex. A cocky display that begs you to look. Dares you to say something.

While my straitlaced neighbors are clutching their pearls, I'm glued to the window. Waiting. Wishing I had the courage to step out and be more than just the skinny redhead from the weird family. I want to feel alive. Normal. Accepted. To see what's on the other side of the ocean. Or in my case, the other side of the river.

The clock by my bed says a quarter past twelve. If I'm really going to do this, now's the time. No more procrastinating. No more excuses.

I hurry to slip on my shortest pair of denim cutoffs and pad down the wooden staircase on bare feet, careful not to wake my sisters as I pass their adjoining rooms. If they knew my plan, Emma would tattle and Dani would beg to go. But this is something I need to do alone.

Instead of making a beeline for the front door, vanity pushes me in the direction of Mama Pearl's beauty shop at the back of the house. Like any good Southerner, I've seen Steel Magnolias enough to know "there is no such thing as natural beauty" and who am I to argue with Dolly? In truth, the pit stop isn't an inconvenience at all. With its petal pink hood dryer and bins of worn-out brush rollers, the spare bedroom-turned-personal salon is one of my favorite places. I like everything about it. The faded clippings of outdated hairstyles thumbtacked to the walls. The lingering scent of perm solution that never fully goes away. The thick layer of hairspray residue covering every surface, crusting brown around Marcel irons and hot rollers. The ancient pot of amber wax with about a million popsicle sticks stuck around the rim.

Crystal ashtrays are scattered around the room, filled to the brim with the powdered remnants of Mama Pearl's lipstick-stained Virginia Slims. A framed certificate with her name on it hangs beside the giant lighted mirror, an achievement earned her senior year of high school. But much like the decor, the license expired sometime in the late sixties.

Some of my earliest memories are of standing on a stool behind the mint green styling chair, my little fingers performing all kinds of questionable treatments on Mama Pearl's thinning, over-processed locks. "That's it, just jab it through. You can't hurt me," she'd say, unflinching as I stabbed a tiny metal crochet needle through the plastic highlighting cap again and again. Wisps of hair covering her head, she'd take a drag of her cigarette with one hand and stir the frothy lightening solution with the other.

My sisters and I would cough and sputter, choking on bleach fumes and dropping most of it on the floor as we took turns frosting Mama Pearl's head like a birthday cake. We'd make the biggest mess of the job. Not rinsing it well enough. Leaving the bleach on so long some strands simply gave up and let go. Toning it to a horrible shade of lavender-gray or hacking more off one side than the other with the sharp silver shears.

No matter the outcome, Mama Pearl would nod and smile as we put the finishing touches on her teased up roller set. "What a fine job you girls did," she'd say, holding up the hand mirror to inspect the back of her fried, lopsided new 'do. "Very fine, indeed. You know, with a good hairdo and the right shade of lipstick, there's no limit to a woman's potential."

Her words roll through my mind as I settle into the styling chair and stare at my reflection in the warm glow of the vanity lights. Yanking the elastic from my hair, the mass falls in the same long, tight curls I've had since the beginning of forever. Curls I tortured into submission with a flat iron during middle school. Having developed a certain tolerance for the unruly copper mop, I fiddle with it for a minute, but the makeup drawer under the vanity is my true destination. It squeaks open, a veritable graveyard of cracked eyeshadow palettes and half-used Estee Lauder foundation from twenty years back.

I wrack my brain, trying to recall tips and tricks from

YouTube tutorials as I pick up a newish bottle of black mascara and apply a couple of coats to my normally invisible blond lashes. A bit of bronzer dusted beneath my cheekbones and on to the lipstick. I sift through at least five tubes before settling on the perfect shade and excitement builds in my stomach as I swipe the bright crimson color across my lips. Rebels always wear red.

All gussied up, as Mama Pearl would say, I slip out of the room with my sandals in hand. Aside from the ever present tick of the grandfather clock, the big, old house is still and quiet, making it hard to discreetly navigate the cluttered hallway in the dark. As Mama Pearl's antique collection expands, the trail narrows, leaving only a thin space of polished oak visible down the long corridor. More is more in her opinion. And this attitude applies to just about everything.

Steps from the front door, my toe snags the edge of a crystal lamp. I catch it in time, but it's a close call. I don't know what I'm scared of, really. Any random excuse would satisfy Mama Pearl. But the truth is I'm a sorry liar and would probably screw it up. I play out the scene in my head. The look of suspicion in her eye. The inevitable disappointment to follow. It's almost enough to make me turn back. But as I pause at her room to listen, the sound of her loud snore causes my shoulders to relax, my resolve to strengthen.

The front door shuts with a quiet click, and I take my first real breath since leaving my bedroom. With the hardest part over, my confidence swells as I bend over my collection of terracotta pots lining the edge of the porch. Lamb's ear and comfrey transplanted from Sister Faye's garden. Lemon balm, rosemary, and spearmint from the feed store. Mullein found growing wild in the back pasture.

I snap off a mint leaf, pop it into my mouth, and run my fingers through the fragrant rosemary before stepping into the lane of shadowed oaks. Standing in rows like ancient soldiers, their dark arms spread wide in silent warning. But all I hear are the words to "Green River," my own personal anthem, as I swish along in the sandy loam. Arms swinging, I spin on one foot, embodying the muse. The barefoot girl dancing in the moonlight.

It's a hypnotic thing, being out here like this. For the first time in my life, I'm making my own decisions and actually following through. I wanted to do something, so I did it. Without permission. Without caring what anyone else thinks. That in itself is a huge step forward. But even as I rejoice, doubt has a way of creeping in. Taking over. Making me wait for the other shoe to drop.

The huge iron gate to my right doesn't help and I say a quick prayer as I pass the pair of stone lions guarding the entrance. Known simply as The Cult, the property and people therein remain a mystery. But not one I'm anxious to solve. To be fair, no one knows if it's an actual cult or just the residence of some intensely private person who happens to have a lot of money. Either way, in a town like ours, privacy equals rudeness and rudeness is the work of the Devil.

Cult or not, the place gives me the creeps. No telling what kinds of unholy things happen inside its walls, especially if you listen to my little sister. As the resident expert on all things surrounding The Cult, Emma spent most of last summer documenting suspicious activity captured through the lenses of her binoculars. Beefy pit bulls staked at the entrance of the estate. Video cameras positioned in the tall pines around the perimeter. Expensive vehicles coming and going at all hours of the night.

Heart thumping in my ears, I slip on my sandals and pick up my pace. I doubt there's a lick of truth to most of the rumors, but now is not the time I want to be proved wrong.

The cut leading to the old oil well site is easy enough to find, but as I fly down the trail, the woods close in tight and doubt wraps its fist around my throat, threatening to choke out the spark of courage that once felt so sure. Maybe I should quit. Just turn around and run while I still can. But then I'll never know what could've been. And not knowing is worst of all.

So I push ahead, urged on by the faint strains of country music drifting through the forest and glimpses of silvery current up ahead. This time of night the narrow bridge spanning the Sabine is nothing more than an inky slash of ragged wood connecting Texas to Louisiana. This world to that. It creaks and groans underfoot, but I'm calmed by the rush of the current, the light breeze on my skin as I cross. Swollen out of its banks, the river's presence below feels like a living thing. Steady and sure. A welcome companion in the dark.

As I climb the bank, flickers of light draw me through the trees until the picture sharpens. Guys shifting around a giant bonfire, drinking beer and laughing. Girls dancing in the bed of a pickup, all legs and hair and hips. Eli and his girlfriend,

Minnie, sitting alone on the tailgate of his Chevy. She laughs at something he says and gives an exaggerated toss of her glossy brown hair. Eli's eyes crinkle at the corners as he pushes a wayward lock away from her face. I touch my own, wondering what it feels like to be so adored, and the pang of jealousy burning hot in my chest incinerates any lingering shyness.

When I step into the light, two guys spot me and whistle.

"Hey, sweet thang. Where'd you come from?" one says, elbowing his friend. "Boy, look at them legs. They go all the way up to her ass."

My face feels like fire as the girls stop dancing to give me dirty looks. But I can't decide what's more embarrassing: running away or staying put.

Before I can do either, Baylee Brown steps forward, lifting her chin in a snarl that tells me to go back where I came from. Like she has room to talk. Baylee doesn't belong out here any more than I do. She's popular in that untouchable, good at everything kind of way. The type of girl that only has to exist to win. Student Council President. Cheerleading Captain. Homecoming Queen. You name it. I know for a fact she has her sights set on the coveted title of Miss Old Salem this year, but from what I can see, this crowd is about the farthest thing from beauty queen royalty I can think of.

"You lost, honey?" she says in a sickly sweet voice.

"I was about to ask you the same thing," I say with a surprising amount of gumption. "Where's Dawson at, anyhow?"

By the look on her face, I've caught Baylee off guard.

Everybody knows she has a thing for slumming it with the River Rats on occasion—everybody except her old money, straight-A, church-going boyfriend, that is. But that's Baylee's thing. Always trying to pretend she's something she's not. She just didn't expect me to have the balls to say it out loud.

When her face hardens, I tense, not sure what's coming but certain it won't be good. I've never been in a real fight and I don't relish the idea of starting now.

I'm saved when a nice-looking senior named Zack steps between us, flashing a confident smile. The same smile I've seen him give a dozen other girls over the years. But never me.

"You look like you could use a beer," he says, his eyes sliding down my body.

I lift my chin and nod, like I belong. But I can feel the others staring. Hear the harsh whispers from the girls in the truck.

Zack leans close and gives me a wink. "Come on, let's get you fixed up," he says, ushering me through the crowd with blatant possessiveness.

I let out a breath, comforted by the sureness of Zack's stride, the warmth of his hand on the small of my back.

The other guys turn away as we pass, feigning lost interest. They know the rules. Approaching me now would mean a fight. Only Eli has the audacity to stare, his eyes tracking our movements despite Minnie's attempt to distract him with a kiss. I bite my lip to keep from smiling at the sight. The victory is small, but it feels good to be the center of his attention for once.

Zack plunges his arm into an icy cooler and pulls out two Bud Lights. He hands me one. And then another and another. Eventually, my shoulders relax and my body sways, the music pulsing through me like waves lapping the shore. We don't talk much. There's nothing to say. But the boys are cute and the music is loud. The Flame is everything I thought it'd be and more.

Eli's eyes continue to follow me as I dance and flirt—I know because I'm watching him, too—and his attention proves just as intoxicating as the beer. It's clear he's shocked by my presence, and that translates into an unhealthy desire to show him just how much he underestimated me. So when Zack pulls me close and squeezes my ass, I let him. And when he whispers an invitation in my ear, I feel a certain amount of satisfaction knowing I've accomplished my goal. This is my chance to leave shy, loner Sunday behind and I'm going to take it.

The ground sways and I stumble a bit as Zack pushes me toward his truck, but Eli's voice is hard as iron. "Come on, Sunday. It's time for you to go home."

I spin around. "What? Why?"

"You've had enough fun for one night. Come on. I mean it."

Zack steps in front of me. "What the hell, man?"

"Just get away from her."

Zack puffs out his chest. "You think you're gonna make me?"

Eli shoves him out of the way and hoists me over his shoulder like a sack of potatoes. I scream and fight and beg him to let me down. He ignores my shouts and shoves me inside his own Chevy like a naughty child.

"Hey you son-of-a-bitch, I'm talkin' to you," Zack says, trailing behind like a buck in rut. "Oh, I see how it is. You want her all to yourself."

I lean out the window and stare in horror as one punch from Eli sends Zack to the ground, writhing in pain.

Baylee screams and rushes to Zack's aid while the rest of the crowd takes a step back. "Get that slut outta here!" she says, pointing to me.

Minnie runs up to the truck with wild eyes. "Wait. Where're you going?"

Eli jumps inside and nods my way. "Takin' her home. Be back in a little while."

"No. Make somebody else take her."

"I'm the one got her into this."

She crosses her arms and huffs. "What if I told you I might not be here when you get back?"

He slams the truck in gear. "Suit yourself, darlin'."

We ride in silence until the gate to Belle Terre comes into view. Usually the ornate entrance to our grand old estate is a welcoming sight, but tonight the metal bars feel more like a prison than a home.

I glare at Eli one last time. "You didn't have to hit him."

"That's the only language Zack understands."

"But he didn't do anything. And even if he did, I can take care of myself."

"Maybe ... if you were sober." Eli lets out a harsh breath.

"Listen, you don't wanna get mixed up with Zack. Trust me. You don't know him like I do."

"Why'd you even ask me to come if you didn't want me to stay?"

"Hey now. I didn't *ask* you to do anything."

I tense as his words hit their mark. "You're right. *Dared* is more like it. You just didn't think I'd have the nerve to show up." I jump out and slam the door. "Have a nice life."

I pick up a rock and hurl it at the truck as Eli drives away. It bounces off the tailgate as he continues on, unfazed by my theatrics.

When he's out of sight, I plop down on the cool grass, angry sobs ripping through my chest until my eyes feel like sandpaper and my throat aches from the effort. Exhausted, I lean back against a sturdy oak, not far from the spot Mama Pearl found me one bright Easter morning sixteen years ago. Abandoned by some faceless kin, so the story goes, swaddled in pink and tucked inside a cardboard box. Like Moses. Or a stray dog.

But what was once front page news, is now just a yellowed newspaper clipping Mama Pearl keeps tucked inside her Bible. I look at it sometimes, wishing for a clue into where I came from. Who I came from. Who I never got the chance to be.

I should probably go inside, but I'm too defeated, too drunk, to move just yet. Nothing matters anyway. Where I go. Where I sleep. It's all pointless.

Darkness wraps around me and my eyelids fall. Minutes turn to hours until the sound of crickets shift into the distant coo of mourning doves and a fiery sunrise breaks through the pines, pushing the soft, lingering fog into the deep recesses of the forest.

As I squint into the light, the memory of my foolishness hits me like a hammer. For as long as I can remember, Mama Pearl has kept to herself, using these landscaped grounds as a gilded cage to keep most of the world out. Now I understand why. The idea that I could go to The Flame and reinvent myself was a pipe dream. A weakness. But it won't happen again. I'm done trying to fit in where I don't belong.

Just as I'm about to crawl out of my pit of self-pity, movement across the street catches my eye. Mr. Pickens stepping onto his porch. Bright yellow spandex stretches across his rotund stomach and tight compression shorts cause his pale thighs to bulge like a busted can of biscuit dough.

I stare as he begins a series of awkward stretches, unable to remember the last time I've seen the cranky old man in workout gear. Or outdoors. Or at all, for that matter.

Done with his stretches, he guzzles from the sport bottle strapped to his waist and bends to check his shoelaces. I plaster myself to the tree, hoping he won't notice my morbid curiosity as he rights himself and fiddles with the watch on his arm. Satisfied with his preparations, he launches into a sluggish jog down his long driveway, arms pumping up and down, white sneakers pounding the pavement at an ever-increasing pace until he's barreling toward the main road at an impressive speed. But just as he reaches the curb, his feet slow, stuttering to a stop. Chest heaving and face pouring sweat, he pulls a pack of Camel's from his running belt and props against the mailbox for a few long drags. Finally, he turns and strolls back up the driveway, his rendezvous with running over as swiftly as it began.

In that way, Mr. Pickens and I are the same. We both took a chance. Stepped out of our comfort zone to try something new. But he'll never be a runner and I'll never be a rebel.

People always go back to what they are. Always.

CHAPTER 2

SIX YEARS LATER

Emma's blond head pops around the corner of the butler's pantry. "Are you gonna help me with this or not?"

I look up from my sandwich. "Help you with what?"

"We have to fill these boxes and drop them off at church, remember? I told you about it last week."

I shove the last bite in my mouth and try not to look annoyed. "Remind me."

"It's for the community garage sale. They need donations."

My little sister might be the baby of the family, but she's never had a problem giving orders. Especially if it involves a good cause.

"Don't you have friends to hang out with or something? You know, like a normal teenager?"

Her eyes narrow. "I *am* a normal teenager. All my friends volunteer."

I'm not immune to the plight of my fellow man, but Emma's do-gooder nature can be a bit much sometimes.

She holds out an empty box. "Come on, Sunday. I've seen your room. There's a ton of stuff up there you don't need anymore."

I hate to admit it, but I know she's right. My room hasn't been touched since I left for college, four years ago. When I crossed the threshold late last night, the experience was like entering a time capsule where withered homecoming corsages hang from canopy bedposts and jars of dried herbs line shelves overflowing with high school annuals, books on naturopathy, and old copies of Texas Teen. The magazines are dated, the corsages yellowed, but the books are my forever keepsakes. Timeless reminders of my first real taste of natural medicine; the pastime that grew into a passion.

I set my plate in the sink and pick up the box. "Fine. What's the fundraiser for this time?"

Emma's eyes light up. "A wilderness camp in Montana that helps troubled kids. The proceeds we raise sponsor kids who want to participate."

"Anybody from Old Salem going?"

"A few. But there's always a waiting list. Not everybody gets in. I got to be a volunteer last year, and I've never felt such a sense of purpose," she says with a conviction well beyond her years. "I just wish ..." She presses her lips together.

"What's wrong?"

"Well, the program is great and all, but when it's over, the kids are just devastated. A lot of them are scared to go home." Tears pool in her eyes. "I remember feeling like that before we came here. It was terrible."

Lucky for us, Mama Pearl is a collector of more than just antiques. I was her first adoption, but certainly not her last. Emma and Dani don't talk much about their life before Belle Terre, but I know enough. Their mama used to be our cleaning lady. A waif of a woman with brassy bleached hair who liked to slip Mama Pearl's lipsticks into her pocket when she thought no one was looking. I always wanted to tell, but then she'd be sent away, along with Dani and Emma. They were my best friends. My only friends. And I wanted them to stay forever. When their sorry mama ran off with a truck driver later that summer, I got my wish.

I flash Emma a smile and try to sound upbeat. "You're doing a lot of good for those kids. Just focus on that."

She gives a hesitant nod. "You're right. I shouldn't worry about things I can't control."

"What you *should* be worrying about is Mama Pearl catching you smuggling her stuff out of Belle Terre. Good cause or not, she'd be fit to be tied if she knew what—"

"Shh!" Emma cranes her neck to look down the hall toward Mama Pearl's bedroom. "Did you hear that?"

"It's just the cuckoo clock. She's still napping."

Emma flaps her hands, ushering me toward the stairs. "Hurry and get what you can before she wakes up. I don't have any room left in my car, so we'll have to use your Jeep. You got all your stuff out, right?"

I nod, thinking of the boxes I brought back from Austin and how Dani now has the apartment all to herself. Unlike me, she's happy there attending cosmetology school and following in Mama Pearl's footsteps. Dani couldn't wait to grow up and get away from Belle Terre. To strike out on her own and conquer the world. On that account, we're as different as night and day. Part of me will forever mourn my childhood. Being free to run and play outside with my sisters until well after dark with no responsibilities. Losing track of time, rummaging through piles of antique jewelry, old fur coats, and used high heels in the big, old mansion. Hunting for treasures tucked away in dusty rooms stuffed floor to ceiling with expensive curiosities. I miss those days in a way I can't explain. In a way that makes leaving without a backward glance unthinkable. But I guess people do it all the time— jetting off to L.A. or New York if they're extra ambitious. Bragging about the move like it's something worthy of an award. In reality, leaving home is never harder than scraping up the money for a bus ticket. The real trick is figuring out how to come back. How to stay.

I hurry to sort through my room and head outside with an overflowing box.

Mr. Lavergne spots me across the yard. "Let me get those for you, sha," he calls in his thick Cajun accent.

He scowls when I wave him away. More of a father figure than a groundskeeper, Mr. Lavergne disapproves of us girls doing anything for ourselves outdoors. I can't blame him for assuming the role. Our family has been patched together, bits at a time, and I wouldn't have it any other way.

When the boxes are loaded, Emma heads back inside, but I follow at a slower pace, stopping short of the back door. It's open and I can hear her talking on the phone.

"Well, I'm not getting in the middle of it," she says, oblivious to my eavesdropping. "Yeah I know, but Mama Pearl has the final say. No, she hasn't asked her yet. Come on Dani, you're freaking out for no reason. Listen, if it'll make you feel better, I'll talk to her when she comes back in. Okay, love you too."

I wait a few moments, taking deep breaths to calm my rattled nerves before walking inside.

Emma sits at the table with her eyebrows drawn together. "Hey. Do you have a minute?"

I nod, bracing myself for what's to come.

She rubs her palms on her jeans, taking her time, choosing her words like always. "Dani doesn't like Jeffrey's idea."

I shake my head, irritated by Dani's stubbornness. "We never should've told her about it. She's such a worrywart."

"But she has a point, Sunday. You've only been together a few months. Don't you think you should get to know him better before making these kinds of plans?"

Emma's judgement feels like a slap in the face. What right does she have to lecture me? She's just a kid. "If I know Jeffrey well enough to marry him, then I certainly know him well enough to start a business with him."

"We just don't want to see you get hurt," she says in a quiet voice. "That's what sisters do. We look out for each other."

"I honestly don't know why we're even having this conversation. It's Mama Pearl's decision. Not mine." I glance toward the hall. "I actually planned on asking her about it today."

As if on cue, Mama Pearl's voice floats down the corridor. "Tea time, girls."

Emma stands. "I'll help her to the porch. You get the tea."

The wheels of the tea service squeak as I push it onto the porch where Mama Pearl waits in her usual spot on the hammock. Her freshly styled hair is teased high on her head and a new floral housedress covers her large form like a tent.

Although prominent in years and an unrepentant chain-smoker, very few wrinkles mar her rosy complexion, a faint reminder of the beauty she once was. The family photo album glitters with evidence of a very different woman than the person before me. She may've been born on the wrong side of the tracks—poor river trash as she calls it—but that didn't stop her from being crowned Miss Old Salem in a borrowed dress and tying the knot with the richest man in town, all before her eighteenth birthday. It was the stuff of fairy tales. But not all fairytales end the same.

Mama Pearl had risen above her station. Married up in a big way. But the whirlwind romance with Hob Frederick sent tongues wagging as the motives of the pretty young hair-dresser who'd caught East Texas' most eligible bachelor came into question. Mama Pearl was in love with the man, not his money. But that didn't stop the town gossips from calling her everything from a whore to a gold digger, none of it true.

As long as she had Hob, Mama Pearl was better equipped to ignore the rumors and public disdain. But when a sudden heart attack took him a few years into their marriage, old biddies reveled in the assumption that their speculations were correct. In their minds, she was a regular black widow, catching a millionaire and killing him off at the first opportunity.

Nothing could be further from the truth.

Mama Pearl was devastated by Hob's death and never fully recovered from the blow. As gossip ran wild, she completely withdrew, shutting herself inside Belle Terre. Childless and alone, depression took hold as she attempted to fill the void with cigarettes and antiques and food. By the time Mr. Lavergne came to live with us, the ashtrays were full, the house was overflowing, and Mama Pearl was barely getting around without help.

She gives me a warm smile and motions to the chair beside her. "Come sit by me, sweet. Tell me what you've been up to with that handsome Jeffrey. I suppose the wedding plans are underway?"

"Everything's going great. My dress should be ready in a couple of weeks, and the flowers we settled on are absolutely gorgeous."

Her head bobs up and down. "I'm so proud of you. I was telling Irene the other day what a good match you made. That Jeffrey's a fine young man, to be sure."

Emma looks at me and clears her throat. "Don't you have something else you want to discuss?"

When Mama Pearl's penciled eyebrows lift, I hesitate.

"Jeffrey wants us to turn Belle Terre into a game ranch," Emma blurts.

"I don't need your help, Emma," I say, shooting her a look.

"A *what* kind of ranch?" Mama Pearl's laugh comes out as a sort of high-pitched fluttering that brings an unexpected wave of guilt.

Established in the days when Texas was still a Republic, Belle Terre is one of the few historical markers in the area that has stood the test of time. Situated on twenty thousand acres, our home has survived with a grace and strength that comes from being needed. Belle Terre is more than a house. It's a haven. A place I can run when things get hard. No matter how many years pass, the sturdy pine floors remain strong, the carved white columns straight and tall. But the world is changing and in order to survive, we must learn to adapt. To compromise.

I give Mama Pearl my most persuasive smile. "A game ranch is a type of resort where people hunt deer and other kinds of exotic animals. Jeffrey came up with the idea as a way to utilize all of the Belle Terre property without having to log it."

"But we don't log the land now, dear. And the gas wells generate enough to pay the taxes and such."

"What I'm trying to say is Jeffrey wants to build a life here. Put down some roots," I say, trying not to sound desperate.

She shakes her head in confusion and holds out a cigarette for Emma to light. "Well now, I thought y'all might want to travel around some while you're both still young. Go do all the things I never got to. Get out of this town and see the world."

Nails biting into my palms, my voice rises against my will.

"But that's just it. I don't want to see the world. I want to come home. But Jeffrey can't sell commercial real estate way out here. He has to make a living, and this game ranch is the perfect solution." I pick up my phone. "Can I show you—"

Mama Pearl turns her attention to a truck rumbling up the driveway. "Look, there he is, right on time," she says, patting my arm in satisfaction. "He said he'd come by today. Would you be a dear and run grab my good lace shawl, Emma Jean?"

Emma darts into the house as I crane my neck to get a better look at the old Chevy rolling to a stop. When a man with sandy hair and leather work boots climbs out, I have to remind myself to breathe.

With several days' worth of stubble and unkempt shoulder-length hair, he's very different from the guy I knew in high school. But with that cocky grin, jacked-up four-wheel drive, and faint scar marring his left cheek, I'd know Eli LeBlanc anywhere.

CHAPTER 3

"Got some good blue cat today," Eli calls, pulling a string of catfish from the bed of his truck. "Where you want 'em?"

Mama Pearl waves her cigarette in excitement. "Oh aren't you a sweetheart. If you don't mind, there's an ice chest around back. Here, Emma Jean can show you."

Just as I'm picking my jaw up off the floor, Eli has the nerve to look me straight in the eye and wink. But as he and Emma disappear around the corner of the house, all I can do is gawk.

Mama Pearl's smile widens. "Ain't he a doll?"

"No. He's actually not," I say, finding my voice. "What on earth is he even *doing* here?"

Mama Pearl snuffs her cigarette and gives a happy sigh. "Oh, he comes over all the time."

"Since when does *Eli LeBlanc* come over *all the time*?"

"Let's see. Guess it started back when his truck broke down a few years ago. Right out on the road there. He came up asking to borrow some tools from Mr. Lavergne and I tell you, we both took a shine to him right away. Turns out, I know some of his people. They used to live down by us when I was a kid. I lost track over the years, but it's sure been good to kind of catch up, you know?"

At the sound of footsteps, I sit up straight as Eli rounds the corner of the porch.

Mama Pearl holds out her hands and gives him an adoring smile. "I was just telling Sunday how much we look forward to your visits."

"Well, that makes two of us. You sure look pretty today, darlin'," he says in his smooth, deep baritone, bending low to kiss the top of her hand like some strange reincarnation of Rhett Butler and Conway Twitty combined into one tall, blond-headed River Rat. He points to the ivory shawl draped around her shoulders. "Ain't that somethin'." He brings the delicate edge into the light for closer inspection. "Tatting, right?"

Mama Pearl lifts her chin, ready to burst with pride. "I made it myself."

"*You* know what tatting is?" I blurt, shifting uncomfortably when Eli's eyes meet mine.

"My grandma used to tat," he says with a nod. "And I remember how mad she'd get if anybody called it by the wrong name. Used to say any fool can learn to crochet, but tatting is an art."

I faintly register Emma's presence at the tea service,

arranging neat slices of pound cake on a platter as if the sight of Eli LeBlanc making himself at home on our front porch were the most normal thing in the world. But I just don't get it. Mama Pearl doesn't make new friends.

Ever.

It may seem odd, but I've always found comfort in this kind of extreme predictability. There are never any surprises. She's the same day in and day out. The glue that holds our family together.

I watch in horrified fascination as Eli takes a seat and leans over to whisper something in her ear. When she laughs and swats his shoulder, I feel unreasonably bereft at how easily he has managed to infiltrate our happy home.

"Are y'all ready for some sweet iced tea and lemon pound cake?" Emma asks in a chipper voice.

As we sip our tea, Mama Pearl turns the conversation to me. "Did you know Miss Sunday just got engaged?"

Eli glances my way and clears his throat. "No, ma'am. Heard she was some kind of fancy doctor now, but I didn't know there was a fella to boot."

Mama Pearl's eyes sparkle with pride. "Jeffrey Frost is his name. I'm sure you've heard of his daddy, Spencer Frost. Big lawyer up in Austin. Maybe you've seen his commercials." She turns to me. "Oh, what is it he calls himself?"

"The Texas Ice Storm," Emma says in a loud voice.

"I know the one you're talkin' 'bout. How does it go again? Oh yeah." Eli's voice takes on a brash tone as he recites the commercials cheesy catch phrase. "Let the Frost Law Firm freeze out the big insurance companies for every dollar you deserve! Nothing stops the Texas Ice Storm!"

I want to crawl in a hole and die as Eli mimics Jeffrey's dad with painful accuracy.

"Spencer's not like that in real life," I say, hoping against hope he believes me.

Eli nods, but his eyes are still laughing. "Is your man a lawyer too?"

When I hesitate, Mama Pearl speaks up. "No. His daddy wanted him to join the firm, of course. But Jeffrey went into commercial real estate, instead."

Certain things aren't talked about in the Frost family, and Jeffrey's failure to get into law school is one of them. His parents were disappointed, but not for the reasons people think. Spencer and Gwendolyn aren't your typical Austin elite. They are some of the kindest, most genuine people I've ever met. And at the end of the day, they just want their son to be happy, no matter his career path. But the overachiever in Jeffrey was devastated. Selling real estate had been an easy second choice, but it isn't his true passion. He has the heart of an entrepreneur and the drive of no one else I've ever met.

"That Jeffrey's a fine boy, I tell you," Mama Pearl says with her usual abundance of pride. "Sunday was just telling me about his new idea for Belle Terre."

Eli inclines his head, waiting for me to explain.

I glance at the notes on my phone and try to steady my voice as I detail the benefits of opening a game ranch. Creating jobs, keeping loggers away from Belle Terre, and sparking the local economy, to name a few. When I finish, everyone is quiet.

Mama Pearl looks at Eli. "What do you think?"

"Guess it don't really matter what I think. It's your land. Do what you want to with it."

"No, I really want the opinion of someone familiar with my property. All of it, I mean."

He nods in understanding, but hesitates to answer. "If I'm bein' honest, I think it's a bad idea."

I bristle, unable to believe he's getting to have a say in what is clearly a family decision. "You don't know anything—"

Mama Pearl cuts in. "No, let Eli explain himself. I've let the locals hunt and fish my land for decades. And you may not realize this, Sunday, but Belle Terre's holdings completely surround the community of Devil's Pocket. It's been over forty years since I left that little river shack, and I've never looked back. But if the people are anything like I remember, I feel it prudent to take their reaction into account."

Eli shifts in his seat. "Listen, I'm not tryin' to be a spokesperson for the Pocket, or anything. And I sure don't want to interfere in your private business ..."

"That's right," I say. "If anything, a game ranch would help the Pocket, not hurt it."

Mama Pearl cuts her eyes my way, as close to stern as she ever gets. "I'd still like Eli to explain why he's not comfortable with the idea."

Properly chastened, I sit back with a huff and wait for Eli to state his case.

"If you really wanna know, I'll tell you. For starters, turnin' twenty thousand acres into a fenced-in resort for rich people ain't gonna go over very well with anybody I know of 'round here. Most of 'em been huntin' and fishin' this land for generations. You'd have one hell of a fight on your hands. And even if you did manage to pull it off, it'd kill the culture in our area."

"Culture?" I cross my arms and glare at him. "I was born and raised here and I have no idea what you're talking about."

"Of course you don't," he scoffs. "Because you're confusin' culture with refinement. And refinement ain't somethin' the river bottom'll ever have. But, to say it has no culture, just shows you don't even know what culture is." I open my mouth, but Eli keeps talking. "The people out in the Pocket ain't like everybody else. They didn't grow up goin' to Old Salem Sunday school picnics and Civic Club meetin's. Just ask Mama Pearl. They stay to themselves. They're a different breed altogether, with different values. Without the land they hunt on and the river they fish out of, they're nothin'."

I stand up. "You're acting like these people would never get to hunt and fish again. And I'm sorry, but that's not true! There's plenty of other places for them to go do that."

"Really? Name one."

"Well ... surely there are ..."

Mama Pearl fans herself, her eyes bouncing between us. "Eli means there are no other free places nearby. Only leases that charge membership."

I shrug. "So let them pay."

Eli's eyes narrow. "You're crazy if you think people are gonna start payin' fifteen hundred a year when they've been doin' the same damn thing for free right in their own back-yard for generations."

"Well, that's not my problem."

"Yes, it is. You just don't know it yet." Eli walks to the front steps and gives Mama Pearl a nod. "Thank you, ma'am, for the tea, but I better get on now."

She stops fanning herself. "So soon? I was hoping you'd stay for supper."

He glances at me. "I appreciate the offer, but I think I've worn out my welcome. Don't worry, I'll bring you some of that sassafras root I was tellin' you 'bout in a couple days." He tips his hat. "Ladies."

The others say goodbye, but I can't bring myself to join in.

CHAPTER 4

The ticking of the hall clock is driving me crazy. It's one thirty in the morning and I can't stop thinking. I've replayed every sentence of my encounter with Eli for hours and he has proven to be just as much of a pompous jackass as I remember.

It infuriates me that Mama Pearl can't see through his charade. She'd probably call me childish and petty for holding a grudge, but I can't help it. The one time I tried to learn more about his so-called 'culture,' Eli was the one to prevent it, humiliating me in the process.

But that night at The Flame was a turning point. Eli may have called the shots back in high school, but those days are over. I'm educated and engaged and on my way to happily-ever-after. He will never intimidate me again.

I pull the quilt over my head and flip over, determined to fall asleep. But all too soon, Emma's voice interrupts.

"Sunday, wake up. Right now."

"What do you want?" I moan, unwilling to open my eyes.

"What I *want* is to go back to bed."

"So go."

"Gladly. Just as soon as you handle the situation downstairs."

"What're you talking about?" I say, forcing myself to sit up.

She points to the window. "See for yourself."

The sight of Jeffrey's sparkling black Land Rover makes my stomach drop. "Shit. Shit. Shit. I'm so stupid." I bolt out of bed in the direction of my closet, hangers clattering to the floor as I search for my favorite maxi dress. "How could I forget he was coming today? He's going to kill me for making him late. He hates being late."

Emma's eyes narrow. "I'm sure it's not that big of a deal."

I jerk the dress over my head and glance at the mirror. With wild curls and a puffy face, I make a sorry picture. But there's no time for anything else.

My hands shake as I struggle to fasten my sandals, but a thought makes me freeze. "You didn't let him in the house did you?"

"Of course not. I asked him to wait on the porch, like always."

I close my eyes in relief. The last thing I need right now is to try to explain the state of the place. Mama Pearl's hoarding has always been a part of our life. A quirky vise that's annoying, yet fairly harmless. But the prospect of inviting my fiancé to step over the threshold has me seeing the collection with fresh eyes. With boxes and crates and trunks and furniture spilling out of every room, the view is less than picturesque.

"You know you're going to have to let him inside one day, right? Might as well get it over with now," Emma says—without sympathy.

The suggestion makes me wince. "I will. Soon. Promise."

She rolls her eyes, spotting the lie as it leaves my mouth. "Guess you better get going, then. Heaven forbid you deviate from your fiancé's *precious* schedule."

I tense at Emma's tone. "What's your deal?"

She turns away but doesn't respond.

"Answer me. Why don't you like him?" I press, knowing it's better to get this over with now rather than let it fester.

She shakes her head. "He calls you like twenty-seven times a day and all he ever talks about is the game ranch this and the game ranch that. It's so annoying. And why wasn't he at your graduation? The least he could've done was show up."

"I told you he had an important meeting he couldn't miss."

Emma crosses her arms and scowls. "You worked hard for that degree and he didn't even know the name of it. I heard him tell somebody you're a nutritionist."

"I think you're being way too hard on him. Naturopathy isn't exactly a word people use every day."

Emma bites her lip.

"Well, what is it? I really have to go," I say, irritated by her attitude.

"I don't know ... it's just like when you're with him you turn into somebody else. Somebody I don't recognize."

I open my mouth to argue, but it'd be a waste of time. Emma's too young, too inexperienced, to understand the nuance of grown up relationships. She can say what she wants, but I know the truth. Meeting Jeffrey and being welcomed into his family is one of the best things that has ever happened to me.

"I don't have time for this," I say, rushing down the staircase and onto the porch where his elegant form leans against a column.

At the sight of my bare face and hastily pulled together outfit, his mouth gapes. "Um, are you sure you're ready to go? I mean ... sorry that came out wrong," he amends, visibly flustered.

Embarrassment washes over me as I take in his own carefully coiffed ensemble. With hair falling in smooth, black waves and expensive-smelling cologne, I seem like the country cousin in comparison.

"Sorry I overslept," I say, trying to tug the wrinkles from my dress. "I forgot you were coming in from Lake Charles today. How'd the meeting go?"

"Better than expected." He gives me a tight smile and glances toward the front door. From his spot on the porch, the rest of the house isn't visible—and I want to keep it that way.

"You know, I'd love to come inside sometime," he says, reading my mind.

I shake my head. "We should really get on the road."

Clutter and chaos has no place in Jeffrey's life. The life

we'll soon share. I know I'll eventually have to let him see the real us. The real me. But not yet.

⬥

OUR TRIP WEST TAKES UP MOST OF THE DAY, SO I OPT TO do my makeup in the car, tracing careful lines and brushing eyeshadow across my lids. I prefer a more natural look, but I know Jeffrey likes it when I'm made up.

Satisfied with my reflection, I flip the sun visor closed and study the giant, stone pillars flanking the entrance of Pecos Ranch Resort.

As we bump over the cattle guard, I squirm in my seat and clamp my thighs together. "Um ... Jeffrey. I really have to pee."

He glances at the GPS on the dashboard. "It's only a couple miles. Can't you wait?"

"No. I gotta go *now*," I say, no longer able to ignore my full bladder as the empty road stretches before us to the West Texas horizon. "Just pull over right here. I'm about to bust."

"What? No. Somebody could see you."

I stare at the cloud of dust trailing behind us. "We haven't seen another car for the last hour."

"I don't care. There's no way I'm letting my future wife relieve herself in a road ditch in broad daylight."

My teeth grit together as sweat beads on my forehead. "I swear, if you don't pull over right now ..." The threat hovers on the tip of my tongue as I eye his beloved Hydro Flask. He thinks he has a problem with me peeing outside? Clearly, he has no idea what I'm capable of accomplishing with a simple open container. Not that I'm bragging.

"Damn it, Jeffrey. *I'm serious.*"

"Please don't curse." He veers to the right with a shake of his head. "Make it fast."

I grab a few napkins from the glove compartment and jump out before we stop rolling.

When I climb back in the Land Rover, Jeffrey's massaging his temples.

"You okay?" I say, feeling much better myself.

"I have a headache," he snaps. When I reach into my purse, he holds up a hand. "No. I'm not in the mood for whatever snake oil remedy you're about to give me. I'm just ready to get to the ranch."

The tension is palpable as he speeds back onto the road and rejects my attempts at small talk. I try to understand his frustration, but after ten hours stuck in the same vehicle, I don't care to justify his mood, headache or not. Hell, if he had any idea how many times I've peed outside growing up, he'd likely take back his engagement ring.

I take a few deep breaths and focus on the rugged landscape out the window. Rocks and cactus and sagebrush, so different from the pine forests I'm accustomed to, stretch out over gently rolling hills of muted color. It's wild and open and unexpectedly beautiful. A lovely escape from the ordinary that I was hoping to enjoy together.

I glance Jeffrey's way. "How many acres do they have here?" I say, hoping a question about the ranch we are visiting will spark his interest.

He hesitates before answering, his voice devoid of emotion. "Eighteen thousand or so. Not as big as Belle Terre, but still a nice-sized spread."

"You know, I don't think I've ever actually seen all of Belle Terre's holdings. I've seen what's right around the house, of course, but Mama Pearl never really explained where the boundaries are. Strange, really, owning something you've never laid eyes on." I know I'm rambling, but I'm desperate to lighten the atmosphere.

Jeffrey's phone dings. He picks it up, hits a button, and drops it back into the cup holder. "Hey, remember not to say anything about Belle Terre up here," he says in a matter-of-fact tone. "The ranch manager thinks we're just coming for a tour."

"Isn't that what we *are* doing?"

"You know what I mean. It's not like we can tell him we're only here for information."

I prop my elbow on the windowsill and rest my head on my hand, my hair brushing against my thigh. "You think we could actually pull something like this off? I always thought game ranches were just a West Texas thing."

"Well, they are ... *right now*." His golden eyes flicker with a spark of genuine excitement. "But that's the genius of it. We'd have the first luxury hunting ranch East Texas has ever seen. There's virtually no competition. I mean, how many other people have twenty thousand acres of untouched private property around there? Nobody. It's all been bought up by the timber companies."

"You forget that Mama Pearl may not go for the idea. She's funny about Belle Terre."

"I'm sure we'll be able to get her on board."

I swallow hard and fiddle with the hem of my dress. "Yeah, but we don't really have to decide anything yet, right? After the wedding we'll have plenty of time to think— "

"That's what I've been meaning to talk to you about. The investors I met with yesterday are anxious to get the ball rolling right now." He reaches over, squeezing my hand. "If we don't strike while the iron's hot, we may lose our chance forever. We can't miss this opportunity."

I'm still a bit unsure about turning Belle Terre into anything other than my childhood haven, but I understand the practicality of his argument. When I left for college, I had no idea how much I'd miss home. Stuck in my Austin apartment, memories would churn in my gut until I was sick with regret. The little things were what I missed most. Sitting on the veranda with a glass of sweet iced tea. Listening to the breeze as it rustled through the oaks. Jeffrey's family has been wonderfully warm and accepting, but Belle Terre is my North Star. No matter where I go or what I do, it's the one place in the world where I feel truly at home.

I worked hard to earn my degree in naturopathy with the intent of returning to Old Salem to practice my craft. But choosing to settle down in a rural area comes with obstacles. Jeffrey can't sell commercial real estate living way out in the sticks. And he refuses to spend the first years of our marriage scraping by. That leaves the game ranch as our only option to do something big. Neither of us know much about running a ranch, but I like the idea of being able to live and work at Belle Terre while preserving the home and property for future generations. "The Lord doesn't care for waste," Mama Pearl always says. "You build a barn and don't use it, it'll rot and fall in a few years' time, sure as the world. But you take that same barn and put just one cow or goat or chicken under it and it'll stand forever. Gives it a purpose. A reason for being."

I wave my hand toward the window and the open land beyond. "How much does a place like this make anyway?"

Jeffrey's eyes brighten as the wheels in his head kick into gear. It's an expression I love seeing on his handsome face. He's so intelligent. So ambitious. The kind of person who makes me feel like anything is possible. Nothing is out of reach.

"I don't know about annually, but the base price for a three-day trophy hunt starts at about six thousand a person." When my jaw drops, he nods. "And there are all sorts of ways to raise profits, like installing our own breeding program. Ranches pay out the nose for trophy bucks. But if we raise our own, that's more money in our pocket."

We slow to a stop in front of a huge building made of log and stone. Massive wooden beams frame the spacious front porch of the lodge where several rockers sit unoccupied. Barns and other outbuildings of the same style are scattered about, with a group of cozy log cabins situated in a horseshoe around a fire pit.

A bowlegged gentleman in a straw cowboy hat ambles toward us as we wait for the dust to settle. Starched and ironed from head to toe, he's worn and western, with eyes closed by the sun and a missing right thumb.

"Welcome to Pecos," he says, eyeing Jeffrey's mint polo and khaki shorts. He gives me a warm smile and tips his hat. "Bill Burton, ranch manager. Glad to make your acquaintance."

"Sorry we're late." Jeffrey shoots me an exasperated look. "We got ... held up."

"No problem. Just follow me and if you have any questions, don't be afraid to ask."

As it turns out, none are needed. Bill is the long-winded sort, unconsciously revealing too much at every turn. Based on Jeffrey's glowing expression, Bill's chatty manner plays well into our plan to gather insider information. But as the minutes pass and Jeffrey consumes the ins and outs of running a successful game ranch, I can't help feeling guilty. We will never be guests at Pecos, spending thousands to hunt white-tail, axis, antelope, and elk. Nor will we refer our friends and family to do the same. We're copycats, plain and simple, seeking only to glean hard-earned knowledge from a man who doesn't know any better.

Jeffrey stops to admire a large elk above the fireplace in the main room as Bill rambles on. "Oh yeah, we have all kinds of exotics. If you have people to impress, like a corporate hunt or something, you're at the right place. We offer skinning, processing, and taxidermy too." He elbows Jeffrey and winks. "See, here at Pecos you get the dream, not the reality."

As we enter the trophy room, I glimpse a woman walking across the yard carrying two buckets filled with oversized baby bottles. Curious, I excuse myself and follow the stone path leading to the barn where the smell of sweet hay lingers.

When my eyes adjust to the dim interior, I spot the woman near the back struggling to balance both buckets while opening a heavy wooden gate.

"Wait," I call, trotting toward her and lifting the latch. "Here, let me help you."

"Gracias. You feed babies?" she asks in broken English, lifting a bucket.

"What kind of babies?"

She frowns, searching for the word. "Bambi?"

I clap my hands together. "Oh, I'd love to!"

She motions for me to follow her through the gate into a large open pen. When I step inside, I can't believe my eyes. Like a scene from a storybook, a dozen beautiful fawns frolic across a floor covered with clean hay.

"Come." The woman waves me forward to a low bench in the middle of the pen where she hands me a bottle and shows me how to position it to allow the baby to nurse.

I gaze down at the fawn, enamored. "I've never seen one up close. They're beautiful."

"We take good care. Pay lots of money."

My head comes up. "What?"

"Money," she repeats, holding her hands beside her head to signify horns. "Big buck one day."

My stomach drops. "Oh ... yes. I didn't think of that."

I stroke the fawn's soft coat and try to justify the ethics of raising an animal in a domestic setting, only to parade it as wild a few years later.

"There you are." I jump at the sound of Jeffrey's voice and spill milk across the floor. His mouth twists in amusement at the fumble. "I thought I'd lost you."

"No, not lost. Just admiring the baby deer."

"Fawns, you mean." He casts an appraising eye. "They're fine specimens, for sure. But we really need to get going. I have a meeting tomorrow. And you have your … ah … "

"New job?"

"Yeah, that," he says, helping me up.

"Are you sure you're okay to drive all the way back? I don't mind switching off," I say, cringing at the idea of the endless ride home.

He just rolls his eyes and gives me a look. When Jeffrey scheduled the tour, I begged him to change the date so I don't show up for my first day of work looking like death warmed over. But he refused, saying we're in this thing together and I'll just have to suck it up.

He takes out his phone. "Siri, make a note to call the architect tomorrow and add a trophy room to the blueprint."

I stop walking. "Blueprint? I thought she was just making a rough sketch."

Jeffrey curses under his breath. "I shouldn't have said anything. I actually wanted it to be a surprise."

"You didn't think I'd want a say in the plans?"

"It's just a starter blueprint. Nothing's set in stone."

Before I can reply, a guy wearing tactical gear and camouflage face paint flies into the yard with a huge buck strapped to the front of his four-wheeler.

"Ohhhh!" he calls to a group of his buddies surrounding

the fire. A few call back, raising their arms over their head to make an O.

I turn to Jeffrey. "What do you think they're doing?"

"Who knows. Bill said they're hosting a fraternity from the University of Texas. Guess that's them."

The guy with the deer notices us and jerks his chin toward the buck. "Would you look at this fucking twelve-point, man?"

I nudge Jeffrey with my elbow and try to whisper without moving my mouth. "Is he talking to us?"

Jeffrey nods and pulls me toward the group. As we near, I notice the guy's shirt reads: *Omicron Kappa Delta—Spring Break —Cowboy Boots and Bathin' Suits—Galveston, Texas.*

Jeffrey eyes the bloody carcass and smiles his approval. "Nice job. Is this what brings y'all to the ranch?"

"Yeah, we wanted to go out with a bang this year," the guy says. "So, we decided to give Pecos a try."

I look at the lifeless buck and wonder if it had been bottle-fed as a baby too.

Jeffrey whistles. "How much did that sucker cost you?"

"You'll have to ask his dad," one of his buddies yells, producing laughter from the group.

"Hey, check out this shit," the guy says, rolling his shirt sleeve up to reveal the letters *OKD* seared into the skin of his shoulder. "We all did it last night," he brags, waving his hand to the guys who are busy setting up a game of beer pong. "We were wasted as fuck."

"You mean you actually ... *branded* each other?" I say, finding my voice.

With yeasty breath and a gleam in his eye, he sidles close. "Stay and do some shots with us."

"Oh ... uh ... we really have to go but thanks for the offer," I say, glaring at Jeffrey in a way I hope he won't ignore.

"Some other time guys." Jeffrey lowers his voice. "But hey, listen. Y'all be on the lookout for a new game ranch opening up in East Texas in the near future. Remember the name Belle Terre."

"You know the owner?"

Jeffrey motions to himself.

"Sweet, man. Thanks for giving us a heads-up."

As Pecos fades in the distance, I think about the twelve-point lying on the four-wheeler and reach for Jeffrey's arm. "Do you think we'll have guests like that at Belle Terre one day?"

"Like what?"

"You know, those guys back there. Frat boys with nothing better to do than spend daddy's money and make a fool of themselves."

"Boys will be boys. Besides, if it's money in our pocket, what do we care?" He sits up straight, rolling his neck until it cracks. "I can just see it now. When we get up and running, everybody who's anybody will be standing in line to stay at our ranch."

I fail to see the allure of rubbing elbows with the upper echelon Jeffrey describes, but the very idea that he's willing to leave his family in Austin and settle in the middle of nowhere makes me want to reciprocate the gesture. If a game ranch is what it'll take to make him happy and content in our new life together, then the least I can do is be supportive.

When I lean over, he covers my hand with his own and gives it a squeeze. "I have a really good feeling about this. As soon as Mama Pearl gives us the nod, it'll be smooth sailing."

CHAPTER 5

My heart feels ready to burst as the florist slides a vase of pink roses onto my desk. There's no card, but I don't need a signature to know exactly who they're from. Becoming a naturopath is a lifelong dream come true, and Jeffrey is just the kind of man who is thoughtful enough to send flowers commemorating my first day on the job.

Bright and early this morning, Jeffrey's mom and dad called to wish me a fantastic first day. Changing the words of the Happy Birthday song to fit the occasion, Spencer and Gwendolyn's voices blared through the speaker, making me laugh at the corny perfection of the gesture. I bury my face in the pink blooms and make a mental note to show them off to Emma. It'll be the ultimate I told you so.

The idea puts a skip in my step as I head back to Doctor Navarre's private office. Dim and cozy, the space is filled with rich furnishings and the thick scent of mahogany, leather, and books. Jars of dried herbs and watery tinctures line the walls, giving the room a mad scientist flare. But after forty years as Old Salem's only local physician, Doc has earned the freedom to be eccentric without much complaint from the community. It's a trait I admire and seek to emulate as the newest member of his team.

I settle into a wingback chair and wait as Doc sifts through the piles of paperwork littering his antique apothecary desk. After pulling out each and every one of the tiny drawers, he presents me with a small handwritten list of plants, herbs, and oddities.

"You're familiar with the Pocket, correct?" he says.

The question catches me off guard. Other than my one foolhardy trip to The Flame, Devil's Pocket is a side of the tracks I've never been brave enough to explore. Curious, I sit up straight. "Uh, kind of ..."

"And here I was thinking it was your old stomping ground." Lined with a thousand shallow wrinkles, Doc's face holds an ever present troubled expression that's easy to mistake for disapproval, but the glint in his eye tells me he's joking. He nods to the list. "That's a few of the things I'd like harvested out of the river bottom. You think you're up to it?"

"Wait. You want *me* to harvest all this?" I say, scanning the list.

"Exactly. With help, of course. I've already got a guide set up to take you everywhere you need to go."

"Why can't you just order these things?"

He massages the back of his neck with one hand. "Well, I

can, but I prefer wildcrafting the plants from their natural environments for optimal potency."

I'm not surprised by Doc's admission. Relying on naturopathy more than Western medicine, he has long since proclaimed his freedom from the pretensions of so-called modern medicine by forever experimenting with unconventional formulas and techniques.

Most things on the list I recognize, but others—like wild hog thyroid—seem a little farfetched, even for Doc.

A bell rings at the front desk, interrupting our conversation.

"I better get that," I say, standing. "Georgia is still out to lunch."

As I round the corner, the blonde receptionist bustles in through the employee entrance.

"Sorry I'm late," she calls, careful not to touch her wet nails as she drops the mail in a heap on her desk.

"I was just coming up here to check ..." My smile fades as I catch sight of Eli LeBlanc standing in the reception area, holding a brown paper bag. He approaches the desk and mumbles something to Georgia.

She gives him a huge smile. "Sure is, honey. Go right on back."

When he brushes past with a coy grin, my blood boils. I stomp over to Georgia and try to keep my voice low. "What's he doing here?"

"Eli? Oh, he comes in every week about this time." She lifts a delicate brow and blows on her nail polish. "I don't dress up on Mondays for nothing, you know."

"What y'all whisperin' 'bout over there?" Eli calls, striding back toward us.

I turn away but keep Georgia in my peripheral.

"You," she says, pushing her cleavage together for maximum effect.

"Well, I'm sure Miss Sunday there had a mouthful to say."

My patience snaps and I whirl around. "If I remember correctly, I've already said everything I wanted to say to your face."

Eli ducks his head. "Listen, I don't wanna rehash all that. It was never my intention to upset you." He nods to the vase of roses on my desk. "I see you got the flowers."

"Wait, what?" I choke out, unwilling to believe his insinuation.

He shrugs. "I wanted to say I'm sorry. We just seem to keep gettin' off on the wrong foot, don't we?"

My brain sputters to a stop.

I desperately want to say something profound. Or sarcastic. Or ... audible. But all I can do is stare like an idiot as the corner of Eli's mouth lifts in that way he knows is charming. That way I've grown to hate.

"So," he says, leaning against my desk like we're old friends. "I've been talking to Doc and I have a proposition for you."

The office phone rings, but Georgia hits a button, silencing it immediately.

Eli looks into my eyes, a hint of pleading in his own. "Before you convince Mama Pearl to go through with this hair-brained ranch idea, all I ask for is one week."

"A week for what?" I finally manage to say.

"Come out to the river with me. Let me show you what you have to lose." Georgia gives a contented sigh, prompting a satisfied smile to spread across Eli's annoyingly handsome face. "If you do that, I'll make sure we find everything Doc needs," he says, pointing to the list in my hand. "What do you say, Sunday? You up for a little adventure?"

I cross my arms, unable to believe Eli's nerve. "No way. I have absolutely no interest in you showing me anything. Not now. Not ever."

His eyes take on a wicked gleam. "Not even if I *dare* you?"

Eli's bold reference to the past makes it hard to lift my chin and look him in the eye. "We aren't in high school anymore."

His mouth twitches as he ponders a moment, then strides toward the door. At the last minute, he turns back. "You'll change your mind."

When he disappears outside, Doc walks up with a clipboard in one hand and a half-eaten donut in the other.

I stare at him, dumbfounded. "Please tell me that's not the guide you were talking about earlier."

Doc stops chewing and frowns. "I'm afraid so. Is there a problem?"

"It's just ... I mean ... why *him*?" I blurt, knowing full well how unprofessional I sound.

"Well, right now, Eli gets just about anything I need. Always has. But now that you're here, I'd really like you to learn how it's done. Where the plants are located and such. You'd be doing me a big favor."

The prospect of exploring our region's untapped potential, full of the widest variety of plants and herbs available in Texas, is tempting, sure. It's a naturopath's dream. But with Eli as my guide … it's downright terrifying.

"You could learn a lot from that boy," Doc continues. "Eli knows that river bottom like the back of his hand. But he won't accept pay, so I hate to keep asking. Of course, if you're not comfortable with the idea, I understand." It may take me a little while to find a different guide, but the decision is yours. Just think about it and let me know."

When Doc walks away, I turn to Georgia. "What'd he mean by that? About Eli not accepting pay."

She pulls her rhinestone reading glasses from the top of her head and slides them on. "Eli won't take it. Says he owes Doc a debt."

"For what?"

"Haven't ever asked." Her eyes narrow. "What's the deal with you and Eli, anyway?"

"We have … history."

Her eyebrows lift as she leans forward. "Go on."

I give her a quick recap of our run-in at The Flame and the events to follow.

"Hot damn, girl," she says, fanning herself. "It'd take a hell of a lot more than that to make me turn down the chance to spend a week with that little cutie."

"I'm *not* interested in Eli LeBlanc."

She gives a loud snort. "Well, you're the only female in this town over eighteen and under eighty who can say that."

I plop down at the desk and put my head in my hands. "I don't know what to do."

"Sit up," she commands with the authority of a judge. "There, that's better. Now, why don't you put on your big girl panties and quit whining."

"I'm not whining."

"Yes you are," she says without a hint of sympathy. "You're making this a lot more complicated than it should be. What happened between you and Eli is water under the bridge. So, if Doc wants you to learn wildcrafting from him, I say go give it a shot. What have you got to lose?"

"Well—"

She shakes her head, unconvinced by my weak excuse before it's even spoken. "You and Eli may not be on the best of terms, but believe me when I say you don't want to head into that river bottom with just anybody. From what I know of Eli, he's trustworthy and he's a gentleman. And that's a hell of a lot more than I can say for most men."

Confident in her closing argument, Georgia purses her lips together as her words sink in. I may not like it, but she has a pretty solid point. Eli makes me uncomfortable, but not in a creepy, serial killer kind of way. He's infuriating, not dangerous.

Maybe Georgia is right. If I have to venture into the wilds of Devil's Pocket, it may as well be with the devil I know.

CHAPTER 6

As I roll down the highway toward the Pocket a few days later, I cuss Georgia for talking me into such an escapade. I should've known better than to listen. She's a romantic. And romantics have a way of inspiring sane people to do insane things.

But I can't put all the blame on her. It's my job to help Doc and I desperately want to make a good impression. To let him see I'm a team player. A professional ready to do what's needed and go where I'm called, even if that means Eli LeBlanc's river camp. And I'd be lying if I said I don't relish the idea of proving the jerk wrong. But first I have to find the damn place.

I dig around in my purse for the scrap of paper with directions. According to Mr. Lavergne's hand-drawn map, I need to make a right onto Chicken Gut Road, another right at the old cemetery, a left when the road splits, cross over the Sabine

River into Louisiana, and take the second road to the left after I pass a blue cowboy camper turned deer stand.

Within spitting distance of my hometown, there's no mistaking Devil's Pocket for any part of Old Salem, where historic homes stand in neat rows around the courthouse square and littering is an unthinkable offense. Small, quaint, picturesque. These are the words clucked over and over by the town leaders before our annual festival. But with that kind of community pride comes a certain level of intolerance.

Sure, Devil's Pocket is geographically close, but it may as well be on another planet. The ugly stepchild no one likes to talk about. A place where the bottom rung of society collect: inbred, backward, and possessing an "almost exotic stupidity" as *Texas Monthly* once reported in a mean-spirited spread about the region. I've never agreed with those ridiculous labels, of course. But I haven't fought them either.

As I get farther and farther from civilization, my tires vibrate over washboard sand, leaving behind a trail of dust. Unlike breadcrumbs, I can't use it to find my way back when every road, every tree, every direction starts to look the same. I don't want to admit I'm lost but something's wrong, I can feel it.

I check the directions again and reluctantly dial Irene Bergeron's number. She's the only person I know who lives in the Pocket besides Eli. And at this point, I'd rather die than ask him for help.

"There ain't no way you'll find that boy's place on your own, map or no map," Irene bellows in her good natured way.

"You just come on over here and let me bring you out there in the boat, you hear?"

Irene's camp turns out to be much easier to find than Eli's, but the trail is still long and dusty and littered with trash. From ancient RVs to moldy school buses, the unusual assortment of dwellings lining each side of the narrow river road is endless. But I can't help feeling intrigued by the dirty, suntanned children who stare suspiciously and old men who wave without looking up.

My Jeep thumps along, glimpses of water flashing through the trees as I'm sucked deeper and deeper into the wilderness. Then the trail opens to a crowded sandbar of people mingling through a summer maze of beer coolers, lawn chairs, and jacked-up pickups. They're a rough-looking bunch, deep-tanned and rawboned, with muscular bodies that speak more of outdoor labor than a gym membership.

But there's something else. Something in the way they move that calls to my basest instincts. Like watching footage of the crowd at Woodstock. I want to get closer. To see and hear and be a part. But the idea that I still feel the pull, after all these years, is disturbing.

I roll to a stop and shift into park, careful to leave the doors unlocked and key in the ignition. Doc made it clear that River Rats view locks and gates as direct insults, silent accusations against their character that, ironically, often leads to theft and vandalism.

I grab my phone and take a screenshot of my current location.

"I'll be at this address if you need me," I type, sending the photo to Jeffrey.

"Is that a B&B?" he replies.

"No, Irene Bergeron offered to be my host," I lie. "She's a family friend."

I hate being dishonest, but I've been dancing around Jeffrey's questions for days. There's no way he'd agree to let me spend a week alone with another man. Ever. But I told Doc I would, so I have to see it through. I console myself with the knowledge that what Jeffrey doesn't know won't hurt him. He has enough on his plate without a new worry. And it's not as if I have anything devious in mind. I'm here to work, plain and simple. There will never be anything between Eli and myself except an affinity to butt heads.

"Give me a week," Eli had said. So, sure. I'll give him a week. I'll hear him out. And then my family and I will do as we damn well please with Belle Terre.

Hoisting my bags, I attempt to slip past a group of men playing horseshoes under the shade of a huge beech tree. One notices me and smiles. Raising his beer high in the air, he elbows his friend and yells something I can't make out. The attention makes my ears burn, but I keep my eyes straight ahead, trying my best to seem nonchalant as I hurry up Irene's front walk.

Irene and Mama Pearl have been friends more than half a century, but Irene's house looks much older. Painted neon green and built mostly of particle board, it sits high off the ground on wooden piers with a tin roof and large front porch. A shabby addition made of black tar paper stretches across the back, and an old blue tarp covers parts of the roof. Faded garden gnomes and ornate miniature windmills sit among flower beds made of old tires, with a prominent display of purple petunias cascading out of what was once a white porcelain toilet.

The front door is wide open, but I knock and wait at the threshold as I eyeball the gallon-sized Ziploc bag filled with water hanging from the doorframe. Everybody says it keeps flies out of the house, but I can't imagine why.

"Come on in," Irene yells, stomping toward me.

Shoeless and sweaty, Irene Bergeron is no beauty. In fact, with her unkempt, mousy hair and florid complexion, she's one of the ugliest women I've ever known. But also one of the most beautiful.

Smiling from ear to ear, she grabs me by the shoulders and kisses me on the lips with a hard, fast peck. "It's 'bout time you made it out my way. Just look at you, all growed up and purty."

"Thanks for offering to bring me out to Eli's."

She waves a hand in the air. "Anytime. Sure never thought I'd see the day when any of you gals set foot in the Pocket. Come on in. I'll make some coffee."

"I'd love to, but we should probably get going."

"How long you plan on bein' out here, baby doll?"

"No more than a week or so. Just long enough to find everything Doc needs."

"Well, come on. Got the boat waitin' over yunder." She points to an area at the far end of the sandbar, away from the crowd.

I slip off my shoes and follow her down the steep bank past broken lawn chairs and chicken wire barrels filled with empty beer cans. When the sparse grass gives way to coarse river sand, I pause at the water's edge, my eyes drifting along with the dark green current as it wraps and curves its way through the bayou country and on toward the brackish estuaries of the Gulf.

The scene is peaceful. Picturesque, even. But I'm jolted back to reality when Irene casts my bags into the boat with a heavy thump.

"Oh!" I say, rushing forward. "My phone's in there. Do you think it's okay?"

She takes a step back, ignoring the question as her narrowed eyes scan my white lacy blouse and light pink shorts. With a shake of her head, she removes her own threadbare Wayne Toups concert T-shirt and slips the faded black fabric over my head. "Don't wanna ruin them good clothes," she says as it balloons around me, falling almost to my knees.

Left wearing only a thin white tank top with no bra, Irene jumps into the tiny aluminum boat and waves me forward. But I stand frozen, wishing I could insist she take back the borrowed shirt that smells like a mixture of moth balls and beef jerky.

Irene puts her hands on her hips. "Come on, we ain't got all day."

The subtle crescendo of summer locusts echo around me in hot waves as I inch forward, sinking into the water bit by bit. Thick mud, murky and warm, tugs at my bare feet, causing me to struggle and Irene to frown.

Outdone with my incompetence, I bite back a shriek as her rough hands drag me into the boat like a hooked catfish. Mortified, I make my way to the bow, stepping over empty Coke cans, tangled balls of faded trotlines, and a plastic milk crate of minnow jars. Weathered shades of green, yellow, and blue paint flake off the vessel's original aluminum, and the splintering plywood floor is stained and smells like fish. But I can't help liking the thin, old boat. It's no frills. Just like Irene.

I watch as she makes herself comfortable, wipes the sweat from her fuzzy upper lip, and cranks the motor in one fluid motion. It smokes and sputters and smells like burning oil. Without warning, we catapult into the strong current and the bow elevates, suspending us in air for just a moment before crashing down. Stunned, I grip the chalky edge and look to Irene for help, but her expression remains unaffected as she continues to strong-arm the aluminum death trap at top speed.

Illusions of gliding peacefully to our destination vanish as my hands slip with each jarring bump and sweat runs down my back. I've never been a coward, but this ride beats anything I experienced as a kid at the county fair. The ultimate trial by fire.

Eyeing the boat floor, I consider lying in the fetal position until we either arrive ... or die.

I'm saved the immediate decision when Irene slows to cross a shallow spot she calls Pebble Island. She adjusts the motor so the propeller won't drag and explains how the curiosity is formed of banked pea gravel and petrified wood, the remains of someone dredging for rocks long ago. The current rushes over the island in the choppy washboard pattern typical of shallow water, making rocks glisten under the surface like fall leaves after a hard rain.

I glance down, enjoying the way my engagement ring glitters right along with the rocks. Nestled in a vintage-style setting Jeffrey's mom designed, the three-carat diamond is the most beautiful piece of jewelry I've ever seen. It's just my style, and I feel lucky to have such an amazing and thoughtful future mother-in-law.

Irene notices my preoccupation and nods to the ring. "Still can't believe it. From what Mama Pearl says, you met one day and was engaged the next."

I laugh, amused by her candor. "No, it wasn't quite that quick. The proposal was a little unexpected, but welcome."

"I know Mama Pearl sure is proud. Ain't the weddin' comin' up pretty soon?"

"Next month. We don't see any reason to wait."

Irene's mouth falls open. "Then what the hell you doin' out here? Ain't you got stuff to do to get ready?"

"Most of it's been covered by our wedding planner. He's been a real lifesaver."

"So, Jeffrey don't mind you goin' to stay with Eli?"

I hesitate. "He knows it's just for work."

Guilt churns in my stomach at the half-truth—and I have a feeling Irene knows I'm lying—but I don't have the energy to explain.

As we continue to drift, I turn away, taking the opportunity to soak in my new surroundings. With steep bluff banks looming over deep rushing water and low hanging willows swaying in the breeze, the river has a simple elegance that is lush and inviting, if not beautiful.

Without the wind to cool me, the sun burns my face. I pull my bag from the foul-smelling compartment under the seat and, finding a bandana, lean over to dunk it in the water. Compact mirror in hand, I dab at my melted makeup but only manage to smear it worse.

I shudder at the image I present with mascara running down my cheeks and lipstick escaping its boundaries. My hair isn't any better as massive red curls soaked with sweat tangle in knots and stick to my forehead. I attempt tying the unruly heap in a tight bun and securing it with the bandana, but it falls after a few seconds.

Always ready to help, Irene reaches into a faded tackle box and pulls out a mangy hairbrush. She makes quick work of removing all the old hair and twists it into a long string she calls a rat. "Here, baby doll, let's tie this 'round your hair. It'll hold better." Gathering my hair on top of my head, she secures the rat around my ponytail with the speed of a rodeo contestant tying a calf's legs in competition.

I open my compact a second time and her eyes brighten with expectation as I touch the hideous new hairdo.

"Well, there you go," I say, at a loss for other words.

She gives me a satisfied smile and holds out a silver flask that I kindly refuse. After a long swig, she resumes her place at the motor. "Alright. Hang on, then."

Before I can get a decent grip, my stomach drops as she

hammers down on the tiller handle. My eyes fix on the flask still in her hand and I berate myself for refusing the offer. If I have to die in this boat, I don't want to do it sober.

"How much farther until we get there?" I yell over the roaring motor.

"Oh, maybe seven bends or so. Don't worry, won't be long."

When Eli's houseboat finally comes into view, my shoulders sag in relief even as I shift in my seat to get a better look. Nestled beneath a roof of rusty v-crimp, traps, hoop nets, and animal hides hang from walls made of rough-cut lumber. It's certainly nothing to write home about, but there is a certain amount of rustic charm to the tiny dwelling.

A large dog lies on the front porch beside a dusty, straight-back chair with a busted out bottom. Bursting into maniacal barking, the dog jumps to his feet and glares at me with peculiar blue eyes that would send a shiver down anyone's spine.

But the thing that really bothers me is the small wooden sign nailed to a porch post:

NO TRESPASSING—VIOLATORS WILL BE SHOT —SURVIVORS WILL BE SHOT AGAIN.

CHAPTER 7

I stare at the sign, hoping it's a joke. But something in my gut tells me it absolutely is not.

Irene tilts her head to the side. "You okay, baby doll? You don't look so good."

I don't feel so good, either. But I sit up straight and lift my chin. I may be out of my element, but I refuse to be seen as some pampered princess on her first trip into the wilderness. I can be brave. Fit in. Wearing Irene's shirt with her hand-me-down hair tying up my own, I'm halfway there.

"Hush up, Bleu." She snaps her fingers at the dog who drops to his belly to gnaw on a small, unidentifiable carcass. "See, he ain't gonna hurt you."

The screen door screeches and Eli emerges, squinting into the bright afternoon sunlight. Wearing only a frayed pair of cut-off Wranglers, the sight of his muscular chest is more distracting than I'd like to admit.

Irene tosses him the rope. "How you been, boy? Seems like it's been a coon's age since I seen you last."

"Aw, fair to middlin', Aunt Irene," he says, rolling out syllables as he ties off the boat.

She steps onto the porch and holds out her arms. "Give me some sugar."

When he obliges, I take the opportunity to stand and attempt pulling myself onto the porch without falling into the water.

Eli relaxes against a porch post, watching. "Well now," he says, with a lopsided grin. "I knew you'd change your mind."

He wants to rile me, but I won't give him the satisfaction. I press my lips together, biting back a retort as I hold up my bags. "Where should I put these?"

Making no move to show me inside like a decent host, Eli nods toward the buckled plywood door. Unsurprisingly, the house is basically just one room with skulls and shells of dead animals hanging on the walls and classic country drifting from a shabby radio on the kitchen counter. A metal bunk bed stands against the far wall with ugly, mismatched linens. Thankfully, they seem clean and in decent shape.

Dropping my bags, I hang my head over the AC unit mounted in the window. Held together by an assortment of duct tape and tinfoil, it blasts cold air into the room with a determination that feels divine. If only I could stay here a while longer, soaking up the cool air until I'm more prepared. More collected. But I can't hide in here forever, no matter how appealing it sounds.

I force my feet toward the door when an unexpected

glimpse of teeth and fur makes me jump back in surprise. A giant bobcat peers from behind the door, sharp teeth bared. The snarl on its face make my heart hammer, and a scream escapes my lips.

Footsteps sound on the porch.

"What the hell?" Eli says, bursting inside with Irene hot on his heels.

I try to hide my shock as I realize the ferocious animal is, in fact ... dead.

Realizing my mistake, a slow smile spreads across Eli's face. "Scared were you, darlin'?"

It's all I can do to bite my tongue and ignore his satisfied smirk as Irene laughs and jabs me in the ribs. "You gonna have a fine time out here! Yes sir!"

If only that were true.

She lifts both arms in a long stretch and mumbles something about getting home before dark. Begging her to stay isn't realistic, but it's on the tip of my tongue as she ambles out the door. When her motor fades in the distance, I'm left without a buffer. I don't know what to say, how to act. But my stomach speaks for me, rumbling loudly.

"There's some leftovers on the stove. Help yourself," Eli offers, lowering into a seat at the table.

Something smothered in a dark gravy simmers under the lid of a heavy black iron skillet. I'm not sure what the concoction is, but it's food and I'm grateful.

Eli takes down a gun from above the door and starts the slow, methodical task of cleaning the rifle as I eat. While he studies the gun, I study him. The furrow in his brow. Cleft in his chin. The scruff and scars. Interesting imperfections he pulls off with ease. His left hand is bare, but I never heard what happened to Minnie. They always seemed so in love. So ready to settle down like most hometown kids who go straight to work instead of college. I itch to ask him about it, but my pride stands in the way.

When the silence stretches to the point of awkwardness, I clear my throat. "Whatever you're thinking, I just want you to know my assignment here has nothing do with our little encounter at the office the other day."

Eli regards me for a long moment. "I still aim to change your mind, one way or another."

"You're wasting your time."

He leans forward, a barely perceptible twitch tugging at the corner of his mouth. "Why don't you let me be the judge of that?"

I shift in my seat and decide to change the subject. "I didn't know Irene was your aunt," I say, at a loss for anything better.

"My aunt?"

"Isn't that what you called her?"

"Oh, yeah. Well, we're dog-kin I guess. Lived with her some before I got this place."

That sounds like Irene. Always ready to help. I think of all the times she's wandered up to Belle Terre with some sort of homemade goodie tucked under her arm. And how much those sweet gestures mean to Mama Pearl. When others called her uppity for marrying Hob, Irene stayed true. She didn't begrudge Mama Pearl's good fortune. She celebrated it by standing up with her at the wedding and never failing to visit as often as she can manage.

Done with the rifle, Eli relaxes back into his chair. "So what's first on Doc's list?"

I check the paper in my pocket. "Looks like swamp lily root," I say, using the common name for Saururus Cernuus. "I brought along some newspaper and plastic bags to keep the roots moist after harvesting."

"Well, it's too late to hunt up any lily root tonight," he says, languidly taking a chew of tobacco. He licks his fingers and wipes them on his cut-off jeans before standing to stretch his back. "Got a Lodge meetin' anyhow. Be back a little later."

"You mean ... you're leaving?"

"Yep."

"But what if I need something? What if I need to get in touch with you?"

He picks up the rifle and pulls out a cabinet drawer, stirring the contents until he finds a Sharpie. Pausing at the door, he writes on the frame in bold script. "There's my number. You'll be fine."

CHAPTER 8

The idea that Eli considers himself above common courtesy makes my blood boil. Jeffrey would never dream of leaving me in such a predicament. I don't know what I expected out of Eli, but it certainly wasn't this.

Now I'm alone, stranded in the middle of nowhere for who knows how long. But other than calling Irene and abandoning the mission, there's not much I can do about it. Doc is depending on me and I loathe the idea of giving Eli a reason to say I can't hang.

As the sun dips lower, I sit in the silence feeling sorry for myself and outdone by the whole stupid situation. When self-pity turns to boredom, I wander to the porch and down a wooden ramp that creaks and sways with each step. The characteristic half-moon of an outhouse stands out against the tree line, so I walk over and lift the latch. The scene isn't surprising. A stained plastic toilet seat mounted over a hole cut into a dusty wooden bench. Toilet paper stuffed into a metal coffee can. A small jelly jar sitting on the floor beside a five-gallon bucket of white powder with LYE - 2 PER SHIT written on the side in all caps. The only suspicious looking item is a stick dangling overhead, hanging from the ceiling by a long string. Its purpose remains a mystery, but not the kind I'm anxious to solve.

If this is the toilet, where's the shower? The other sheds and outbuildings turn up a couple of freezers, a few hand tools, and a rusty push mower, but not much else.

Turning back, the terrifying possibility of not bathing for days on end takes root in my mind like a bad weed. I can go without a lot of things, but soap and water is a necessity. I plop down on the porch and put my head in my hands. What kind of backwoods nightmare have I gotten myself into?

Bleu whines and nudges my arm, begging me to throw a ball. I grip it until my knuckles turn white and hurl it far into the river. He dives into the water and retrieves it, jumping and wiggling, anxious for another round. That's when I notice the bar of soap on the floor next to a ladder extending into the water. A lightbulb goes off and I wonder why I didn't consider it before. It's not an ideal situation, but anything is better than nothing.

As dusk falls, a small sense of adventure prompts me to pull off my clothes and step to the edge. I want to cast caution to the wind and dive in, but I hesitate, suddenly unsure. I've never skinny dipped in the river before. Heck,

I've never skinny dipped, period. But there's a first time for everything, right?

I step onto the ladder with shaking knees and ease into the rushing current. It pulls me downstream, so I loop a leg through the rung and lean back, letting the water cradle me in its cool embrace. My mind stills and time fades as I lie suspended, lost in the freedom to just be.

The sky darkens and the dim glow from the kitchen window casts eerie shadows on the water, bringing to mind childhood tales of nutria rats the size of small dogs. I visualize the vile creatures circling, waiting to attack with wicked, yellow teeth and long, bony tails. I hate my overactive imagination, but unfortunately it's not something I'm likely to outgrow.

In a panic, I grasp the sides of the thin ladder, ready to ascend. Then I feel it. A small nibble on my right ankle. I squeal and kick my legs to shake off the villain even as common sense tells me it's probably just a tiny perch. Nothing to be afraid of. But try as I might, paranoia wins and I fly up the ladder, slipping on the wet rungs and almost breaking my neck in the process.

My heart pounds in my ears, almost drowning out the faint ring from inside the house. I run toward it, but miss the call. Several, in fact. Jeffrey has called nine times, left four voicemails, and seven text messages ... all in the past hour.

"Oh boy," I murmur, wrapping a towel around me as I dial his number.

He answers on the first ring. "Are you okay?" he practically shouts.

"Yeah. Fine. Service is just sketchy out here."

"I don't like not being able to get in touch with you. Can you send me the number of the place you're staying? Mom and Dad are worried sick."

"Um ... I don't think Irene has a phone," I say, crossing my fingers behind my back. "But I'll check my messages as often as I can. There's nothing to worry about. Promise."

Jeffrey sighs. "I looked up Irene's house on Google Earth and the pictures show some kind of junkyard or landfill or something. Are you sure you gave me the right address?"

"Yeah, it's just a poor area."

"It doesn't look safe. I can only imagine what the accommodations are like."

I slide a toe across the gritty plywood floor. "It's nothing fancy, but I'll live."

Jeffrey makes a sound that tells me he isn't so sure. "Listen, while I have you on the phone, can we talk about the cake tasting? Dean's been calling me like every two minutes since you left, and I don't know how much more I can take."

"You know I'm not picky. Just get whatever you think tastes good."

"Why do I have to go at all? Can't the wedding planner do it for us? Isn't that what we're *paying* him for?"

"Come on, Jeffrey. I hate to ask Dean for anything else. He's stressed enough as it is with the time limit."

BOOM! A gunshot in the distance makes me jump.

"Sunday? You there?" Jeffrey says.

"Yeah, I just ... I think I heard a gunshot outside."

"What! Are you okay?"

"Yeah, hang on a minute," I say, cracking the door to listen.

An owl hoots. The sound of rushing water. Crickets. Then the faint rumble of a truck engine.

Gathering my bath towel tightly around my body, I tiptoe onto the porch and peek around the corner of the houseboat. A truck pulls up with the lights off and the air crackles with anticipation as the engine dies. A door slams and I freeze, ready to run. But when Bleu whines and thumps his tail on the porch, relief washes over me. It's just Eli.

"Hey, I gotta go," I whisper into the phone.

"I really don't think that's a good—"

I hang up and put my phone on silent before Jeffrey can protest further. I'm not sure what Eli is up to, but the last thing I need is Jeffrey hearing his voice in the background.

With the darkness hiding my state of undress, I rush down the ramp to the bank. "What on earth are you doing, scaring me like that?" I yell.

"Shh. Tell you in a minute."

The tailgate squeaks and something heavy hits the ground with a dull thud.

"Tell me what's going on," I demand.

"Got me a good size buck. Stepped right out in my light. Help me drag him to the skinnin' shed," he says as if this kind of thing is an everyday occurrence.

"Absolutely not. You're crazy. You could go to jail for that."

"Come on, I need help."

I consider calling the game warden, but Eli reads my mind.

"You know, if you don't help me and we get caught out here, I'm gonna say you pulled the trigger."

"That's ridiculous! You wouldn't!"

"You really wanna take that chance?"

As much as I'd love to tell him to shove it, the image of Jeffrey's reaction to my face on the six o'clock news—guilty or not—is enough to make me step forward.

"Grab him right there. That's it," Eli says as if nothing's wrong.

I grit my teeth and grip the horns with one hand, gagging as blood trickles onto my skin. Together, we drag the deer into a dark shed that smells like mildew and dirt and who knows what else.

Eli twists the single bulb attached to a rafter and light floods the area. "Now you can help me jerk the hide off."

I take a step back, pulling the towel tighter around my body. "If you think I'm gonna help you skin that thing, you've lost your damn mind."

He turns to look at me for the first time and smiles. "Have I now? Least I got all my clothes on."

My face feels like fire as embarrassment wars with anger. I shake my head at his ignorance and spin on my heel, his throaty laughter mocking me all the way back to the houseboat. He thinks he's won. But I still have every right to turn him in to the authorities. I flex my hand against the uncomfortable tightness of dried blood and consider the notion. As much as I'd love to, it would be my word against his. And with the authorities involved, it wouldn't be long before Jeffrey—and the rest of the town—would know every sordid detail. It's not worth it. Not right now, anyhow.

I scrub my hands raw and change into my nightclothes, hating the way the top bunk squeaks as I settle in for the night. One glance at my phone shows Jeffrey's in a full-blown panic. I send a quick text to calm his nerves. But I'm dying to tell someone the truth about this nightmarish adventure, so I dial Dani's number.

"Hey, what's up?" she says, her voice muffled over music and voices in the background.

"You can't even imagine."

"Hang on. Let me walk outside. Okay, that's better. Emma told me you're out in Devil's Pocket. Is it really that bad? Should I tell her to come get you?"

"No ... I'm fine, really. But did she happen to mention who my guide is?"

"Who?"

"Now you can't breathe a word to Jeffrey, but it's *Eli LeBlanc*."

Dani makes a strangled sound. "The same Eli LeBlanc that put a live coon inside Mrs. King's mailbox that time?"

I think back to the narrow-minded English teacher who seemed to delight in humiliating students who struggled with the subject. "She *did* kind of deserve it."

Dani laughs. "Well you're right not to tell Jeffrey. He'd blow a fuse if he found out. Especially if he got a look at the competition."

"*Competition*? You're insane."

"Am I? You should've seen Eli at the benefit rodeo last year. Back there working the chutes with that Stetson pulled low." Dani lets out a whistle. " I mean cowboys aren't my thing, but hot damn. I'd let that one saddle me up any day of the week. Bend me over and fuck me—"

"Don't be vulgar," I interject.

"Okay, *Jeffrey*."

"What's that supposed to mean?"

"He gave you a twenty-minute lecture for saying shit."

"That was *one time*."

"Whatever. Let's get back to Eli."

"It's a long story."

"I've got time."

When our conversation ends an hour later, Dani is properly scandalized and begging for more. In her mind, Eli is a young Robert Redford character, flawed yet redeemable in a sexy outlaw kind of way. The trouble is, Dani's taste in men is even worse than her comparison. The only thing Eli will ever have in common with a silver screen legend is his rugged good looks.

I flop over on the lumpy mattress, the satin edge of the cheap coverlet brushing against my face in an irritating manner. No matter how hard I try, I can't relax. My mind won't stop. The cold jar of water I saw in the ice box calls my name, but just as I venture from my perch to pour myself a small glass, Eli steps inside.

"You okay?" he says, glimpsing my expression.

I stare at him, too angry to pretend everything is fine. "What do you think?"

His forehead wrinkles, but I turn away and lift my glass, not in the mood to hear some lame excuse. I gulp the water, determined to get back to bed as quickly as possible. But instead of the refreshing drink I was expecting, heat races down my throat, taking my breath. I double over, gasping for air.

"Third run's the best," Eli coolly observes as I cough and sputter. "That right there'll put hair on your chest. Strongest moonshine Lil' Bit's ever made."

Moonshine. I should have known. I sit the glass down with a quiet clink, determined to bite my tongue. But when Eli's laughter turns to a self-satisfied smirk, my temper flares and I grab the abandoned drink, finishing it off in one painful gulp.

When I slam the empty glass on the counter, Eli's eyes widen and a huge smile emerges. "That a girl."

He studies my face, waiting for a reaction. But the best thing I can do is refuse to comply. I'm too old to engage in any more of the childishness Eli seems to thrive on. Without a backward glance, I tuck myself into my bunk and ignore the slam of the screen door as he waltzes onto the porch a moment later.

After a lot of splashing, I crack one eye long enough to see his naked ass amble across the floor and fall into bed with a contented groan. I bury my face in my pillow to keep from screaming. What kind of person walks around butt naked in front of someone they barely know? It's rude and arrogant and totally an Eli move. He's trying to shock me, but I'm not playing his game. Not this time.

"You sure have an odd way of winning me over," I say, slurring a bit thanks to the shine.

His soft chuckle floats through the darkness, easy and sure. "Aw, but think of how disappointed you'd be if I went about it the normal way."

CHAPTER 9

The familiar aroma of fresh coffee fills the houseboat long before the sun rises. I open my eyes to a single bulb swaying back and forth over the kitchen sink, illuminating Eli's shirtless form and washing his hair and skin in a golden glow. He's more muscular than I remember and has a tattoo of a capital G surrounded by a square and compasses on his left shoulder.

Clanking two coffee cups on the counter, he walks to the icebox.

"How many eggs you want?" he says without turning around.

I jump at the sound, surprised he knows I'm awake.

"Two," I say, easing into a sitting position and eyeballing the rickety metal ladder.

After spending yesterday in Irene's makeshift cover-up, I'm thankful to climb down and dart into the dressing area where I pull on my own tank top and favorite jean shorts. A long braid and plenty of SPF are in order, as well as some light makeup. Satisfied with my reflection and feeling much more confident than yesterday, I walk back into the kitchen.

"Made some coffee," Eli says, nodding to the pot.

I pour myself a cup and take a seat at the table while bacon sizzles in the frying pan, turning brown around the edges. Eli fiddles with the flame under the eggs and slaps a few slices of buttered bread on a flat, black iron skillet.

He doesn't seem in the mood to talk, but I have plenty to say. Yesterday was a complete shit show and last night's stunt was the grand finale.

I lean forward, ready to do battle. "So, did you get that deer added to one of your many freezers, or did you just chop off the horns and leave the meat out for the buzzards?"

Eli's head jerks around. "What kinda chicken shit person would do a thing like that?"

"Outlaw hunters. Why else would you need to sneak around?"

He takes a long breath in through his nose. "Looks like you got your pretty li'l mind all made up. So, why should I try to change it?"

"I'm glad you're catching on."

We eat in silence, broken by the occasional sound of Bleu crunching on slices of bacon Eli tosses his way. The dog's enthusiasm for the treat makes me smile despite my sour mood.

I glance up to find Eli watching me. His mouth opens, then clamps shut.

"What?" I say, hating words left unsaid.

He stands abruptly. "You 'bout ready? We got work to do."

With my bag of supplies and brand-new LaCrosse rubber boots, I follow him outside to a boat that's much bigger and nicer than Irene's, with a large motor and a spacious front deck.

I point to the words "Wampus Cat" painted on the side in scrawling letters. "Is that a type of fish, or something?"

"No," he says, offering his hand. It's warm and rough with a strong grip, but as soon as I'm on board, he's quick to let go.

I settle onto the bow and bend to pull on my new rubber boots.

Eli frowns. "Don't do that."

"What?"

"Them boots. You fall out, they'll pull you right to the bottom."

"So what shoes am I supposed to wear?"

"Ain't gonna need any."

I pull them on anyhow, daring him to argue.

Eli watches my rebellion with narrowed eyes, but cranks the motor without a word. He remains standing as we head downriver, the muscles of his forearm flexing as he maneuvers into the fast-moving current. As the boat picks up speed, I grip the edge until my knuckles turn white and prepare myself for the worst while trying to maintain a neutral expression.

Eli notices and slows a little. "What's wrong?"

"I'm just not used to riding in boats," I say, unwilling to let go.

"Come 'ere."

I stiffen. "Why?"

At his irritated stare, I relent, making my way to the back-seat with careful steps. But icy panic fills my veins when he shoves the tiller handle into my hand.

"We're gonna have a little drivin' lesson," he says, shaking his head when I try to argue. "I don't wanna hear why you can't, 'cause I know you can. Now twist the handle to the right, like this."

I jerk my hand back. "No."

He eases into a squatting position in front of me and lets out a breath. "Listen, if somethin' were to happen to me out here and you needed to get help, what would you do?"

I shake my phone in the air. "Call someone, of course."

He nods, considering my answer. "Now what happens when your phone ain't got no service?"

One glance at the expensive piece of equipment and I know I've been caught. With zero bars of service, my argument is dead in the water. Literally.

"But I don't understand," I say, squinting at the screen in disbelief. "I talked to Jeffrey last night with no problems." Defeated, I shove the phone in my pocket and bite my lip until it hurts. "Fine, just show me the basics."

Eli explains how to accelerate and swivel left and right to steer. Despite his careful instructions, my hand shakes as I grip the tiller handle. Growing up, I was never even allowed to drive the lawnmower.

"You sure you understand?"

I don't have a clue what I'm doing, but I lift my chin with more confidence than I feel. "Yeah. Let's go."

My initial panic subsides as the boat slides forward, cutting through the water's surface like butter. As we gradually pick up speed, I feel oddly at ease as warm, fresh air fills my lungs with the kind of early morning sweetness found only in remote places. Maybe I can do this after all.

We glide past egrets poking along the shallows where tree roots stretch long, mysterious fingers into hidden depths along the banks. In this remote expanse of pine forest, the river thrives with a life all its own. A life I've glimpsed but never really seen.

"Be sure to stay on the willow side," Eli says, indicating the bend's inner curve where willow trees hang low. "The bluff side's where all the trash is, deadheads and snags and stuff. That's it, you got it. Give 'er a little more gas."

Feeling brave, I twist the handle harder and as we vault forward, I have the sudden wish for Jeffrey to see how well I maneuver through the water without so much as a steering wheel for comfort. Here I am, captain of the ship, with raw talent my only resource. Hell, I'm a natural.

Lost in my daydream, I make a sharp left to avoid a snag. But the bank straight ahead is too close for comfort and my relief is short-lived.

Eli shouts to slow down, so I let go of the handle, assuming it'll spin back to the original slow position on its own.

I couldn't be more wrong.

CHAPTER 10

I've always assumed that when faced with a near-death experience, thoughts of importance would surface. A bit of clarity, providing superior insight into the meaning of life. An inspired moment to change my outlook and bring me closer to God. The memory of loved ones, perhaps accompanied by a single tear and poetic verse.

But no. Not me. No epiphanies. No beautiful last words. As our boat smashes into the serene tree-lined bank with a dull crunch, my mind chooses to focus on one brutally inelegant idea.

Rubber boots.

The same rubber boots Eli told me not to wear. But did I listen? Absolutely not. And now all I can think about is them filling up and pulling me to a watery grave to drown from my own stubbornness.

Before my nightmare can materialize, Eli rushes over and

grabs the tiller handle. While I'm still struggling to wrap my head around this horrifying turn of events, he's casually trolling to a sandbar as if everything is fine.

When he jumps out to view the damage with a mystifying calmness, I attempt to swallow the bile in my throat as I tug off my newly offensive boots. "I'm so sorry. Is it bad?"

Eli glances at my bare socks and grins. "Just a li'l dent. Nothin' to worry 'bout. This time twist 'er to the left when you wanna slow down."

He jumps back inside and I catch his arm in disbelief. "But ... I don't want to try again."

He lifts a brow, recognizing the lie as it escapes my lips. "Drive."

Whether pleased or irritated by Eli's unusual confidence in my abilities, I can't decide. But I suppose my second attempt can't be any worse than my first.

When we safely pull into a shady cut several bends later, I can't keep the smile off my face. Eli shows me how to kill and raise the motor before stepping out into the knee-high water. It's a bit clearer here, with golden sand merging to brown then black as the warm surface gives way to cooler depths. A swarm of tiny yellow butterflies flutters over it, spiraling upward, touching down a moment, then back up. Like children at play, running here and there, never still and always joyous in their endeavor.

I'm reluctant to leave them behind as we trudge up the bank to a sandy path where deer flies buzz thick in the air. We hurry single file down the narrow trail, trying to escape the constant sting, but they're persistent little suckers.

"Where're we headed?" I say, swatting one off my leg.

"Yellow Bluff. Gonna go see Romance."

"Romance?"

"Yeah. I hear he's the one to see if you want swamp lily root."

"So, Doc's never asked for it before?"

"Nope. Gives me a different list almost every time."

"Does Romance grow it?"

Eli shakes his head. "Just knows where it's at. Never heard of nobody bein' able to grow it. Heard he digs it mostly for folks with teethin' babies."

The flies eventually disperse and the air turns cool and damp with hints of wisteria complimenting the ever present pine. I breathe deep, enjoying the small respite from the hot sun despite Eli's unrelenting pace.

When the trail opens to an overgrown clearing, he stops and points. "There it is."

A ramshackle camp sits on the edge of a bluff bank, surrounded by a halo of junk.

Wild grass tickles my legs as we near, picking our way around old tools, rusty car parts, and stacks of worn-out tires. You name it, it's here. Four-wheelers up on blocks. Gutted washing machines serving as live wells for fish. Clotheslines made of polyester mule tape stretching from any object high enough to hold.

Based on the appearance of the yard, I'm not sure what to expect of the owner. But when the man called Romance steps onto the porch, I like him immediately. He's a small man, probably in his sixties, with tan, leathery skin, and the bluest eyes I've ever seen. Leather moccasins peek from beneath sun-bleached Wranglers rolled high, and a pack of Marlboro Reds are tucked into the pocket of his sleeveless, faded army shirt left unbuttoned to reveal a pot belly and dog tags hanging from his neck.

Before we can be introduced, a barking rat terrier bounds out of a trash can lying on its side by the porch. "Get outta there 'fore I give you a trompin'!" Romance yells, eyeing the dog's handiwork littering the ground. "Ain't nothin' that bitch likes better'n strowin' trash all over hell's half acre."

It's all I can do not to laugh when the feisty little dog ignores the threat and keeps barking.

Romance shakes his head in dismay and pulls a plastic comb from his back pocket to sweep his yellow-tinged gray hair away from his face. Thick and wavy, it shines with an abundance of pomade and radiates a mixture of Old Spice and cigarette smoke as I step forward to shake his hand.

"Come on in and I'll make some coffee," he says, leading the way into a house made of weathered brown particle board with felt hanging in the windows in place of glass. At my whispered question, Eli explains how the felt is saturated with water to keep the interior cool in the absence of electricity. I stare at him, a little taken aback. Even the poorest people I've come in contact with have electricity. Especially in Texas, where temperatures regularly reach triple digits.

We take seats at a flimsy vinyl card table in the middle of the room as Romance sets to work making coffee in an old-fashioned drip pot. He starts a kettle to boil and removes the cloth coffee filter from the pot, emptying the old grounds into a milk jug full of garden scraps.

I turn to Eli, keeping my voice low. "Do we really have time for this? I mean, shouldn't we get started looking for the swamp lily root?"

"That ain't how it works out here. You can't ask Romance for a favor if you ain't even willin' to have a cup of coffee with him."

"I'm not trying to be rude. I just think we should use our time wisely."

Eli keeps his eyes on Romance, ignoring my concerns. "You like strong coffee?"

"Yeah. Why?"

"You ain't gonna like this."

My eyes fly to the porcelain sink where Romance gently rinses the cloth filter under the tap.

Eli nudges me with his elbow. "Recognize anything?"

I squint my eyes and gasp. "Is that what I think it is?"

He smiles and gives a barely perceptible nod.

Stained deep brown, the filter is none other than the recycled toe of an old sock.

I stare in disbelief as Romance presses the sock back into the pot, minding the raveled edges as he measures out four heaping scoops of Seaport. I'm willing to put up with a lot, but the idea of enduring sock coffee is more than I can bear. I try to think of a good excuse to abstain, but nothing believable comes to mind. So I sit in silent trepidation while Eli and Romance exchange pleasantries.

At the mention of our quest for swamp lily root, Romance

insists on showing us himself and moves the subject to other things. Eager to extend the company, he entertains us with exaggerated hunting tales and old reminiscences, with Eli providing his own share of tall tales. But I only half listen as I sit mesmerized by the odd ritual taking place at the stove.

Sliding the coffee pot in slow methodical circles over the burner, Romance speaks to it in hushed tones.

"Come on, little feller, drip for Pawpaw. Doin' good, little feller. Drip now. That's it, drip for Pawpaw," he hums over and over, the cigarette on his lip bobbing up and down as his chin nearly meets his nose.

Just as I settle into the comfortable rhythm of his gentle words, I jump when he slams the pot down and gives it a hard glare. "Drip, you little some'a bitch!"

The room goes quiet for a tense moment before he heaves a sigh, dabs his brow with a greasy-looking dishrag, and settles into the crooning ritual once more.

Amused, I glance at Eli. He gives me a wink.

"There's you a cup of coonass, li'l gal," Romance says placing the finished product before me with great pride.

"Uh, thanks," I say, staring at the darkest coffee I've ever seen. The brew reminds me of Mr. Lavergne's old adage about coffee that's too thick to drink and too thin to plow.

I attempt a small sip and choke back a cough. My eyes water and my throat burns. This can't be coffee. It tastes more like radiator scrapings. However, I do like Romance's name for the brew. Cajuns are a tough bunch of people with strong personalities and an uncanny ability to make the most of life. "People either love us or they hate us. There's no in-between, sha," Mr. Lavergne always says, and Romance's coffee is a shining example of this belief.

I watch as he pours his own portion into a saucer and props both elbows on the table. Bringing the saucer to his lips, he takes his time slurping loudly, a sign of true enjoyment and compliments to the cook by older generations.

"Drink up, li'l gal," he says, eyeing my full cup when he stands to bring his own to the sink.

I resent Eli's ability to finish his quickly and without complaint. Lucky bastard.

"Lookin' a little green 'round the gills," he teases, enjoying my discomfort.

I make no reply, choosing to glare at him instead. But when he grabs my cup and downs the bitter contents before Romance notices, my mouth falls open in disbelief. It's quite possibly the nicest thing anyone has ever done for me.

"Let me try and get these on and we'll head out," Romance says, retrieving a pair of rubber boots from beside the door. He bends to pull on the first boot, but stops, wincing and cursing under his breath.

"What's the matter?" I say, rushing to his side.

He pulls the boot off and shakes his head. "Aw ain't nothin'—"

"Let me see," I demand, lifting the hem of his jeans to reveal a swollen leg wrapped in an Ace bandage.

I turn to Eli and motion to the row of cots draped in mosquito netting along the far wall. "I need to get his leg elevated so I can take a better look."

The sore beneath the bandage is worse than I expect, but Romance refuses my advice to pay Doc a visit in town.

"He ain't goin' to the doctor, so don't even waste your breath," Eli whispers as I dump the dirty dressing in the garbage.

I glance back at the golf ball-sized sore weeping yellow pus and my stomach drops. "But he needs antibiotics. He needs—"

"I'm tellin' you, if you go to talkin' like that he won't listen to a word you have to say. I've known him all my life. See that scar across his ribs? Got it in a knife fight down at Foster's Bluff when I was a kid. Wouldn't let nobody take him to the hospital. Ended up makin' Aunt Irene staple him back together with a surgical gun we use for huntin' emergencies."

"So what do you want me to do?" I hiss, frustrated with the situation.

Eli holds up his hands. "Thought you was a natural doctor."

"I am, but—"

"It's real simple. Either you can help him or you can't."

I clench my jaw as my mind whirls with possibilities. I'm not used to such limited resources, but it looks like I don't have a choice. I'll have to make do.

"Be right back," I say, heading for the patch of comfrey I spotted in the yard when we arrived.

"What else you need?" Eli calls.

"Put on a pot of water to boil. And see if you can find some vinegar, salt, and cayenne pepper. Oh, and there's a bottle of tea tree oil in my bag."

When I return from the yard, Eli has the water boiling and my supplies arranged on the table. I drop the comfrey leaves into the pot along with the other ingredients and turn off the fire. After the brew steeps, I apply the poultice to the wound and cover it with a fresh bandage.

"It may burn at first," I warn. "But hopefully it'll kill the bacteria and speed up the healing process. I want you to reapply this poultice three times a day using the recipe I'll write down." I wag my finger in his face. "And if this isn't better in a day or two, you'll have to go see Doc. There's no way around it."

Romance sits up and smiles. "Well, I'm much obliged, li'l gal. How can I repay you?"

"Just point us in the direction of the swamp lily root, and we'll call it even."

Romance directs us to a slough behind his house where Eli and I spend the rest of the day harvesting. The work is hard, sweaty, and hot. But I enjoy the thrill of the hunt, the feel of the cool dirt on my fingers as we pull and wrap the white roots in damp newspaper.

Dusk has fallen when the last bit is loaded into the ice chest, and the accomplishment makes me stand a little straighter. I've studied herbs for years, but nothing compares to the satisfaction of retrieving something from the wild.

We're too exhausted to make the trip back to Eli's houseboat, so we accept Romance's hospitality for the night, much to his delight. Seated by the campfire on school bus seats worn with age and missing most of their upholstery, we linger over a simple supper of eggs and deer sausage that's as unpretentious and inviting as the host himself.

When Romance goes inside for the evening, Eli stands. "Guess I better hit the hay, too."

I give him a nod and watch as he heads toward the house with a bit of a limp. "What's the matter with your leg?"

He stops and gives me a questioning look.

"You're limping."

"What happens when you get throwed too many times, I guess."

"Throwed?" I say, amused by the word.

"Used to ride bulls a little. Gets worse at night."

At my nod, he disappears inside the house, but I stay out a little longer, enjoying my time alone. The feisty rat terrier Romance pretends to hate makes herself at home on my lap, and I close my eyes, stroking her soft ears as the pleasing sound of rushing water converges with the crack and pop of dying embers.

When the fire burns low, I rise with regret and ease into the house where Eli is sprawled face down on the farthest cot, mosquito netting draped around him, his back rising and falling in a slow, steady rhythm. Romance sits cross-legged on the adjacent cot, staring into space and enjoying a cigarette. Cradling it in time-worn fingers, he takes a long drag and exhales slowly, thumping the ash through various burned out holes in the netting.

I don't want to disturb him, so I tiptoe to the nearest bed and lie down. I'm asleep as soon as my eyelids fall, and the next thing I know, it's morning and my phone is ringing at an obnoxious volume. I fight my way through mosquito netting in a blind attempt to find it.

"Right here," Eli says, grabbing it from the kitchen table and tossing it my way.

"Why didn't you tell me your dress is pink?" Jeffrey practically shouts when I answer.

"Just a minute," I say, stumbling onto the porch out of earshot. "Who told you that?"

He lets out a heavy breath. "Dean called asking about my tux and let it slip."

"Well, there goes the surprise," I say, thinking of my beautiful, blush Vera Wang wedding gown Gwendolyn helped me choose.

"I don't want to upset you, but now that I know ... can we discuss the color choice?"

"Color choice?" I repeat, trying to wrap my mind around the words.

Jeffrey hesitates. "I just don't understand why you didn't choose white. It's classic."

I shake my head, unable to believe I'm actually having this conversation. "Styles change, Jeffrey. These days people wear any color they want."

"Yeah, if they want it to look like it's their fourth marriage."

I grip the phone tighter. "What did you say?"

"Look, I'm not trying to be the bad guy here. I just don't want people to think ..."

"Wait. Are you trying to say you're worried about my *reputation?*"

"Come on, Sunday. You know we have a lot of important guests coming. The last thing I want are nasty rumors floating around."

I love my dress and the thought of Jeffrey disliking it in any way makes my throat constrict.

"Who cares what anyone else thinks?" I declare. "I swear, you act like you're running for office or something."

"Well, who says I won't in the future?"

Stunned, it takes me a moment to respond. "You can't be serious."

"What if I am?"

My brain fogs as I grapple with the revelation. "But you've never mentioned anything about politics. I thought your dream was to own a game ranch. I thought—"

"It is, sweetheart. But that may just be a stepping stone. Entrepreneurs go into politics all the time. Especially with the right people behind them. And I'd want to start at the local level. Work my way up. Now do you see why I'm questioning the dress?"

"But ... I don't have time to change it. It's already being altered."

"I'll take you to any shop you want to find a replacement, and you can wear the other one to the spring art gala Mom is hosting."

"I don't want to wear it to the spring art gala. I want to wear it to my *wedding*!"

"Fine. Have it your way. It's not like it's my wedding too or anything."

When he hangs up, it takes me a moment to remember to

breathe. He's never spoken to me like that. Ever. My mind whirls and my stomach hurts. I want to scream and cry and punch holes in something.

But the rational side of me says to calm down and think. Maybe it's not really about the dress at all. Maybe his reaction is just the result of stress. Between the wedding and the game ranch, he has a lot on his plate and I'm not there to help with any of it. Instead of tending to my obligations, I'm off galli-vanting in the woods. Sure, this is my job. But maybe I'm expecting too much out of Jeffrey as a result.

A tear slides down my face. I wipe at it with the back of my hand and turn to see Eli watching me from a few feet away.

"You okay, pasquale?" he says in a gentle voice.

I frown at the unusual nickname, but I'm not in the mood to decipher the meaning.

"Fine," I say, brushing past him into the house.

My quarrel with Jeffrey is not something I feel like discussing right now. Or ever. And especially not with Eli. So, I busy myself helping Romance reapply a fresh poultice before we say our goodbyes.

Eli asks if I'm okay a few more times during the ride back to the houseboat, but I don't feel like talking. My personal life is none of his business and I want to keep it that way.

As soon as we arrive, I rush inside and send Jeffrey a text asking him to call. When the read receipt pops up and the minutes tick by, my heart sinks as I wait for a call that never comes.

CHAPTER 11

I'm being punished. Plain and simple. Jeffrey's a master at giving the silent treatment, but I'll be damned if I'm going to stare at this phone a moment longer. I extended an olive branch and that's all I can do for now.

I toss the overpriced piece of technology on the top bunk and paste a smile on my face as I step onto the porch. "Where're we going to look for saw palmetto?" I say in an upbeat voice I hope doesn't sound artificial. I'm determined not to let this get me down. Feelings ebb and flow. It'll all work out in the end. And until then, I can fake it as good as the next person.

Eli's face brightens. "I take it you're feelin' better, then?"

"Much."

"Good." He bends to load a second ice chest into the boat. "We're gonna head over to Cat's Island. But we gotta make a quick stop first. Won't take long."

He doesn't elaborate and doesn't invite me to come with him when we pull up to a sandbar a few minutes later. Hoisting the ice chest in his arms, he heads toward an unfamiliar camp in the distance. "Be right back."

When his tall form emerges from the trees a little while later, he climbs into the boat without a word.

"So?" I say.

"So, what?"

"Aren't you going to tell me where you went?"

"Got rid of that deer."

"You mean the deer you murdered illegally?"

"What's it to you?"

"I can't stand waste."

"I guarantee you, ain't none of that deer gone to waste."

"Oh, really? So, what did you do with it? Sell it for profit?"

Eli turns to me and stares until I shift in my seat. But I manage to hold his gaze as I wait for an explanation.

"No I didn't sell it," he says slowly. "Gave it away. You remember Tonya Y'Barbo?"

I think of the shy girl who got pregnant her freshman year of high school. "Yeah. Mama Pearl used to send her our hand-me-downs."

"Well, she lives up there with her four kids now." Eli nods toward the camp. "Her ol' man run off a few months ago with some lot lizard he picked up over at the Flying J. She does the best she can without him, but it ain't always enough. 'Course her pride won't let her take no money off anybody. But deer, fish, squirrel—anything like that's a different story. That buck'll last 'em a couple months, I figure. Long as there's land to hunt on, ain't nobody 'round here gonna let those babies go hungry."

I know he's referring to Belle Terre—and our plan to restrict access. But his rudeness is unnerving.

"It still doesn't justify breaking the law."

He gives a short laugh. "It's all about rules with you, ain't it? When you gonna learn to think for yourself, woman?"

"I do think for myself!"

"Then you tell me, what's more important? Followin' the law or four hungry kids?"

"It's not that simple."

"Let me get this straight. You're tellin' me what I did isn't okay. But you're totally fine with 'legal' huntin', like the kind all those rich assholes do out in West Texas. The kind that pay thousands to shoot bottle-fed deer. Oh, they love to brag about the big'ns they get openin' mornin'. And they make sure to hang 'em on the livin' room wall, front and center for everybody to see. Then they post a few pictures of fried back-strap on Facebook to impress all their buddies." He shakes his head. "'Livin' off the land,' they write. Then, they stick the rest of that deer out in some deep freeze in the garage, and by the time they look at it again, it's all freezer burnt. But hey, it's okay. There's plenty more where that came from, 'specially if you have the money to pay for it. You wanna talk about waste? Well, it don't get much more wasteful than that."

I think of the frat boys we saw at Pecos—exactly the kind of people Eli describes.

He reaches back to crank the motor. "If you're lookin' for

an apology for what I did with that deer, you're gonna be waitin' a long damn time."

I want to say something. To fight back. But I'm out of arguments. I mean, is he right? Would we be depriving these people of a major food source? I know what Jeffrey would say. That there are other resources out there and people just need to pull themselves up by the bootstraps and make their own way. But after hearing Eli's point of view ... I'm not so sure.

We ride in silence until we arrive at Cat's Island where saw palmettos fill the landscape. The shady spot has an exotic feel —an unconventional sort of paradise. But with plants ranging from very small to four feet wide and eight feet tall, the work is grueling. Mosquitos swarm and the thick mud and ferns covering the forest floor make walking difficult.

"What's this shit good for anyways?" Eli says, rummaging through the leafy green plants in search of dark purple berries.

"Don't you know? I thought you did this all the time."

"I do. But I just get what's on the list. Never said I knew what it's for."

I drop a berry into the basket and my frustration with him fades a bit as I focus on my area of expertise. "Well, it has lots of uses. But seems to be the most beneficial to men's urinary and prostate health. And ah ... libido."

Eli whistles. "Must be worth a mint."

"It's actually pretty affordable."

"People eat 'em raw?"

"No, they're either made into an extract or dried and put into capsules."

He holds a ripe berry between two fingers. "Wonder what it tastes like straight off the vine."

"I dare you," I say slowly, enjoying Eli's look of surprise at my statement.

"Oh, so you're the one daring me now?"

"I should probably warn you I've heard the flavor described as 'rotten cheese steeped in tobacco juice.'"

He drops the berry as if it were poison and makes a comical show of backing away.

"Wasting good product," I tease.

"Plenty here. Island's always been full of 'em." He picks up another berry and frowns. "What made you wanna study this stuff, anyhow?"

"I don't know. I guess growing up around Doc had a lot to do with it." I smile at the memory of his visits over the years. Rarely following his advice, Mama Pearl hasn't been an easy patient, but that hasn't stopped Doc from trying. No matter how many trips he's made or how many orders she's ignored, he's never given up. Never lost hope that one day she'll listen.

I stand to stretch my back. "I remember when I was five or six, I fell and scraped my knee on the front steps. Doc walked over to the aloe vera plant sitting on the porch and snapped off a leaf. He squeezed the juice on my scrape and explained that plants and medicine are the same thing and how they've been used by people since the beginning of time. I asked about a million questions, so the next week he brought me a picture book about Native American medicine and I was hooked. I started an herb garden and wanted to learn everything there was to know about natural healing."

Eli nods, his eyes growing distant. "Doc has a fine soul. I think some of the greatest people in the world ain't the ones you read about in history books. They're everyday people like you and me. The good things they do might seem little, but they add up. And it's them things you remember for a lifetime."

We return to our work in comfortable silence, both lost in thought as the sun climbs high.

"Why is this place called Cat's Island?" I say, wiping my damp forehead with the back of my hand.

"Named after a man who moved out here an' claimed the island as his own."

"So, this isn't Belle Terre land?"

"Naw, we're right on the edge. All this is part of a national park now. The government took it from Cat a while back."

"Should we be harvesting here, then?"

"Prob'ly not. But I still think of this place as belongin' to Cat and he'd of never cared."

"What happened? Why did the government take it?"

"Because they could. And that's the long and short of it. Cat held his own for a while and he didn't mind playin' dirty. But neither did they and 'fore it was over, there was dead bodies on both sides of the fight. 'Course in the end, the little people always lose. It didn't matter to the government that they'd had lived on this land for generations. All they cared 'bout was gettin' their way no matter who they had to step on in the process." Eli turns to me with raised brows. "Sound familiar?"

I force a smile and bat my lashes. "You're trying to bait me, but it's not going to work."

"Gonna take the high road, eh?"

"Did Cat have a family?"

"Yeah, a wife and a few kids. They always called him Polecat."

"Why?"

"You sure you wanna know?"

"How could I not?"

"Cat did a lot of trappin' out in the woods in the wintertime. Used to spend weeks away from home, campin' out at night. He mostly caught nutria rat and coon and fox and sometimes a bobcat, but he got a lot of skunks too."

"Ew, what did he want those for?"

"Ha, well he didn't eat 'em or nothin' like that. And I don't know if he kept the hides or not, but the main reason he wanted 'em was for their musk glands."

"You're kidding."

"No, ma'am. I tell you, he'd cut out them two little glands, bein' real careful not to puncture 'em. Then he'd keep 'em in a leather pouch tied to his belt and use 'em to start fires. Lay that shit over some wood and it works just like lighter fluid." Eli laughs and fans himself. "But damn it, that fire must've stunk to high heaven."

"Why didn't he use lighter fluid like you said?"

"Good question. Or just regular ol' kindlin' from a pine knot. Would'a smelled a hell of a lot better too."

I laugh until my vision blurs. "That has to be the most peculiar and disgusting thing I've ever heard."

"Cat was both of them things, for sure. After he died, the family all left. Moved on over to the Bottom Loop Road out in Caney Head."

Part of me is disappointed that the mysterious island is vacant. From Eli's description, Cat and his family seem like interesting folks. "Well, can't the family continue to fight for their land?"

"Tried that. Not worth it."

"Well, if they got a really good lawyer, I'm sure they could get something done. And if —"

"And if a frog had holsters, he'd tote pistols and shoot snakes."

I roll my eyes but can't help smiling. "You're stupid."

He squints into the distance. "Think the ol' house might still be out here somewhere. But I ain't been there since Cat died. Park Service might'a bulldozed it by now."

"Oh, I hope not. Can you take me to see if it's still there?"

He points to the basket brimming with berries. "Think we got enough of this shit to quit?"

"Yeah, come on. I'm curious."

Eli sets the basket in the boat and grabs a black-handled machete. "Let's see if I can remember how to get there."

After a couple of false starts, we head toward the east side of the island with Eli chopping a path through the trees. The jungle-thick brush pushes back, with gumbo mud weighing our feet and twisted rattan vines scraping our arms. Spiraling like snakes around the larger trunks, they remind me of the kind Tarzan used to swing from tree to tree. I grasp one and pull, surprised that it holds my weight without the slightest threat of breaking.

Eli doesn't notice me stop, so I hurry to catch up. Just as I round a large pine, something catches my foot and I fall hard on the cool, moist earth.

"Oof!" I look back to see a strand of rusty barbed wire sagging close to the ground between two trees.

Eli stops and turns around. "You alright, pasquale?

"Yeah. Just tripped," I call, trying to sit up.

Before I know it, he's on his knees, checking my ankle for cuts. His rough fingers are surprisingly gentle, but my breath catches in my throat when he lingers a bit too long.

I pull back and jump to my feet. "I'm fine, really," I say, dusting the dirt from my legs with shaking hands.

Eli stays on the ground, his eyes on the wire. "Ain't seen one of these in years."

On closer inspection, I see the wire is one of several strands forming a crude sort of fence using trees as posts. We follow the fence down to where it encompasses part of a stream and a small portion of woods.

"What is it?" I say, unable to solve the mystery.

"Looks like an ol' mule pen. Loggers used 'em wherever they were workin' to hold their teams at night. That's why it's over the water here, so they'd have somethin' to drink."

Up until the sixties, mule teams were a staple in the logging woods of East Texas. The industry has changed a lot over the years, but with over seven billion trees planted for harvest at any given time, timber is still king.

We continue on and come to a shallow hill where a tall sycamore holds the tattered remains of a tire swing.

"That's it," Eli says, motioning to the wooden house beyond. It's old and unusual, with a rusty tin roof and an open hallway about ten feet wide separating the left side from the right, like two different dwellings under the same roof.

The grass thickens with a tamer quality as we near the front steps. But I jump back in surprise when a wiry red sow with black spots rushes from beneath, followed by a multitude of piglets.

"Shoo," Eli calls, stomping and waving his arms.

"Look at them!" I say as the rambunctious lot scatter into the woods, grunting with each step. "I've never seen so many different colors before. Are they all like that out here?"

"Most of 'em." Eli hesitates before continuing. "Had one as a pet for a while when I was little. My uncle brought him to me after one of his dogs caught him and hurt his leg. I doctored him up and hid him upstairs in my closet ... 'til Mama found out, at least."

"What'd she do?"

"Tore me up and made me turn him back loose in the woods." He turns away before I can react, taking the front steps two at a time. "Careful," he says, motioning to the floor covered in dried leaves and debris, with daylight visible through a number of gaping holes.

An old wooden swing hangs by a rusty chain at the far end of the porch, giving the home a haunted, eerie feel. But I'm eager to explore all the dim recesses and secret nooks.

"Why does it have this kind of hallway?" I say as we cross from one side to the other.

"Called a dogtrot. Some call it a breezeway or dog run. The hall always faces north and south to funnel the wind. People used to sleep on 'em to get some air in the summer."

I pause at the kitchen, envisioning a woman pulling a steaming pan of cornbread from the oven. Children and dogs running in the yard; a man chopping kindling by the barn; neighbors arriving from down river for supper. How marvelous and simple life must have been for these people to have an island of their very own, away from the turmoil of the outside world.

A tiny door off the porch sits half open, so I peak inside expecting a broom closet but find a narrow staircase, instead.

Eli cranes his neck to see. "That's where the boys used to sleep. Go on up and take a look."

"You first," I say, eyeing the dark passage.

Eli eases up the creaking steps to the landing with me close behind. Light filters through open doors at each end of the room, illuminating a dusty space full of cobwebs but little else. A beefy, wooden four-poster bed with ancient-looking wire springs is the only item left.

I venture toward it, but stop when the floor begins to dip halfway across. It feels a bit spongy and unstable, so I turn with the intention of retracing my steps.

"Yeah, that's prob'ly a good idea," Eli says with a nod.

I'm almost to the landing when a board cracks under my foot, threatening to give way. My heart jumps into my throat as I lurch to the left, arms swinging wildly. When I catch my balance, I stand frozen as a million dreadful possibilities clank around in my head. Should I go forward? Backward? Stay completely still?

Eli's talking. Saying something in his slow, steady way. But I can't hear over the pounding in my ears. I'm afraid to move. To breathe. And even if I could, every choice seems wrong. A risk not worth taking.

Before I can make a decision, I'm off the floor with Eli's arms clamped around me. "I gotcha," he says, keeping me close.

He strokes my hair, whispering low as I sag against his chest. I feel like a fool but this is nice. More than nice, if I'm being honest ... I'm reluctant to pull away, but staying could prove more dangerous than falling to my death.

"We better get back to the boat," I say, forcing my feet down the stairs and out the door before I can change my mind.

Thump, thump, thump, comes a sound from under the porch.

I turn back to Eli, glad for the excuse to talk about something other than the elephant in the room. "What's that?"

He bends to peer through a hole in the floor. "Prob'ly just them hogs back."

"What're they doing under there?"

"Pullin' cover. Beddin' down for the night."

He steps around me and offers a hand down the steps, but I pretend not to see. After our encounter in the attic, I simply don't trust myself. Being out here is messing with my head. Carving a need that's stronger than logic.

But I know this song and dance. I've been here before. So on the ride back to the houseboat, I focus on another kind of hunger. The emptiness in my stomach. There's leftover deer hash in the icebox, but I have something better in mind.

While Eli is busy cleaning out the boat, I gather the ingredients for a gumbo and set about making a roux in a black iron skillet. The task brings back the memory of Mr. Lavergne's loving instruction, and in no time, a rich fragrance fills the air.

Eli stomps through the door and peeks over my shoulder. "Is that what I think it is? Sure smells good."

"It tastes even better."

After polishing off two bowls, he leans back in his chair with a smile. "You really didn't have to cook, but that was damn good. I'm full as a tick. You know, keepin' house with you ain't half bad. That Jeffrey's a lucky man."

I should feel flattered, but the compliment makes me uncomfortable. I shake my head. "Based on this meal, I doubt he'd agree."

"Why's that?"

"He's not into Cajun food. Or anything too spicy."

Eli's eyebrows shoot up in amusement. "How'd you two meet, anyway?"

"Through a mutual friend," I say, standing to clear the table.

He puts out a hand. "No, no. I'll get all this in a minute. Tell me 'bout it. Did ol' Jeffrey wine and dine you?"

I eye Eli for a moment and sit back down. "I don't know

about wine and dine, but we ... uh ... grew on each other I guess you could say."

"Sounds romantic," Eli mumbles, unimpressed.

"Have you ever been on a blind date?"

"That bad, eh?"

"Worse." I smile at the memory of our disastrous first date.

Jeffrey was just my type. Or so my friend promised. Apparently "my type" shows up an hour late, straight off the green and still in his golf clothes. We missed our reservation and ended up eating at the bar where Jeffrey spent most of the night slamming back drinks and making lame jokes. Later, he apologized for that awful first impression, explaining how he had just been through a bad breakup and initially wasn't even sure he wanted to come.

Eli sits up, his eyes sparkling with interest. "What happened?"

"Vomit happened. All over my floorboard, to be exact. Jeffrey blamed the sushi, but I think the eight mojitos probably had a lot to do with it."

"Wait. So, you're tellin' me this fool puked in your car on the first date and you gave him a second one?"

"Yeah. I mean, I guess I felt bad for him. He was so embarrassed. Luckily, the second date was a thousand times better. His family was hosting a benefit barbecue and they were so warm and welcoming. It was the first time since moving to Austin that I felt at home. And Jeffrey kept apologizing for being such an idiot. He was so cute, I couldn't help being charmed."

"If you say so." Eli tilts his head. "You didn't seem too happy with him this mornin'."

My chest squeezes at the thought. "It was just a disagreement. Nothing important."

"What you fightin' over?"

"We're not fighting."

Eli holds up his hands. "Okay, okay. What was the *disagreement* over?"

"Nothing."

"Tell me," he says, sincerely.

"It's just ... Jeffrey wants me to choose a different wedding dress," I admit.

"What's wrong with the one you have?"

"It's not white."

Eli stares at me and blinks.

"Well? Aren't you going to say anything?"

"I was just waitin' for you to finish tellin' me what's wrong with the dress."

"I already did."

"I guess I'm not followin'."

I throw my hands in the air. "I chose pink, or blush, or whatever it's called when I was supposed to choose white. Now Jeffrey's having a fit that people are going to think I'm ..."

Eli's brows shoot up. "Soiled?"

When I don't say anything, he kicks back his head and laughs.

"It's not funny."

He wipes his eyes. "So, you told him to go to hell, right?"

"Not exactly."

"You need to tell him you'll show up wearin' a burlap sack if you have a mind to ... In fact, you need to tell him he'll be *damn* lucky if you show up at all."

I look away. "That's a little much. Besides, Jeffrey has a valid point. I'm probably just being too hard on him."

"You're kiddin', right?"

Eli's opinion of Jeffrey makes me uncomfortable ... makes me question my own feelings about the man I'll soon vow to love and cherish, till death do us part.

"What about you? Why aren't you married?" I toss back.

"Ain't no gal ever blew my dress up, I don't guess."

"What about Minnie?"

"Who?"

"Never mind."

Eli brows come together. "You mean Minnie Harris from high school?"

I nod and look away, embarrassed I remembered her name.

"Ain't seen that girl in years."

"But you two were together for so long. Surely you came close to marriage."

"Close only counts in horseshoes and hand grenades."

"Don't you want a family one day? Or at least a ... wife?" I venture. Might as well get all my burning questions out at once.

He shrugs. "Used to think 'bout it, some. But that life ain't for me. Hell, my truck is more reliable than most of the women I've met."

I bristle at his rude generalization, but the whir of a motor outside interrupts. I follow Eli to the porch and squint into the darkness as the porch bulb sways, casting enough light to make out a boat pulling up. There are two men, both in sun-bleached overalls left unbuttoned to reveal trim waistlines shimmering with sweat.

"Hey, doll," one calls to Eli, who lifts a hand in greeting.

The man in front loops his arm around a post and tilts his head to the side, grinning as he glances from Eli to me.

The pair make small talk for a few minutes, but keep their eyes on me the majority of the time. Their bold curiosity makes me uncomfortable, so I retreat to a seat on the swing and fiddle with a loose string on my shorts.

When they ask us to join them at Foster's Bluff, Eli grins and takes a chew of tobacco. "Naw, think we'll pass this time."

"Guess you got better things to do," the man in front says with a nod in my direction.

Eli ignores the insinuation and bends to shove their boat out into the current. "You boys try not to get in too much trouble."

The pair laugh loudly and make a show of gunning the motor as they speed away.

"You don't want to go with them?" I say.

Eli shakes his head, staring after them. "They're a rowdy bunch. Remember the first time I met them two boys. I was prob'ly fourteen or so, back on Horseshoe Lake checkin' limb lines early one mornin'."

I lean back and set the swing in motion with a gentle

push, enjoying the cadence Eli's voice takes on as he begins the tale.

"It was February and damn cold, so I built me a li'l fire there on the bank and waited for it to get daylight. There'd been some ice 'round the pirogue that mornin' and I had to make me a little fire in a coffee can to keep warm once I got out on the water."

"A coffee can? Really?"

"Yeah. You just put a roll of toilet paper inside and pour rubbin' alcohol over it. But there's other ways too."

"And it really works?"

"Works good enough when you're freezin' to death." He laughs. "Anyhow, I was out there checkin' lines when I heard a man holler, 'Whoop! Hey, doll baby!'"

"I heard them call you that. What's it mean?"

He shrugs. "Just somethin' them boys over in Caney Head've always called each other."

"Well, it's better than what you've been calling *me*."

Eli grins. "So anyways, I looked up and saw two men walkin' up waist deep in that cold-ass water with them li'l boys swimmin' right behind 'em, tryin' to keep up. They was in there hog huntin' them ridges. Said they lost a dog and wanted to know if I'd seen it."

"Let me get this straight, those two little boys were the same guys I just met?"

"Yeah, but they was real li'l, maybe six or seven."

The idea hurts my heart. I stop the swing and lean closer. "What happened?"

"I asked if they needed any help. They said yeah and asked

to borrow my pirogue. Wanted me to get out and wait for 'em since it wouldn't hold all of us. I told 'em it'd flip with any more'n two people in it, but they wouldn't listen. I offered to take them kids over to the bank, one at a time, where I could build a fire and let 'em warm up. Told 'em they could pick up the boys on their way back through. But they wouldn't have it. Hardheaded sons-a-bitches. Said they'd get on just like they had been. But I swear them two li'l boys was some of the toughest kids I ever saw."

"Sounds like they didn't have much choice."

CHAPTER 12

Fluttering overhead catches my eye. A tiny screech owl up in the porch rafters.

Eli walks to where it sits and raises an arm. After a moment, the owl steps onto his hand.

"How did you get it to do that?" I whisper, afraid of scaring it away.

"Are there any pieces of raw chicken left?" Eli says in a low voice.

I grab some and watch as Eli offers it to the owl. My jaw drops when the bird eats its fill from his fingertips and flies out into the night.

"That was amazing," I breathe. "It wasn't scared at all. I had no idea they would do that."

"They don't." He steps to the sink and washes his hands. "Raised that one from a baby. Found him out in the woods a while back. He still comes 'round every now and then lookin' for a handout."

Something inside me softens at the thought. It's a side of Eli I didn't expect to see and don't want to acknowledge. Doing so would mean I might be wrong about him. About everything.

He pulls a fifth of Jack out of the cooler and holds it out. When I wave it away, he takes a seat beside me on the swing, his long body draped casually, the scent of whiskey more enticing than any cologne on the market.

I don't want to think about the feel of his knee pressed against mine. Or the way that one little touch is able to make my mouth go dry, my insides quivering in anticipation of something that can never, will never, be.

I pull my phone from my pocket and stare at the screen where my unanswered texts are a sad reminder of my fight with Jeffrey. He's had plenty of time to cool off. To see that he's being completely unreasonable. But he's not giving an inch and the idea that he's avoiding me on purpose stokes a fire in the pit of my stomach I've been fighting to keep at bay.

"Hey," Eli says, nudging me gently. "What you say we go huntin' tonight?"

"Hunting for what?"

"It's a surprise."

"I don't know ... "

"Come on, pasquale. You'll have fun, promise."

Not in the mood for joking, I bristle. "Why do you keep calling me that? What's it even mean?"

"Pissin' dog."

"You're lying."

"Well ... I prob'ly am. But we got better things to do than argue 'bout it." He stands, reaching into the rafters for a spear that looks like a miniature pitchfork.

"Unless you plan on hunting up some snakeroot with that thing, shouldn't we be turning in for the night?" I say, a bit wary of whatever mystery adventure Eli has in mind.

"We'll have plenty of time for that tomorrow. You say you wanna open a big game ranch, so why don't you let me show what real huntin's like?"

"Fine," I concede. I'll never admit it to him, but I'm intrigued by the invitation to do ... well, whatever it is we're about to do.

With only the moon to light our way, we fly through the muggy night air across water that feels like glass. Crouched low in his seat, Eli holds the tiller handle in his left hand and the bottle of Jack in his right.

"How can you see out here?" I yell into his ear.

He points to the darkened tree line visible against the night sky. "Shows me the way the river's goin'. Long as I stay on the willow side, a floatin' log's the only thing I gotta worry 'bout in the dark."

"So how do you see those?"

"You don't."

I slide myself off the seat and onto the plywood floor for safe measure.

He nudges my shoulder. "Aw, I ain't gonna let nothin' happen to you and you know it."

I realize Eli has the river memorized. Every bend. Every

danger. But I stay where I am, just in case. "Where're we headed, anyhow?"

"Gig some frogs."

I've heard of people gigging frogs and I'm certainly no stranger to crispy fried frog legs. But I prefer to view them as a delicacy, not some slimy creature plucked off the bank of a dirty river.

I wrinkle my nose. "You're going to eat them?"

"'Course I am," he huffs. "I ain't like them little city boys you're used to. I don't kill nothin' just to watch it die."

I swallow hard, knowing he's right. Most of our future ranch guests will be hunting for sport, not survival. It's a fact I chose to overlook in the past. But as I face the reality of such a venture, Eli's words leave me with a healthy amount of guilt.

We slow to turn into a small channel leading to a place Eli calls Sally Wither's Lake. He explains how the river cuts through the land to form a backwater lake from a low spot. "B'lieve it or not, best fishin' you'll find anywhere is right here."

I slide back up on my seat and lean over to let my fingers skim the inky surface, wondering what secrets might lie in the deep stillness. Calm and steady, the backwater isn't a fast-paced showboat like the main river, nor is it shallow and empty like a slough. It's an unassuming place most people will never notice. Never see. But like all things worthwhile, the backwater's offerings are only exceeded by its humility.

As we troll around the lake, Eli entertains me with the intriguing tale of Sally Wither's ghost seen hovering over the water. Shivering, I feel inclined to believe him as I look at the spooky and beautiful Spanish moss hanging in big, soft clumps from ancient cypress trees surrounded by knees. Narrow on top and wide on bottom, the trees have velvety green moss growing around the base above the waterline and long, thin leaves, airy like a cedar, but softer to the touch.

I point to two big stumps with notches cut deep into the flesh of the trunk, about eight or ten inches. "What's that from? Do you know?"

"Just another ghost of the Piney Woods ... 'bout like them mule pens we seen."

"But, why would they do that to the trees?"

"To hold spring boards for the loggers to stand on back in the old days."

"Wow. It must've been hard for them to work in an area constantly covered with water."

"They was a tough bunch, that's for sure." Eli spits a stream of tobacco juice over the edge of the boat.

I wrinkle my nose. "That's really gross, you know. And unhealthy. And ..."

He looks at me like I'm crazy. "And what?"

"Unattractive," I blurt. "No woman wants to kiss a man with that crap in his mouth."

"So, you've thought 'bout kissin' me, huh?"

"What? No!"

"But you've thought about somebody else kissing me?"

"Stop trying to aggravate me."

He holds both hands up. "Hey, you're the one who brought it up."

"Whatever," I say, turning to lock eyes with a giant brown

spider clinging to the silvery green bark of the nearest tree. Its resemblance to a tarantula makes me suck in my breath.

Eli notices too and reaches around to grab at the vile creature. I squeal and claw my way onto his lap, away from the predator who skitters up the tree and out of sight.

Eli's arms settle around me, his chest shaking with laughter. But white hot rage makes me stand abruptly, knocking him off his seat with a satisfying thump.

"Well, that was just plain hateful," he says, clambering back to his perch. "That lil' ol' spider wouldn't hurt nobody."

"Don't try to piss on my leg and tell me it's raining, Eli LeBlanc," I say, testing one of Mr. Lavergne's favorite sayings.

His eyebrows shoot up and a slow grin spreads across his face. "Well, ain't you gettin' sassy."

I scoot as far away from Eli as I can manage and swat a mosquito that lands on my neck. They swarm much thicker here than on the main river. Rarely seen over moving water, the backwater is a breeding ground for the little varmints, and the knowledge makes me want to bathe in a pool of DEET, side effects be damned.

In the dim glow of Eli's headlight, I find a half-used bottle of insect repellent and the strong fragrance makes me cough as it mingles with the smell of his chewing tobacco and the thick scent of stagnant mud.

Rolling down my sleeves, I stare at my stained denim work shirt. "I must look awful."

"Why you say that, pasquale?"

"Well, just look at me ..."

Eli grows still as his eyes soften with unquestioning acceptance. River Rats don't care about appearances. Never have. Never will. To them, sweat and grime means progress. A sign of hard work. A badge of honor. But Eli's gaze holds more than that. More than I'm prepared to acknowledge.

I stand and make for the front bow, but he asks me to wait and shoves a silver spotlight into my hand, its long spiral cord plugged into the 12-volt battery sitting on the floor. He points to the bank and tells me to shine the waterline looking for "white Styrofoam cups."

"I thought we were looking for frogs ..."

"We are. Their bellies are white like a cup. Just keep shinin' and you'll see 'em."

I wave the light left and right, traveling the bank as we troll down the waterway for what feels like forever. Then I spot it. A small glimpse of white next to a cypress knee.

"There! Over there!"

"You're blindin' me, woman," Eli says with a laugh when I accidentally cast the beam his way. He takes the light and hands me the tiny pitchfork. "Okay, when we get close enough, stick 'em."

I stare at the frog and start to take aim, but doubt creeps in. "You do it and I'll drive," I say, losing my nerve.

He silently takes the gig, but the disappointment on his face is evident. Does he think I'm a big chicken? Should I even care?

Before I can overthink it even more, I grab the gig from his hand. "I've changed my mind."

As the boat inches closer to the bank, I'm shocked to see the frog hasn't moved a muscle. Gathering all my courage, I draw in a deep breath, take aim, and let it fly. Instead of hitting my target, the gig lodges itself deep into the sticky mud about a foot from the frog and just out of reach.

"Just grab him with your hands," Eli hollers. "You can reach him. Hurry!"

With a rush of adrenaline, I pounce out of the boat like an awkward cat and manage to flatten the frog to the ground. But the clammy prey is high strung and it takes quite a bit of effort to keep it from escaping.

"Yeah! You got him! Here let's put him in this." Eli holds open a burlap bag and gives me a big smile. "You just might turn out after all, pasquale."

I'm covered in mud, but grinning from ear to ear. "You think so?"

"I *know* so. You're doin' a damn sight better than most for your first time. Hell, there was a time when me and my buddies couldn't even manage to get out on the water, much less gig frogs."

"Really?" I say, clambering back into the boat.

"Oh yeah. Remember one night when me and Gator and Colorado went giggin' in a li'l slough behind my pawpaw's house. I brought along my brand-new gig for the occasion, but we didn't see nothin', not even one. So, we figured we'd borrow Pawpaw's boat and try our luck in a backwater lake. But that ol' boat was dry docked in the woods across the slough and it needed a battery. So, we took the one off Gator's truck and headed through the slough on foot. Gator had hold of the battery, Colorado had the gig, a gun, and the light, and I had the ice chest full of beer."

"Naturally," I smirk.

"I tell ya we didn't get twenty feet 'fore Gator decides to go and get bit by a damn snake. Just a li'l ol' water snake, but he yelled like he was dyin' and ended up throwin' the battery out in the slough tryin' to get away from it. So, Colorado spends forever pokin' 'round with the gig tryin' to find the battery and ended up loosin' the gig too."

Eli's story brings a smile to my face as we continue through the backwater, filling our bags. One low lying area is too shallow for the boat, so we pull on our rubber boots and take our time, weaving down the narrow banks on foot. With practice, I get pretty good using my hands, as well as the gig. But I'm more taken with the atmosphere of the forest, all blue and black and silver in the moonlight.

Lightning bugs glisten in the underbrush as the sound of crickets and frogs fill the air. From the deep throaty groan of the bullfrog to the high-pitched "*naaa, dirk, dirk, dirk*" of the rain frog, the night echoes nature's lullaby in a song too ordinary to praise, too intricate to replicate.

"How do we know when we've caught the legal limit?" I say, stepping over a fallen log.

Eli gives a short laugh. "Don't worry 'bout that. Out here we make our own rules."

I can appreciate what he did to help Tonya and her kids, but I can't justify disregarding the law at every turn. "So you're telling me you just take as much as you want without answering to anyone?"

"Yep."

"Isn't that kind of greedy?"

He stops walking and turns. "Listen, I never take more'n I need or more'n I can use. But I'll be damned if anybody, short of the Lord himself, is gonna tell me how much that is."

I wait a moment before speaking, trying to choose my words while standing firm. "I can see that making sense if this was your property. But it's not. It's mine."

"That's right. This is your land and you have every right to tell me to hit the road. But that ain't the point."

"Well, what *is* your point? I'd really like to know." The words come out harsher than I intend, but I can't bring myself to calm down.

"The point is, you may own this land, but you don't know a damn thing about it." I open my mouth to argue, but Eli holds up a hand. "It's the people like me, and all the other families 'round here that really care 'bout it. Understand it. No, it ain't legally ours, but we love it just the same. And sure, we hunt and fish a lot, but we also keep an eye on the game. If you look, you'll see most every house in the Pocket has a hog pen out back. If the herds start to thin, we'll pen some up. Raise a few litters until we get the numbers back up. See we take our responsibility to the land seriously. Because it's a part of who we are. Who we've always been." His head drops and when he clears his throat, my own squeezes tight. "Listen, Sunday. You have every right to fence this place off and turn it into some fancy resort for rich people, but I'm askin' you to think long and hard about how it would affect the rest of us. You might hold the deed, but it's *our* home too."

His words sting, but I'm not ready to give in. "Have you thought about the fact that we'd be creating jobs? That this whole area would become a tourist destination? We'd be doing the community a favor."

"Sure you might create a few jobs, but not enough to quench the anger you're gonna stir up. Just look at what happened with Cat's Island. Hell, you'd have a damn war on your hands."

"You don't have to be so dramatic."

"I'm just tellin' you the truth." He grabs my hand and holds tight. "Listen to me, Sunday. You're smart. And you have so much to offer. So much to give. If you want to do good for the community, then do it. Do somethin' truly *good*. Not this."

CHAPTER 13

As we poke along the bank, Eli's words take root in my chest, dangerously close to my heart. He has a way of making me question myself that I despise. But also crave. It's a crazy feeling. Like being under water too long and not knowing which way is up.

Lost in thought, I crash into his back when he skids to a stop. He spins, catches me, and signals to be quiet.

In the distant water, baby ducklings flutter to and fro in a panic as a large bobcat relaxes on a log overhead. He casually swats at them from the perch, enjoying his game of cat and mouse in hopes of catching one for dinner.

We stare in silence a moment before Eli yells and waves his arms causing the confused cat to shoot off into the darkness.

"In all my years, I ain't never seen one do that..." he breathes, shaking his head, "...and prob'ly never will again."

"What about that stuffed one at your house?"

"Ha, well I caught him trappin' one winter."

"You trap a lot?"

"Some. It's decent money now that the market's gettin' a li'l better. Won't never be as good as it was when we were kids, though. Caught that bobcat with a number three coil spring trap baited with a rabbit head in a dirt hole set—"

"Dirt hole set?"

"It's where you dig a hole and throw the bait inside. Then you set the trap out beside the hole that way when the varmint comes nosyin' around, he'll walk right into it."

"That sounds like the opening scene of a horror movie."

"I tell ya it felt like one too when I went back the next mornin' and the damn trap was gone way up in the woods and I couldn't see what had it. I crawled up in them briars a li'l ways and found me a big ol' stick that I'd throw and listen for the chain to rattle, tryin' to see where it was. 'Bout that second throw, the chain rattled alright, and the damn thing jumped at me. Liked to scared me to death. Luckily, the drag was hung up and it caught about two feet away from gettin' me. Only critter ever scared me that bad in my life."

"Is that why you kept him?"

"S'pect so. Remember the first time I ever saw a bobcat. Must've been 'bout three or four. Uncle Wyatt called him a swamp cat but when I tried to say it, it came out 'wampus cat.' Everybody got a good laugh, and it stuck."

"Ah, so that explains it," I say, thinking of the inscription on the side of his boat. Out here like this, it's easy to envision a young, towheaded Eli balancing on his uncle's back, hunting along these same misty banks all those years ago. It's only a small glimpse into his childhood, but part of me longs to have known that little boy—to have grown up with him, running wild through these same woods, catching lightning bugs at dusk on summer evenings and swinging from rattan vines in the cool shade of the tall pines.

"You've mentioned your uncle a few times, but I haven't heard you talk about your dad much."

"Don't know who he is."

"Oh ... I'm sorry ... I didn't realize," I fumble, hoping I haven't overstepped my bounds.

He shakes his head. "I was touchy 'bout it when I was a kid, but not no more. It was always just me and Mama. 'Course, she ain't real easy to deal with. My uncle was the one I could tie off to."

"Where's your mom now?"

Eli's lips form a tight line. "Don't know. Ain't seen her since the night I graduated and don't 'spect I ever will again."

MY PHONE DINGS AND I'M INSTANTLY AWAKE, GRABBING AT it through the bedsheets, anxious to see Jeffrey's name on the screen. It's completely unlike him to stay mad for so long, and I hate being the cause.

But as I read Emma's short text, my heart sinks to a new low. She wants to know how I'm doing.

I'm quick to say I'm fine, but it's far from the truth. It would take more than a text to explain my current emotional state. I'd love to focus on nothing but my work, but Jeffrey's silence is wearing on me. Hard.

The way I see it, I have two choices. I can fight him to the death. Or give in.

Fighting seems utterly pointless. What's the use of getting my way if it makes him so unhappy? Shouldn't I want to please my soul mate more than myself, especially on our wedding day? Good relationships are about compromise. Choosing your battles. So, if the dress means that much to him, I can bend. Better to bend than to break.

I click Jeffrey's name and send yet another message, this time begging him to forgive me and agreeing to a new dress for the ceremony. Anything to make him happy. Anything to start our marriage out on the right foot.

"You up yet?" Eli calls from outside.

He's anxious to get on the road and so am I. It's much easier to focus on locating snakeroot for Doc, than obsessing over my personal problems.

"You know how to get to Charlie Shankle's?" I say, sliding into the passenger seat of Eli's Chevy.

"'Bout a mile East of Belle Terre, right?"

Charlie and Sister Faye's tiny blue wood frame house was one of the few places I felt comfortable visiting as a kid. Filled to the brim with grandchildren and bright laughter, it was always okay to drop by unannounced after school for a healthy slice of Sister Faye's lemon meringue pie and a 'word' from the Lord if she felt so inclined.

"Are you sure Charlie's the person to ask about snakeroot?" I say, unable to envision the weathered pulpwood driver as having a penchant for herbs.

Eli eyebrows shoot up. "If anybody'll have it, it'll be Charlie. His granddaddy was part Coushatta, you know. Come from a long line of medicine men."

"What? You're kidding."

"Charlie's not one to brag, but he's sharp as a tack 'bout that stuff."

When we pull up, Charlie is busy loading a washing machine onto a lowboy trailer. Eli hops out and offers to help, but Charlie waves him off with a flash of his dazzling white teeth. "I got it," he says, wrapping his muscular arms around the machine and lifting it onto the trailer with impressive ease. I can't recall ever seeing such a rugged display of brute strength and sheer testosterone by any man, let alone a grandfather. However, no wrinkles are visible on his dark, glistening skin, making it impossible to tell his true age.

"Is that you, Miss Sunday?" Charlie asks, still smiling as he steps off the trailer.

"Yes, sir. It's nice to see you again." I give him a hug. "Is Sister Faye home?"

He shakes his head. "She's workin' today, but I'll tell 'er you asked after 'er, sure will."

As the longtime head waitress at Dorothy's Café on Main Street, Sister Faye's welcoming smile is as much a part of the establishment's fabric as the fresh biscuits, sticky table cloths, and low hum of daytime soaps from the television over the bar. I make a mental note to stop in for breakfast one morning. Catch up. Maybe bring Jeffrey along to meet everyone.

Or then again, maybe not.

After a recent trip to my favorite hole-in-the-wall barbecue joint ended with him calling the health department, I vowed to never make the same mistake. I can't blame Jeffrey for having high standards, but the fate of the oldest and most beloved diner in Old Salem is certainly not worth the risk.

Charlie bends forward to dab his brow with a handkerchief before shaking Eli's hand. "What can I help you with, Mr. LeBlanc?"

"Lookin' for some snakeroot, Charlie. You know where we can get some?"

"Well, I sure do. Y'all just come up on the porch." Charlie motions for us to follow. "How much you need? I'll go bag it up."

Eli hesitates. "No, sir. What we mean to say is we need to know where it grows. What it looks like. And we'd pay you for your time, of course."

Charlie purses his lips and looks at the ground, shaking his head back and forth. "I'd sure love to show you. Yes, sir. But I can't give away my honey hole. My granddaddy give it to me 'fore he died, and I gotta keep it in the family."

"Well, I sure can respect that," Eli says with a nod even as I shake my head. "Thank you for your time."

"Wait a minute," Charlie says, eyeing us. "You ever try snakeroot?"

"No, sir," we say in unison.

"Oh, you gots to be careful with snakeroot." He holds up his hands. "See, it'll grab you." He fists one hand to demonstrate, then pauses dramatically. "And it'll let you go," he says, releasing his fist. He repeats the action. "And it'll grab you ... and it'll let you go."

The side effects of snake root are one thing, but my true concern is Eli's reluctance to press the issue as Charlie waves goodbye.

"You gave up too easy," I whisper, sprinting to keep up with Eli's long strides.

"Got another idea."

❧

AS WE LIE ON THE DAMP GROUND SHROUDED IN DARKNESS later that night, Eli's meaning becomes clear. From our lookout, Charlie's house stands illuminated in the distance. But I can't help squirming as I imagine spiders—or worse—crawling over my skin, and I'm certain something is inching its way up my leg.

"Be still," Eli whispers.

"I'm trying. Can't we go back to the truck? We've been out here forever."

"Shh, think I see him."

Charlie's dark figure strolls off the porch and out to the main road with a shovel in one hand and a bucket in the other.

"How do you know he's even getting snakeroot tonight?" I say. "He could be headed anywhere."

"Just a hunch."

Eli helps me to my feet, and we creep through the woods, keeping an eye on Charlie's shadow walking along the moonlit dirt road. After about half a mile, his figure disappears into a dark alcove of woods.

Eli motions to stop walking. "That brush is too thick for us to follow without making a bunch of noise," he whispers.

"Well that was a waste of time," I say, irritated to be a part of such a wild goose chase.

"It doesn't have to be."

"What do you mean?"

"Look," he says, pointing to the outline of the large iron gate looming directly to our left. "You up for a little bit of fun?"

I take a step back. "Oh *hell* no!"

"What's the matter?"

"What's the matter with *me*? What's the matter with *you*?" I shriek. "We need to get out of here."

Eli laughs. "You know this place, then?"

"Everybody knows The Cult."

"Aw, come on. You really gonna b'lieve a bunch of rumors?"

"In this instance, I'm willing to wholeheartedly embrace any and all rumors," I say as childhood tales flood back, making me sweat.

Logic tells me The Cult is nothing more than the private residence of some reclusive millionaire who decided Old Salem, Texas was as near to the middle of nowhere as a person can possibly get. But after more than a decade of listening to Emma's intense speculation, another part of me says something more sinister is at play. When she was no more than ten or eleven, she managed to set up an interview with the local sheriff to record his account of a rather disturbing visit he had made to The Cult a few years prior. She would sit and listen to it for hours, jotting notes in her little pink notebook. But the shrewd young investigator didn't stop there. Sightings from surrounding residents were also taken into account, with a favorite being the tale of a beautiful woman in an expensive evening gown sighted crouching at the front gate, hysterical and sobbing. She was said to have denied distress and refused help—a common occurrence among cult members who were thought to be held captive under penalty of corporal punishment involving an infamous wooden paddle. Emma was also convinced the property had large underground fortresses, existing for unknown reasons, all connected by a series of tunnels; a white stone sacrificial altar; a helicopter landing pad; white tigers who roamed freely; and men armed with machine guns who patrolled the perimeter, ready to chase down intruders, most of which were local thrill-seeking teenagers. As a result, legends surrounding The Cult expanded over the years, providing more delightful entertainment and speculation than our community could possibly hope for and certainly ever keep straight.

There was a time when I believed these spectacular tales were all too sensational to be real. But that was before the era of reality television, where documentaries featuring cults seem to dominate. Now I'm inclined to think literally anything is possible.

"Come on, I know where there's a hole in the fence," Eli whispers, unfazed by my concerns.

Before I can answer, he grabs my hand and pulls me forward.

Thanks to Emma, I know the perimeter of the twenty-acre compound consists of two separate fences, five strands of barbed wire each, placed eight feet apart and running parallel to one another. Inside the gap, wild roses are planted among many layers of relocated tree stumps with their root systems intact.

But this doesn't stop Eli from barreling toward the back fence like there's nothing to fear. As I'm dragged along, I look up at the silhouettes of the tall pines and envision cameras documenting our every move. Security guards with inflated egos and high powered rifles waiting to pounce. The thought of being captured is absolutely terrifying. But if I'm being perfectly honest, it's also kind of fun.

Who have I become? Maybe I'm going crazy. Temporary insanity or something like that. That's probably why hermits are so odd; leave someone in the woods long enough and they turn into a lunatic.

Eli indicates a bare spot in the roses and I feel myself nod as if I have no control over my body. I take a step forward, but before I get far, he pulls me back, flush against his hard chest. His hands settle on my hips and he's saying something. Telling me to wait. I try to focus on his words, but I haven't felt this lightheaded … well … ever, come to think of it.

Since that disastrous night at The Flame, I've developed strict views on physical affection prior to wedding vows. And no amount of begging from Jeffrey will change my mind. Sure, I'll allow the occasional kiss, but I'm proud of my restraint and never feel the need to go further.

But Eli's touch is different. Electric in a way that makes

me sure it isn't real. It's simply a side effect of the situation. Adrenaline affects the brain in the same manner as falling in love. That's why a first date to a scary movie works like a charm. It's an illusion. A trick.

I freeze as Eli's head bends toward my neck, his breath tickling my ear. "There, got it," he whispers, breaking the spell as he untangles a vine from my hair.

A wave of disappointment crashes over me, but Eli continues on, oblivious to the direction of my wayward thoughts.

No security lights are visible when we break through the thick barrier of roses. But as we inch away from the fence, I'm able to make out the dark shapes of buildings in the distance. The largest stands off by itself, with turrets and gables reaching into the sky like something out of a Brontë novel.

"Let's get out of here, before someone catches us," I hiss, anxious for our little adventure to be over.

"Come on, Sunday. I have a surprise I want to show you."

Car lights flash at the front gate and a bell sounds, making me nearly jump out of my skin.

"I'm not staying here a minute longer!" Not waiting for his reply, I take off running toward the fence. If Eli wants to hang around and get himself killed, that's his choice. I don't have to participate. Or care.

Fear and anticipation build in my stomach like a balloon ready to pop as I fight my way back through the vines and run down the edge of the road toward his Chevy. Years of wear are evident in the many scratches and dents, and I'm convinced the old flatbed is the same ragged-out truck Eli had in high school—complete with a long CB antenna, stray shotgun shells, and half-empty whiskey bottles rolling around on the floorboard. Slipping inside, I sit twisting the fibers of the navy and brown saddle blanket seat covers, too frightened to start the engine.

I check my phone. No service, as usual.

"Damn it," I say, holding it up to every window, hoping for a miracle.

I squint through the dirty windshield and try to spot movement outside. But my eyes rest on a peculiar necklace made of leather cord hanging from the rearview mirror. It holds a small, glass bottle that rattles when I touch it, but I can't risk turning on the lights to see what's inside.

So I sit waiting. And waiting. And waiting.

With no sign of Eli, my nerves are shot. I don't know what to do. He could be in trouble. And if that's the case, I can't waste any more time. I have to go for help.

Gathering my courage, I slide into the driver's seat. With only rudimentary knowledge of how to drive a standard, my left foot finds the clutch and my right the brake. I try to crank the engine, but the key won't budge. I shake it up and down, back and forth, until it finally turns, and the truck rumbles to life. I rev the engine and when I release the clutch, the truck lurches forward.

"Shit!"

Still in first gear, the engine growls as I attempt to accelerate and the speedometer wobbles back and forth between six and seven miles per hour. At this rate, I'll never make it all the way to Irene's, so I head to Belle Terre, only a half-mile away. But I don't get far before a flicker of movement catches my eye. Straining to see, I slow the truck to a crawl and the engine lurches a few times before stalling. Whatever it is has disappeared into the shallow road ditch up ahead to the left. Rattling the keys, I attempt to breathe life back into the sleepy pickup by pulling and prodding every lever I can find as my feet work the pedals. Beads of sweat run down my face and coat my shaking hands, making it almost impossible to grip the wheel as I envision the sinister form tracking my every move with steely gray eyes, just waiting for the perfect opportunity to pounce.

Something slaps the window by my head and I scream. I make for the rifle in the gun rack, but the door opens and a hand covers my mouth.

This is it. They've got me. I'm dead. I just hope it's quick.

"It's me. Scoot over," comes a low, familiar voice.

Relief washes over me as Eli pushes his way inside the cab and deftly cranks the engine. I sag against him, both loving and hating him as I try to catch my breath.

"Why didn't you wait for me, pasquale?"

"Stop calling me that, unless you plan on telling me what the hell it means, for real," I shriek. "What on earth took you so long?"

He wipes his forearm across his brow and changes gears. "If you would've stayed I could've showed you."

"You're crazy you know that? I don't know why I let you talk me into going in there in the first place. We were supposed to be looking for snakeroot not gallivanting around trying to get ourselves killed!"

"Believe me when I say I'd never let anything happen to you. And I'm sure Doc'll understand about the snakeroot."

I want to give him a healthy piece of my mind, but decide not to press the issue. If I get started, I might not be able to stop.

"I just have one question," Eli asks after a few moments. "Where in hell did you learn to drive a standard?"

I glare at him. "It's your fault for staying gone so long."

"Yeah, I guess it is." He lifts an eyebrow. "But I think you might owe me a new clutch."

"What you need is a whole new truck. This one's falling apart."

Eli clutches his chest. "Me and Lucille have made a lot of miles together. Been to almost every state in the country. Can't just throw 'er away now," he says, patting the dash.

"All over the country, eh? If you were that good of a bull rider, why'd you quit?"

"Naw, I'm not talkin' 'bout that. Never was too good at the rodeo life, but I'm a damn good welder." He jerks his head toward the truck bed. "Don't have my machine on the back right now, though."

"Why aren't you off working then?"

"That's the beauty of construction. Only work when I feel like it."

"Is that why you live on the river? Because it's cheap?" I regret the words the second they leave my mouth. But, as usual, couth has taken a backseat to curiosity.

"Cheap ain't got nothin' to do with it, pasquale."

I pause and try to choose my words more carefully. "I'm sorry. I wasn't trying to be offensive but... "

"But what?"

"Well ... don't you want to make something more of your life? Rise to new heights?"

"Why?"

His question is simple, but I struggle to come up with an answer. "Lots of reasons."

"Name one."

"Respect." I smile, proud of myself for not dropping the ball.

Eli rolls his window down just low enough to spit. "Only kind of respect I want is the kind I already have. People 'round here respect me 'cause I've earned it." He turns to me and his brows pinch together. "Don't you ever get tired of all the bullshit? Everybody tellin' you how to live and how to think. Out here I'm free to be myself and it's enough."

The air leaves my lungs as his words hit their mark, sharp and swift as an arrow.

"Is that why you went to school? For respect?" he continues.

"I guess ... in a way. Mama Pearl always expected me to go. Wanted me to do all the things she missed out on, you know? But I'm glad I went. I can't imagine doing anything else."

"What about Jeffrey?" Eli says.

"What about him?"

"What does he want out of life? Besides your inheritance, that is."

I flinch. "Now you're just being rude."

"It's the truth."

"No it's not! Why does everybody keep saying that?"

Eli's eyes widen. "Oh, so I ain't the only one?"

I bite the inside of my lip until it hurts. "I'm not discussing this with you."

"Hey, if you wanna be his sugar mama, get after it."

"That's preposterous. Jeffrey comes from a very wealthy family."

"That's right. His *family* has money. Not him. And why wouldn't he want to play the big Texas rancher with somebody else's inheritance? Hell, you made it easy for him."

My eyes sting. "I don't know why you're being so hateful."

"I tell you what, I'll give you the chance to shut me up once and for all."

"I don't believe you."

He puts his hand over his heart. "Give you my word. It all hinges on one question."

"Which is?"

"Did Jeffrey propose *before* or *after* he found out about your inheritance?"

My mouth goes dry and it's suddenly very hard to breathe.

"So it *was* after." Eli's words are slow and deliberate and needlessly cruel. "Tell me, how long did he wait? A week? Maybe two? No, it wouldn't have been that long, I don't reckon."

Jeffrey proposed three days after his first trip to Belle Terre, but I've never connected the two events. Honestly, the idea that Eli would make such an assumption is absurd. To Eli, Jeffrey's nothing more than an outsider, and outsiders are not to be trusted. This small-minded redneck attitude is blinding him to Jeffrey's better qualities. And perhaps even sparking a bit of jealousy. Eli may be strong in his own way, free out on the river. But Jeffrey is refined, educated, and ambitious—everything Eli will never be.

My relationship with Jeffrey may not have been love at first sight, but I learned a long time ago not to believe in fairy tales. That's not how the real world works.

CHAPTER 14

The shrill sound of the CB radio interrupts Eli's rude assumptions and stifles my retort.

"How 'bout you, Wampus Cat?" a man's voice asks. "You got your ears on? Can I get a radio check?"

Eli picks up the mic. "Your check's in the mail, Colorado."

"What am I puttin' on you?" the man asks.

"Got me pinned out. You runnin' barefoot?"

"Yes, sir, need a new linear. Listen, we goin' on a li'l ride tonight. Meet us over on the pipeline."

"Ten-four, good buddy." Eli hangs up. "You up for a ride, pasquale?"

I remain silent, staring out the passenger window.

Eli leans over and elbows me. "Aw, come on. Don't be like that."

I'm aggravated and it's getting late. I want to make him take me back to the houseboat. To tell him I'm done playing nice. But I can't help cutting my eyes to the left. "What kind of ride?"

"Mud ride. Gonna meet up with some friends. You'll like it, I promise."

"Are you sure I'm *allowed* to go this time?"

Eli faces me, but I refuse to look him in the eye. "What're you talkin' 'bout?"

The old memory is as clear in my mind as when it happened. "You know exactly what I'm talking about. Don't act like you can't remember that night at The Flame."

Eli shifts in his seat and hesitates before responding. "Hey, I'm sure sorry 'bout how all that happened. I just did what I had to do to keep you safe."

"Safe from what? A good time?"

"Have you ever thought that maybe I knew somethin' 'bout Zack that you didn't?"

I swallow hard. "What do you mean?" Besides hearing the news of his shotgun wedding to Baylee Brown, I haven't thought about Zack VanPelt in years.

Eli makes a U-turn and pulls the truck over in the ditch. "What do you think I mean? Sweet little virgin shows up, gets shitfaced, and lets a guy like Zack drag her off to his truck. Have you ever stopped to think what might've happened if I hadn't been there? Just look at what happened to Baylee. We didn't call him Bareback Zack for nothin', you know."

My cheeks burn as his words sink in.

If what Eli says is correct, I'm embarrassed for how I've treated him. But I'm not ready to beg for his forgiveness either.

"Well, that was for me to decide. Not you."

"If you say so, pasquale."

I shake my head, done with his games. "Tell me what pasquale means. What it really means."

"It's prob'ly an old Indian word for a stubborn woman who likes to hold grudges."

I growl in frustration and smack at his chest. He avoids me by jumping out and heading toward the ice chest in the bed of the truck.

"Peace offerin'?" he asks, holding up a beer when he returns.

Knowing he's unlikely to relent any time soon, I reach for the ice-cold can, and my arm brushes against the necklace I noticed earlier.

I point to the small bottle. "What's that?"

"Just somethin' I found a long time ago," he says, turing up the radio.

I take a sip of beer and close my eyes, resting an arm on the open window as the clear rhythm of Lynyrd Skynyrd's "Simple Man" brings me back. I must've played this record a thousand times growing up. But alone in my room, it wasn't the same. Wasn't as real. This is the way it was meant to be enjoyed, thumping along a narrow backroad, pitted with holes and washouts as the notes mingle with the fresh fragrance of summer, sweet and green and warm.

Eli slows to study a clear-cut where loggers have stripped the land bare, leaving a jumbled span of earth and debris. "Hand me that one-eyed dog, would you?" he says, keeping his eyes on the cut.

I pass him a silver spotlight that's plugged into the cigarette lighter. "What're you doing?"

"Shinin' for deer."

I scoot to the middle seat and peer over his shoulder as the thin beam bounces along the distant tree line. "How do you see them?"

"At night the deer's eyes glow when you shine 'em. They'll stand there, real still, starin' at the light. And that's how you get 'em."

I slide back to the passenger seat. "So basically, it's just a lot easier this way?"

"Poor people have poor ways."

"Obviously."

Eli's face hardens. "We may not always be on the up and up, but we certainly aren't wasteful. We don't have that privilege."

A mile or so farther, we turn onto a smaller trail and, after much maneuvering through the thick woods, come to the pipeline. Headlights appear in the distance surrounded by shadowed forms weaving in and out. ZZ Top plays from someone's radio, and a woman's laughter rings through the night air.

Eli cuts off his headlights and rolls to a stop beside the biggest bonfire I've ever seen. A trailer house sits beyond and I realize we're parked in someone's backyard that adjoins the pipeline.

"Why'd we come this way?" I say, thinking there must surely be a regular road leading to the home.

"That's how everybody gets to Bobby Joe's. Place is landlocked. If he couldn't cut up through Belle Terre land, he wouldn't have access at all."

When Eli kills the engine, people holding beer cans turn to stare. A little self-conscious, I start to follow Eli out the driver's side door, but he holds up a hand. "Wait right there."

He pulls our rubber boots from the space between the cab and truck bed. I tug mine on and we join the crowd that's gathered to watch a young man in a stained ball cap shoot skeet from a machine set up for the occasion. I can't imagine how he's able to see the tiny clay pigeons in the dim light of the fire, but he seems to have no trouble hitting his target.

When he sees us, he sets the rifle down and walks over. "Now there's a sight for sore eyes. Where the hell you been, son?"

"Man, I been catchin' 'em faster'n I can string 'em." Eli pulls me up beside him and grabs the man's shoulder, giving him a playful shake. "This here no good some'a bitch is Colorado."

I offer my hand and introduce myself.

"Got ourselves a city gal here. Needs some initiation if you know what I mean?" Eli says in a conspiring tone.

I frown. "I'm not a city girl."

"So, you've been muddin' before?"

"Well ... not exactly."

"We gonna fix that," Colorado announces to all within hearing distance. He's obviously drunk and more than a little pleased for an excuse to show off.

A pretty young blonde in a camouflage bikini top and tattered jean shorts introduces herself as his girlfriend, Jess.

She lights a cigarette and looks me over with an appraising eye. "How long you and Eli been together?"

"No, no. We aren't together," I protest. "We just went to high school together. I live over in Old Salem."

Jess frowns. "Ain't never had much to do with that Old Salem bunch. But you seem alright. How long you gonna be in the Pocket?"

"A few days. I'm only staying with Eli until I'm done with my work." I cringe at my lame explanation. I sound more like a prostitute than a professional.

Jess bumps me with her elbow. "You ain't gotta explain it to me. Eli's a nice lookin' man. You'd be a fool to miss that."

"No, I—"

"Come on, let's do a shot." She grabs my hand and drags me through the crowd to a two-door Jeep with an ice chest attached to the rear bumper. "Here," she says, handing me a bottle of tequila while she pulls out some salt and a few limes. She looks at a man standing next to us. "Gimme your pocket knife," she says, holding out her hand. He pulls out a yellow-bone Case knife and opens it before handing it to Jess. She cuts the lime in half and hands it back to him with the blade left open as superstition demands. Just like eating peas and collard greens on New Year's Day, painting your porch ceiling haint blue, or not cutting your baby's hair before their first birthday, it's considered bad luck to hand a knife back any different than how it is originally received.

I mimic Jess as she licks the back of her hand and sprinkles it with salt. The tequila burns, but the salt and lime make it bearable.

"Let's do another one!" Jess says, pouring more salt on her hand. She chats in a rambling, familiar manner as we drink, filling me in on the details of the people around us without restraint. Before long, I know who's having an affair, who's trustworthy, who's a cheat, and to whom each person is related. In addition to knowing each individual's personal history, she also knows that of their ancestors. It's odd listening to her detail the comings and goings of people long dead, but I can't help enjoying myself. I speculate she's in her early twenties, but her speech is filled with colloquialisms common of a generation or two before her time.

Just as Jess is finishing up a story, Eli walks up and grabs the tequila bottle, examining its contents with raised brows.

"Slow down, woman. We got all night you know," he whispers, leaning close. His tone sends a jolt of electricity through me, and I can't help smiling as he studies my face. "Now, if I didn't know any better, I'd say you were havin' a good time."

My heart speeds up. Eli is clearly flirting with me. But the moment is cut short by the sound of someone squealing his name. I step back in time for some skinny thing to throw her arms around his neck, bouncing up and down in delight. Her stained white shorts are a size too small, and a tight-fitting red shirt reveals the swell of very large breasts. She has straight black hair and looks a few years older than Eli, but is still very attractive.

"Hey, Cheyenne," Eli says, leaning back in a way that tells me he's uncomfortable.

Engines rumble to life around us, signaling it's time to go.

But Cheyenne stays put, batting her lashes at Eli with blatant desire. "What you say we make a beer run, me and you?"

He loosens her hold around his neck with a grimace. "Got plenty of beer in my cooler."

She giggles and swats his shoulder. "Since when does that have anything to do with it?"

"You better watch Cheyenne. She has her cap set for Eli," Jess whispers.

Eli manages to untangle himself from Cheyenne's grip and nods in my direction. "You ready, pasquale?"

"Pasquale?" Cheyenne eyes me up and down. "What an unusual name."

"It's Sunday, actually," I correct.

She lets out a laugh of mock hysteria. "You're a hoot!" She turns back to Eli and runs her hand up and down his arm. "Your friend is so funny."

He gives me a meaningful look. "You ready?"

"Of course I am!" Cheyenne interjects, pulling him toward the truck.

"Well, I … uh, don't have a lot a room …" Eli says, sounding a bit strangled.

"Oh, that's fine. I don't mind squeezin' in the middle."

Skipping ahead, Cheyenne scrambles into the driver's side of the truck.

When I head for the passenger side, Eli's strong grip pulls me back. "Oh no you don't," he says, leading me to the driver's side door.

"I really don't mind sitting—"

"Hush!" he demands, covering my mouth with his hand. I

consider biting him but don't want to cause a scene. "Please get in," he whispers in a pitiful tone. "I need you to be in the middle."

"Fine. But you owe me."

When Cheyenne sees my intention, she gives me a glare and slides over with jerky movements. I can't figure out why Eli would go through so much trouble to avoid sitting beside her, but regardless of the reason, I play along for his sake. He is my friend, after all. Sort of.

I slip into the middle seat and straddle the stick shift, my face heating as Eli slams the truck into gear between my legs. Cheyenne's eyes fix on his hand as it brushes against my knee and I suppress the urge to laugh at her angry sigh. The two obviously have history, but Eli shows no signs of acknowledging it.

In an effort to ignore them, I turn my attention to the merriment around us as we ease along the trail. This isn't some group of college kids on spring break. The crowd has no age limit and no dress code. Everyone is welcome, with vehicles of all makes, models, and conditions charging down the pipeline. Four-wheelers, Jeeps, side-by-sides, old jacked-up trucks, and even the occasional three-wheeler take turns revving their engines and doing donuts as their headlights cast bouncing shadows on the ground ahead.

Muddy kids line the tattered tailgate of the old Willys Jeep in front of us like chickens perched on a roost. As we bounce along, they delight in the novelty of falling into every hole, whether big or small, with each one taking a turn and relying on their comrades to pull them back onto the slow-moving vehicle while their parents pretend not to notice.

At first, I'm alarmed by the dangerous-looking game, but Eli assures me the adults are aware of the goings on behind the Jeep and are keeping a close eye. I study the happy faces of the children, coated from head to toe in soured gumbo mud, with only the whites of their eyes and teeth visible, and remorse fills my chest. Theirs is a childhood spent enjoying the outdoors and the simple pleasures of life. If we build the hunting ranch, where will they go? What will they do? I'd love to think we could open the ranch and still grant these people access, but it isn't realistic. Jeffrey would never allow it. But what right do we have to take this away from them? Dirt, mud, sunshine, pine tree forests, and deep flowing rivers may not seem like necessities to the outside world, but to these children, they are the very essence of childhood. Of life.

I look around and try to imagine how our wealthy resort guests would view this colorful crowd. Disdain is the only word that comes to mind.

The river people don't play by the rules in any way. They live without a care for society's standards or the approval of the outside world. Holding fast to their convictions, they can't be bribed or persuaded in their opinions. The powerful are always irked by this kind of mentality because it's beyond their control. Beyond their influence. If we build the ranch and allow the locals to keep access to Belle Terre, there would be a constant smoldering between the two worlds. And pissed off guests are the last thing Jeffrey would want.

Eli slows to a stop at a gigantic hole where people are

lined up and eager to cross. Others are content to watch from the sidelines while enjoying a beer and the good company of familiar faces. We join the bystanders as one young man dives into the deep mud, gunning his four-wheeler's engine until he gets to the middle of the hole. His bright yellow CanAm has a welded aluminum marine radio strapped to the front and a snorkel on the exhaust. Slowing down, he stands up, rocking from side to side while gently accelerating. Inch by inch, he makes his way out, grinning with pleasure as the crowd cheers.

Several more take a turn, anxious to show off their back-woods driving skills.

"You ever been to the Hog Waller?" a husky voice says beside me.

A heavy-set woman in tight black yoga pants and a stained Eeyore T-shirt stands to my left. She doesn't make eye contact, but I assume the question is for me.

"Can't say that I have. What is it?"

"Mud races over in Newton." The woman tilts her chin away, jutting out her bottom lip to exhale a long breath of cigarette smoke. "Have 'em there every month. That's where we been all day." She takes another drag and nods toward a navy blue, jacked-up Ford with tractor tires. "That's our baby, right there."

Her beloved truck has busted out windows and "Big Blue Bitch" airbrushed in large, fancy script across the tailgate beside a pair of smoking pistols. The fender wells are cut high, with shackles and straps dangling from the huge pipe bumpers. A marine gas tank serves as a fuel cell, and a radiator is positioned on top of the hood.

The long-haired man in the driver's seat wears a dingy white welder's cap, positioned backward with the brim folded up against his head. As he eases through the hole, he leans out the window to admire how well his tires are pulling. Making it to the other side, he shifts into park and uses his pointer finger as a hook to remove the lump of Skoal from his bottom lip.

I nod to the man as he flings the wad out the truck window. "Is that your husband?"

The woman glances at the man with indifference. "Naw, me and Vicky Dale is just common-law."

"So, how do the mud races work?" I ask, grappling for a different subject. "Do you win money?"

The woman gives me a conspiring look and pulls down her blouse to reveal a sweaty, white envelope tucked inside her bra. "First Prize: $200" is written on the outside. She says nothing as I read the envelope, but the gleam of pride in her eyes as she awaits my reaction is unmistakable.

When I congratulate her accomplishment, she nods and glances around, jealously guarding her prize as a young girl covered in mud splatters runs up and whispers something into her ear.

"Hell no, I ain't givin' you none of mine!" the woman exclaims, her face turning red. "You're almost thirteen years old now. If you wanna smoke, you'll have to buy your own damn cigarettes!"

I blink in astonishment and absently wonder if I'm stuck in some kind of absurd dream.

At the look of horror on my face, the woman seems embarrassed. "I ain't tryin' to be mean to her, or nothin'. It's just them damn things cost so much 'n all."

I have to remind myself I'm an observer, not a judge. But it's all I can do not to laugh as the woman shakes her head in dismay.

People around us begin to laugh and shout as Colorado and Jess plunge their Jeep into the wallowed-out puddle. When they start spinning in place, Colorado calls out to Eli. "Gonna need a li'l help from that pick 'em up truck, good buddy."

"Done gilflirted that some'a bitch!" a man yells from the crowd.

Colorado throws his hands in the air and shakes his head at Eli. "You got some come-a-longs?"

Eli gives me a cocky grin. "Here, hold my beer and watch this shit."

He positions his truck in front of the Jeep, and jumps out to secure the wench cable.

With Eli occupied, Cheyenne eases up beside me. "So how do you and Eli know each other?"

As much as I want to help Eli out, I can't bring myself to say I'm his girlfriend. "We ... work together."

Her eyes light up at the news. "Listen, I'd like to apologize for the horrible condition of that houseboat. I mean, I'm so embarrassed. But let me just tell you, when I get all settled in, there'll be some major redecoratin' takin' place." She moves her hands in the air like she's shaking water from her fingertips. "Get all those animal skulls out and put up some quality decor," she says in a sad attempt to mark her territory.

"Really? What kind?"

I bite my lip as she describes furniture that is predictably tacky. But no matter how much Cheyenne gets on my nerves, I can't help feeling like an ass for judging her taste. I could use a lesson from Jeffrey's mom in that respect.

Just last Saturday, we spent the day registering for wedding gifts with Gwendolyn's help. Our last stop had been a quirky new boutique where I fell in love with a mid-century style sofa upholstered in emerald green velvet. I could tell Gwendolyn was eyeing a very safe, very beige, tweed sofa with traditional, clean lines and an extremely high price tag. But she pasted on a huge smile and pulled out a gold credit card. "That shade of green matches your eyes perfectly. They told me it's the last one in stock, so I think you need it right now. Just call it an early wedding present!"

Gwendolyn's gesture was the epitome of grace, and I feel lucky to be a part of such a top-notch family. They always know just how to make me feel loved and supported. And if I'm being honest, Jeffrey has bent over backward to please me too. He's uprooting his life, leaving everything behind, including his family, just so I can be near mine. Well, now it's my turn to please him. On our wedding day, I'll walk down the aisle in a dress white enough to blind the audience.

My mind snaps back to the present as Eli pulls Colorado out of the hole.

"Shit," Eli says, staring at the exhaust pipe of his truck.

I step forward. "What's wrong?"

"Full of mud and I can't fit my arm inside to get it out."

"I'll do it," I say before I can think.

Cheyenne glares at me, but Eli grins and rocks back on his heels. "Get after it, then."

Swallowing hard, I crouch low and inspect the pipe. The stagnant smell of mud assaults my senses, but I plunge ahead. Easing my hand inside, I'm careful to stay to one side so as not to shove the muck farther into the exhaust. The mud is warm and moves easily, but the pipe is longer than I expect. So, I drop to my knees, ignoring the hoots from the crowd. When I'm up to my shoulder, I rake the slop out, slow and steady, then repeat the action until the pipe is clear.

When I stand back up, Jess looks at Eli and whistles. "You sure she ain't a Pocket girl?"

I laugh, flattered by the compliment.

Eli gives me a warm smile, but his admiration turns to irritation when a young man with large brown eyes drops to one knee before me in mock gallantry. "Oh, fair lady, would you do me the great honor of becoming my wife? For your value this day has been proven and your skill unmatched."

"Well, kind sir, what gifts do you offer?" I say, playing along with the lanky young man who seems more suited for the stage than a muddy pipeline in Devil's Pocket.

He jumps to his feet and grabs a Bud Light from his cooler. "Will you accept the King of Beers?"

I pretend to consider the offer for a moment. "I have decided to accept your gift. But I cannot marry you. Alas, I am promised to another."

The crowd rolls with laughter.

"Well met," the young man says, handing me the beer. "Plenty more where that came from, darlin'. Help yourself."

"That's enough, Bobby Joe," Eli says, shaking the man's hand. "How you been, son?"

"Stayin' outta trouble."

Eli slaps him on the back and turns to me. "You ready to head back?"

I nod, but before we leave, Eli leans close to the man and whispers something about meeting up later.

"Who was that?" I ask when the guy walks away.

"Name's Bobby Joe. Good kid," Eli says, then hesitates. "Went off to college and got in some trouble ... Got a job out at the sawmill a while back. I'm proud of him, though. He's been workin' real hard to get his life straight."

Cheyenne snorts. "Nothin' but a meth-head, I'd say."

Eli gives her a hard look. "Well, it takes one to know one, don't it?"

She jerks her head back as if he slapped her. "What the hell is that supposed to mean?"

"Oh, I think you know exactly what I mean." Eli's eyes are hard and cold. "Remember that money you borrowed the other day? Said you was short on your light bill. Did you really think I wouldn't find out you spent it all on a bottle of pills?"

Cheyenne's mouth falls open and mine does the same.

Eli leans forward to tower over Cheyenne. "You forget, I got friends in low places too, sweetheart."

Her face turns red. "Well, if that's the way you're gonna treat me, then ... then we're through!"

"There weren't no 'we' to begin with," he calls as she walks away.

With Cheyenne no longer squeezed into the truck, Eli fumes in silence as we bump along behind the caravan of revelers. But it's not long before I'm squirming in my seat. I've had a lot to drink and my bladder isn't exactly known for its capacity.

"Um, this might be the wrong time to ask, but can you pull over?"

"Yeah, why?"

I grip the door handle and fumble with the lock. "I gotta pee. You don't mind, do you?" I say, remembering Jeffrey's reaction to the same question.

"Why the hell should I care if you pee?"

"Never mind." I give a nervous laugh and start to jump out, but stop short. "Hey do you have any napkins or something I can use for toilet paper?"

Eli checks behind the seat and rummages through the glove compartment. "Don't see any, but hold on a minute." He reaches into the pocket of his jeans and pulls out his Case knife. Opening the blade, he takes the bottom of his gray T-shirt in his left hand and twists the fabric in front of him until his stomach is exposed.

"What on earth are you doing?"

The fabric makes a ripping sound in reply as he slices through his shirt with the knife. "Here you go," he says, holding up the wad of fabric.

I should probably take it, but I'm unable to tear my eyes away from his bizarre new crop top.

"You said you wanted a napkin or somethin'."

"So you cut off a piece of your shirt?"

"Would you rather drip dry?"

I hurry to do my business behind the truck, but just as I'm zipping up, a burly fellow with shaggy dark hair and a pitted complexion pounds on Eli's window.

"You got some kinda nerve upsettin' my sister like that," the man roars, rage making his eyes shine black.

Eli pulls off the remains of his tattered shirt and steps out. "Listen, I ain't got no quarrel with you. And as for Cheyenne, we both know she was askin' for it."

"Why you arrogant son of a ..." The man throws the first punch, but Eli ducks just in time.

Swinging and spitting, I can tell they aren't going to stop until one of them is on the ground. Eli dodges a few times, then lands a hard blow to the man's face, knocking him flat. Blood gushes from his nose, which is now hanging at an odd angle.

I hightail it into the truck with Eli right behind. "Let's get outta here 'fore somebody calls the law," he says, slamming it into gear.

"What was all that about?"

"Aw, Cheyenne's family's always been crazy. But liquor makes it worse."

"Sounds like some real classy folks." I tilt my head to the side with a grin. "Tell me again why Jeffrey and I should give up our hopes and dreams for these people?"

"There's a bad apple in every bunch. You know that." Eli

cuts his eyes my way. "And you can say what you want, but I can tell this place is startin' to grow on you."

I toss my head to the side, not ready to admit he's right. "Oh really?"

"Yeah, really. You're havin' a ball out here." He lowers his voice to a timbre that makes me shiver. "And there's nothin' more beautiful than a woman enjoyin' herself."

CHAPTER 15

After a quick dip in the river back at Eli's camp, I slip inside and tiptoe across the gritty plywood floor. He sits at the table with his eyes closed, listening to Keith Whitley on the kitchen radio. I watch him for a moment, the slight flutter of dark blond lashes in rhythm with his slow, shallow breaths. His hand is bruised and swollen from the fight, so I touch his arm softly to get his attention.

He flinches and his eyes fly open.

"Sorry. Didn't mean to scare you," I say, taking a step back. "I just wanted to take a look at your hand."

He shakes his head. "I ain't hurt. Just a li'l scratch. It'll heal up and hair over in a day or two. Why, I've had worse on my ..." Noticing my wide-eyed anticipation of the vulgar statement, he trails off and clears his throat. "I should go get washed up."

I put my hands on my hips. "Not until you let me take a look."

His mouth opens to argue.

"I mean it," I say, cutting off whatever tactic of evasion he's about to employ.

His lip twitches, but he leans back in the chair. "Hurry up, then."

I take his hand in mine, turning it over to inspect the damage from the fight. I can feel his eyes on me as I inspect his bloody knuckles, and the knowledge makes it hard to breathe. Heart hammering in my chest, I clean the wounds and do my best to keep it professional.

Covering both my hands with one of his own, Eli puts a stop to my fussing. "That's enough. Get on to bed now."

Flustered, I pull away. But my foot catches a chair leg, causing me to lurch forward, only to be caught by two strong arms around my waist.

For a moment, time slows and I enjoy the guilty pleasure of being held tight.

"Aw damn. I'm sorry," he says, releasing me.

He's still covered in mud, and now so am I.

"No problem. I will ... uh ... go get changed," I say, glad for an excuse to escape his confusing nearness.

The mirror in the dressing area shows the evidence of our brief encounter in the form of several muddy hand prints. As I touch each one, my chest tightens at the delicious memory of Eli's possessive grip.

Outdone with myself, I splash cold water on my face and

stare at my reflection. "What the fuck is wrong with you?" I whisper. "A few more days and he won't even remember your name. Act like a damn professional."

When I step from behind the curtain, I'm relieved to see that Eli is gone, no doubt taking a bath himself.

I scurry up the ladder and face the wall, lest he decide to walk in stark naked and shatter my dwindling self-restraint.

When I hear his bunk creak a little while later, I flip over and stare at the ceiling, trying hard to picture Jeffrey's face instead of the man beneath me. He never responded to my last text and I can't figure out why. I thought he'd be pleased. Overjoyed, actually. He got what he wanted, so why is he still pissed? Tonight I even left a long voice message apologizing, yet again, for my stubbornness and begging him to respond. To let me know everything will be okay. But my mind won't stop spinning. Won't stop telling me I've gone too far.

What if Jeffrey's done with me? What will everyone think? They'll probably say that I've turned out exactly as they always expected. Odd and alone.

"You awake?" I ask the darkness, unsure if I want Eli's response. It would be so much easier—and smarter—to just fall asleep.

"Yeah."

His husky voice is like a soothing balm and the desire to get closer is strong. To be held and told everything is going to be alright. But I can't let that happen. Not now. Not ever.

"Tell me a story," I say, releasing a long breath.

"A story? What kind?"

"Anything. Tell me about Lucille."

"My truck? Well, there ain't much to say."

"Sure there is. Tell me how old you were when you bought her."

"Damn, let me think. Guess I was 'bout fourteen or fifteen. I know it was before I ever got my license. Didn't get that 'til after high school. And only because Aunt Irene found out and made me."

"What took you so long?"

His laugh is warm and full. "Let's just say payin' for driver's ed weren't high up on my list of priorities back then."

I suddenly feel a twinge of pity for the boy he used to be. "Your mom didn't help you?"

"Naw." He pauses. "And I wouldn't let Aunt Irene. I've been payin' my own way since I was old enough to work. Bought my school clothes and everything since I was 'bout twelve or thirteen. Mostly doin' odd jobs for people. Haulin' hay in the summer, mowin' grass, and pickin' peas and whatever. That's how I got Lucille."

"You got Lucille by picking peas?"

"Ha, not exactly."

He takes a deep breath and I roll over, settling in. He's a great storyteller, and I can picture the scenes in detail as he speaks.

"See, Ol' Man Ross had 'er for sale up there at the main red light in town, and I just had to have 'er. So, I went by his house one day after school to see how much he was askin'. You might guess it was more'n I could afford back then, so I shook his hand and thanked him for his time. But as I was walkin' away, he stopped me. Told me he knew I was a hard worker and he could sure use a good hand to help him on a job he had comin' up. He was a carpenter by trade, and did a lot of remodelin' and handyman work around town. So, I jumped on the offer, thinkin' I'd work that job with him and the truck would be mine. Well, he was smarter than that. See, when he saw I was good with a hammer and a chop saw, he didn't wanna give me up. So, when the job was over, he told me that since I was only half growed, he reckoned I only deserved half a grown man's wages. Well, I wanted that truck so bad I could taste it, so I agreed. Worst mistake I ever made, in my life."

"Why's that?"

"'Cause it's been over ten years now, and I still ain't got that damn thing paid off." At my laughter, Eli chuckles. "To tell you the truth, I don't mind helpin' him out. He's gettin' up in years and I'm the closest thing he has to a son. I'd go check on him even if I didn't owe him a dime ... but it'd sure be nice to get my hands on that damn title one day."

I smile into the darkness as Eli sits up. "What're you doing?"

"Got some business to tend to." He gets to his feet and pulls on a pair of jeans. "Be back in a li'l while. You go on to sleep now."

I assume he's is referring to a trip to the outhouse. But as the minutes tick by, I recall his suspicious conversation with Bobby Joe, and my eyes fly open.

Whatever they're planning, I'm sure it's illegal. Moonshine, firearms trafficking, outlaw hunting, a meth lab stationed in the woods ... Well, maybe that last one is a little farfetched, but I can't help myself. My mind whirls with possibilities until the churning in my stomach forces me out of bed. I need sleep. But I need to know what's going on more.

CHAPTER 16

The eerie brightness of a full moon makes managing without a flashlight easy as I creep onto the bank, listening for signs of the men. Low voices are barely audible from the south edge of the forest, so I head in that direction, picking my way around pine saplings and Chinese tallows. Stumps and underbrush try to trip me up, but I keep going even as mosquitos feast on my arms and legs.

The voices grow louder as I reach a small clearing and crouch low. Two dark figures are in the distance; one sitting on a tree stump and the other leaning against a wide trunk. I'm close enough to hear their conversation and I focus on Eli's words.

"Now, Bobby Joe, the next part we're gonna work on is the Dedication. I'll say it all once through, then we can break it down into smaller parts."

"I appreciate you takin' the time to teach me."

Eli laughs. "Somebody's got to keep your ass in line."

"You're right about that."

Eli pauses a moment, his voice taking on the tone and cadence typical of one reciting a well-loved verse from a Sunday school lesson. But as I listen to his rich baritone, I can tell this is not something found in the Bible.

"Our ancient brethren dedicated their Lodges to King Solomon because he was our Most Excellent Grand Master, but modern Masons dedicate theirs to St. John the Baptist and St. John the Evangelist, who were two eminent patrons of Masonry."

I gasp. It seems I've walked up on some sort of secret Masonic meeting. I think back to the emblem tattooed on Eli's shoulder and feel a little stupid for not seeing this coming.

Eli continues explaining the principle tenets of Masonry and how they are taught to regard the whole human species as one family—the high and low, the rich and poor, men of every country, sect, and opinion. And how true friendship is fostered among those who might otherwise have remained at a perpetual distance.

The lesson continues and, while I know it's wrong to eavesdrop, I can't pull myself away from Eli's words. There is something powerful and mysterious and honorable emanating from the ancient principles that draws me in and makes me think of Mama Pearl's late husband, Hob. He had also been a member of the mystical order and the accomplishment is a point of pride for Mama Pearl, who proudly displays a large portrait of him wearing the traditional white lambskin apron over the fireplace.

Bobby Joe recites various paragraphs several times, with Eli correcting mistakes along the way. "Would you say a prayer?" Bobby Joe says as the lesson concludes. "What I mean is, would you say a Masonic prayer? I remember my grandpa used to say some real pretty ones."

I can't make out Eli's reply, but a moment later, his voice is strong. "Most holy and glorious Lord God, the great Architect of the universe, the Giver of all good gifts and graces; Thou hast promised that where two or three are gathered together in Thy name, Thou wilt be in the midst of them. In Thy name we assemble, most humbly beseeching Thee to bless us in all our undertakings, that we may know and serve Thee aright, and that all our actions may tend to Thy glory, and to our advancement in knowledge and virtue: and we beseech Thee, O Lord God, to bless this our present assembling, and to illuminate our minds by the divine precepts of Thy holy word, and teach us to walk in the light of Thy countenance, and when the trials of our probationary state are over be admitted into The Temple not made with hands, eternal in the heavens. Amen."

A lump forms in my throat at the elegant words spoken by such an inarticulate man. With Eli's help, Bobby Joe is on the right track to a better life. And no matter our differences, I find myself wishing there were more Eli's in the world.

It's an idea that stays with me through the night until I wake to a poke in the ribs.

"Knock it off," I say, squirming away from Eli's prodding.

"Here," he says, holding out a blond cup of coffee.

I sit up and shake my head to clear the cobwebs.

"What time is it?" I say after a few sips.

"Mornin' time," he says, turning up The Cajun Jamboree on the kitchen radio.

Growing up, John "Tee Bruce" Broussard's Sunday morning show was a staple at our house. Hearing the man's heavy Cajun accent, halting with the effects of age, still filtering through the airwaves after all these years, is something I didn't realize I've missed.

As Eli pours himself a second cup of coffee, my eyes fall to his bandaged knuckles. "How's your hand?"

He shrugs and rubs his temples. "They ain't nothin' compared to the headache I got. Don't know what's wrong with me. I didn't drink a whole lot last night."

"Well, I can fix that too!" I jump down from my perch, glad for an excuse to feel useful as I hand him a glass of water. "Drink this. All of it. Then put this under your tongue and hold it there. It's just plain table salt."

Eli complies with a doubtful look.

I push him into a chair and set to work. "Now I'm going to open up a few meridians that will allow your body to heal itself."

Eli jumps back in surprise. "You're gonna what?"

I put my hand on his shoulder and try to speak in soothing tones. "Settle down, I'm not gonna hurt you ... much."

Eli moves to stand up, but I push him down and apply pressure to the inner points of his eyebrows.

"Tell me when it hurts," I say, working my way out over each eye.

"It all hurts, damn it!"

After a few minutes, I move to the pressure points on his ears, neck, and shoulders.

Eli gets very quiet and beads of sweat glisten on his forehead. "Shit, I don't know how much more of this I can take," he whispers. "You tryin' to kill me, woman?"

"Nope. I'm trying to heal you," I say, unable to contain a small laugh.

"I don't see nothin' funny 'bout this."

"Just breathe. I'm almost done."

When I finish my ministrations, I put my hands on his shoulders. "There now. All done."

"I ain't never let somebody hurt me that bad in all my life," he says, opening his eyes in relief.

I give him a coy smile. "But do you still have a headache?"

He crosses his arms. "Alright. Alright. You win."

"A simple thank you will do."

He stands and gives a sweeping bow. "Thank you very much. Now come on, we better get movin'. Figure we'll leave right after breakfast. Shouldn't take us too long with the water as warm as it is. Talked to Aunt Irene yesterday and she's gonna drive the catch boat."

"Catch boat?" I am fairly certain harvesting papaya has nothing to do with any of these things.

"Gotta have a catch boat for this kinda fishin', pasquale."

"But ... what about the papaya?"

"We worked all day yesterday. Figured we could take the day off."

Normally, I'd be anxious to stay on task. To complete my mission as quickly as possible and go home. Back to Belle Terre. But the longer I stay on the river, the more I don't want to leave. It's a perplexing emotion that's easier to shove to the back of my mind than face head-on. So, I'll go along with what Eli wants. The list can wait for now. In the words of Scarlett O'Hara, "I'll think about that tomorrow."

❧

"Yeah, I've set many a limb line using either Zote soap or clabbered steer's blood," Irene says around a mouthful of bacon.

Seated at Eli's kitchen table, I push away my breakfast plate, no longer hungry. "Is ... that what we're doing today?" Please, please say it's not.

"Naw, that only works when the river's outta its banks. Get you 'bout five feet of string with a swivel hook and find you a low hangin' limb. If it's jerkin' in the mornin', you know you got a fish."

I wrinkle my nose. "Why do they like soap and blood?"

Eli sits up straight. "The soap leaves a kind of oil sheen that attracts the fish. And the blood ... well, they can smell that a mile away."

"Caught me a big ol' blue cat one year," Irene brags. "Partial albino, colored up like a damn Holstein cow."

"Well now, I don't seem to remember that," Eli says with a wink in my direction.

"I shit you not," she proclaims. "Even got my picture in the paper to prove it. Ask anybody. They'll tell you."

As she and Eli continue exchanging lighthearted banter, the pair seem more like family than friends. Though Irene has no children of her own, I'm glad to see she has found someone to mother.

I linger over a second cup of coffee as they swap tales of people and places passed down for generations. Shaped and molded by practiced telling, the stories come alive through animated gestures, a dramatic pause, or emphasis on the perfect word. The cadence of speech is entertaining by itself, rising and falling with colloquialisms and cuss words sprinkled throughout. I listen, enraptured by the bonds formed through friendship, loyalty, and hard times.

Eli gives Irene a grin. "Remember how we used to catch shiners in minnow jars?"

"How's that?" I say.

He leans forward, using his hands to demonstrate. "First, you take a mason jar and put the top of a Coke bottle upside down inside it to make a funnel. Screw the ring back on and bait it with some cornmeal. Put it down in the water with the ass end up river and push a stick in the sandbar to mark it. Throw out a lil' more cornmeal upriver and them minnows come right to it. Used to catch them red-tail shiners years ago, but they're all gone now, I guess."

"Oh, them was the best ones too. Maybe the cataba

worms carried 'em off," Irene jokes. "I finally gave up and cut down all my cataba trees after the worms quit comin'."

I smile at the local pronunciation of "catalpa" and ask Irene about the purpose of the worms.

"Best fishin' worms you'll ever find," she says. "Used to go underground all winter and come out again in the summer. Eat all the leaves off them cataba trees and get real fat."

"Hey, you remember that ol' gotch-eyed man that used to sell cataba worms at the red light in town?" Eli says to Irene. "Nice ol' man, can't remember his name though."

Her head bobs. "Mr. Williams. Heard he died a few years back."

The pair go on to explain how to catch large fish on the main river using hoop nets baited with "cheese." Eli enjoys describing the process of making the rotten cheese and how the maggots make a loud clicking sound in the fermenting bucket, a signal it's ready for use. I gag and vow to never, ever fish with hoop nets.

Eli gets a kick out of my disgust but assures me there were other ways of using the nets such as fishing "blind" in a process that involves sinking weighted hoop nets to the bottom of a narrow cut. With no way around, the fish swim inside the nets, which are later retrieved with big steel drags. This form of fishing sounds more my style.

"Why haven't I ever seen anyone try it?" I say.

"Oh, they've been outlawed in Texas for years," Irene says with a shake of her head. "Remember when they took our deer dogs too. That was somethin' else, I tell you. Men 'round here started settin' the woods on fire in protest, they was so upset. See, them bigwigs at the timber companies wanted to make all this land into huntin' clubs for city folks and charge a pretty penny for membership. But they was plumb ignorant of how we hunt."

Eli gives me a pointed look, a warning of what might happen if our plans for Belle Terre move forward. "All because a dog can't read a 'no trespassing' sign. Boils down to it bein' easier to outlaw a practice rather than take time and learn the facts. Bunch of ignorant, greedy sons-a-bitches."

I stay quiet, keeping my eyes on my lap.

"That's right," Irene says. "They don't know nothin' 'bout deer dogs or anything other than how to set out a corn feeder, lure the deer up like a kid to candy, then shoot 'em when they least expect it. Now, you tell me, how in the hell is that more 'humane?' It ain't," she declares, pounding her fist on the table.

Clearly upset, Eli stands to his feet and signals it's time to leave. I try not to take what they've said personally. But it's hard not to.

In a somber mood, we gather our things and head to the waiting boats.

"We forgot the fishing poles," I say, reaching for the ones stored in the porch rafters.

Eli looks up from fiddling with the motor. "Don't need 'em."

The idea of using some sort of rotten, maggot cheese like Eli described makes me shudder. Maybe I should fake an illness and stay home. After all, my stomach *is* roiling with guilt and second-guessing about the ranch. But as much as I'd love to avoid further scrutiny, I don't want to seem weak.

We travel upriver about five bends before stopping at a sandbar to swim. I lay out my book and towel while Irene stakes her chair in shallow water and makes herself comfortable.

From my vantage point, I'm able to covertly watch as Eli removes his shirt and dives into the current. He stays under a long time before his head pops up about ten yards away. The idea of swimming that far into the depths of the river has always frightened me. I fight the urge to scream at him as childhood tales of dangerous whirlpools and bodies found in old, tangled trot lines come to mind.

Irene watches as Eli makes his way to the opposite bank. "Been doin' that since he was a kid."

The idea that any mother would let their child do something so dangerous is disturbing, and I'm quick to let Irene know.

"I can see you ain't never met his mama," Irene huffs. "Claudette weren't never right in the head. Came from a whole family of crazies. She was one a them you can't tell nothin' to that they don't already know. You know the kind. She didn't know shit from Shinola, but she sure was good at makin' up stories. If somebody was talkin' about babies, she'd claim to be a delivery nurse. And that's how it'd go every time. One day she'd be a hairdresser, the next a truck driver, then a CPA, feed store owner, roofer ... Hell, one time she even told somebody she was a professional boxer."

"You're kidding!"

"Wish I was." Irene smiles but her eyes are sad.

"Eli mentioned her, but said they don't talk anymore."

Irene looks away. "Claudette's been burnin' bridges with him his whole life, poor baby. Used to go get him as much as I could when he was a kid. But she'd never let him stay for long. Remember one time I saw 'em up at the grocery store. Eli weren't more'n 'bout four or five at the time. Well, he was lookin' at somethin' or other in the store, and Claudette was ready to go. So, she calls out to him how if he don't come right then, that she was leavin' him. Then she heads on out to her car. Without ever lookin' back, she cranked that car right up and drove off. I'll never forget the look on that baby's face when he realized his mama had left him. Cut me to the bone. But 'fore I could tell him I'd take him on home, he struck out runnin'. I got in my truck and tried to find him, but he was fast and too hard to track. Come to find out, he ran all the way across town and through 'bout two miles of woods 'fore he made it home that day."

My heart squeezes. "I had no idea."

Irene snorts. "That weren't nowhere near the worst Eli went through growin' up. He won't talk 'bout most of it, but stories get 'round."

I check to make sure Eli is still out of earshot. "Since you've known him so long, there's something I've been meaning to ask. Georgia told me he won't accept any pay from Doc. Do you know why that is?"

"Yeah. I know why. See, when Eli was a baby he had real bad ear infections. Used to scream his head off. Claudette hauled him over to Doc's office, but 'course she didn't have no money to pay. So, Doc ended up treatin' him free of charge for years. Once Eli growed up, he tried to settle up, but Doc wouldn't have it. Guess Eli figures gatherin' a few herbs is the least he can do to repay him." We watch as Eli pulls himself out of the water on the opposite side of the river. "He's a good boy. I just pray one day he'll finally get the kind of family he deserves."

Irene's nurturing spirit is evident. She has a way of showing up even when the world looks the other way. I try to find the words to thank her for all the kindness she's given. To Eli. To me. To Mama Pearl. But my throat constricts each time I try to open my mouth.

Eli waves to us then dives back into the water's murky depths. I count the seconds until he surfaces and sigh in relief as he easily swims the remaining distance.

He splashes water our way, a blast of cold that makes me squeal and Irene cuss, and my first impulse is to run. But the cool droplets actually feel great in the heat, so I decide to take a dip myself.

Revealing my newest bikini, I step out into the swift water. Eli's busy splashing Irene and doesn't seem to notice. I give them space, sinking slowly, letting the current carry me downstream.

Fluffy white clouds drift overhead as I lie suspended, my hands cupping water, my body loose and free. I close my eyes and drift, intoxicated by the weightlessness until something grabs my leg and holds tight.

I scream and struggle against the unseen threat, but it wins and pulls me under. I fight the monster with all my might, too scared to realize I don't feel any teeth. Then I'm plunged up into the light, gasping for breath and clawing at Eli's chest.

He laughs and gives me a tight squeeze, silencing my body but not my mouth. "You rat bastard! Why'd you do that?"

He sets me on my feet and inclines his head. "Did I just hear the words 'rat bastard' come outta that pretty little mouth?"

I give him a glare and a hard shove.

"Look," he says, eyes twinkling with mirth. He points upriver to the sandbar where Irene sits waving.

I've drifted a lot farther downstream than I intended, almost to the point of no return. But I still don't like admitting I needed saving.

"I'm a big girl, you know," I say, standing to my full height.

Eli throws me over his shoulder like a sack of potatoes. "No, you're not. You're as skinny as a lizard-eatin' cat."

When he takes off walking through the shallow water, I pound his back with my fists. "Put me down! Right now!"

"Only if you promise not to run away again."

"I didn't run away!"

He keeps walking.

"Fine! Whatever, just put me down!"

He plops me onto the sand next to Irene's umbrella and gives her a wink.

"You findin' everything you need for Doc?" she asks when Eli dives back into the water.

Still panting, I smooth the wet hair from my eyes and try to regain my composure. "We weren't able to get the snakeroot. But we're making good headway on everything else."

"What all you got left?"

"Wild hog thyroid and papaya. Eli says he has the thyroid covered but I'm not sure where to find the papaya. I'd love to find an organic supplier, but I don't know if anyone has had luck growing them in this area."

Irene snorts. "Got plenty right in my own backyard. Been growin' 'em for years."

"Really? That's wonderful! Could we come by tomorrow and take a look?"

"Sure thing, baby doll. Got more'n I'll ever eat."

"Is eight or nine too early?"

"Too early?" She frowns. "You can't come too early for me. What on earth does Doc need papayas for, anyways?"

"They contain an enzyme called papain that's good for all kinds of things. But it's especially helpful in digesting rotting flesh. Like gangrene."

Eli lifts his head from where he relaxes in the water and wiggles his eyebrows. "On that note, I think it's time to eat." He hoists a watermelon from where it chills in the water by the boat and places it on the bow. Using his pocket knife, he slices off large pieces and passes them around.

The bright red flesh is sweet and cool, a perfect reprieve from the sweltering heat. Lying on my stomach in the shallow water, I feel like a kid spitting seeds into the current and watching as they float downstream. I bury my face in the slice and my engagement ring catches the light, jolting me back to reality. The fact is, I'm not a kid and never will be again. I'm an adult with adult problems. And no amount of running around this river with Eli is going to make them go away.

I scramble to my feet and grab my bag out of the boat. Tired of waiting for Jeffrey to quit pouting, I've ignored my phone all morning. But something in my gut tells me it's time to check.

When I read the screen, I know my instinct was right. Jeffrey has finally answered. I am forgiven.

CHAPTER 17

The sun is high when we prepare to leave the sandbar, and there's a bounce in my step as we gather our things. After Jeffrey's message, my heart is light and I pat myself on the back for my ability to compromise. If sacrificing one pink wedding dress is all it takes to secure a lifetime of happiness, I will gladly accept the terms and be grateful.

Just as we are about to shove off, a boat with a long shaft and funny-looking prop rounds the bend. Standing in the middle, a lone man balances, his long dark hair blowing behind him.

"Well, I'll be damned if it ain't Li'l Bit," Irene says. "Ain't seen him in years, don't b'lieve."

I turn to Eli. "Who's Li'l Bit?"

"Man from Sheffield's Ferry. Way up river. Ain't been right

since his wife died a few years ago, so you'll have to excuse him if he seems a little off."

The boat pulls up to reveal one of the largest men I've ever seen. He has a long, crooked nose and a fifth of whiskey tucked under one gigantic bicep. Native American symbols cover his body, and a woman's name and date is inscribed over his heart. A lone warrior on horseback stretches across his back, but the arrow shooting across his stomach draws the most attention. Clearly meant as humorous, the tattoo pierces the right side of his large pot belly, revealing itself on the left. I stare at the ridiculous marking and try not to grin as he clambers from his boat like a drunk bear.

"Drunker'n a fiddler's bitch," Irene whispers, reading my mind. "Almost as bad as the time he pistol-whipped Buddy Collie over at Foster's Bluff for callin' him by his given name."

"Where you been, boy?" Li'l Bit slurs, pulling Eli to him as they shake hands.

Eli gestures to me in a charismatic manner. "Man, this woman's got me bowed up."

Li'l Bit's glassy eyes gleam with pleasure. "Well, I'll be damned," he says, slapping Eli on the back. "It's 'bout damn time you tied the knot. What'd you tell her she was pregnant?" he jokes, grabbing my hand to examine my engagement ring.

My cheeks flame at the common assumption that Eli and I are 'together,' and I decide to speak up. "No, sir. I am engaged ... to a man named Jeffrey Frost."

Li'l Bit jerks his head around to give Eli a challenging stare. "You gonna stand for that, boy?"

Eli plays it cool with a slight grin and a shrug, but I'm desperate for Li'l Bit to understand. "Eli and I just work together," I clarify, going on to explain the nature of my assignment.

Li'l Bit shakes his head and starts pacing back and forth. Alarmed when he pauses to take a long drink from his whiskey bottle, I shoot Eli a pleading look.

He takes the hint and puts his arm around the big, sensitive man. "Listen, I promised this gal a mess of fish tonight. And I sure could use your help callin' 'em up."

At this bit of news, Li'l Bit's head comes up and his eyes sparkle.

"See, she's a li'l green and gonna need some help in the catch boat," Eli explains.

Li'l Bit beams with pleasure. "Well, why didn't you say somethin'? It's a damn good day for shockin'."

I'm relieved to see Li'l Bit back in high spirits, but I sure hope Eli's language isn't literal. When he begins to fiddle with various red, green, and black wires hanging from a Skoal can, I have a sinking feeling my first assumption was correct. Before I can ask, a whoosh of air takes my breath as the boat picks up speed.

After a few bends, we slow and come side by side—Eli alone in his boat and the rest of us in the other. I learn the Skoal can device is called a "gizmo" and it's powerful enough to call up some of the biggest fish in the river. Eli sticks two 9-volt batteries to each other, then attaches the wires from the gizmo. The remaining wires are attached to the boat and hooked to an extension cord with a braided chain on the end to give it weight.

When Eli casts the cord into the water behind the boat, we're ready to fish ... I guess.

In my opinion, Eli seems more likely to electrocute himself than catch a fish—not to mention the method's legality. What am I thinking, being associated with this kind of behavior? Jeffrey would have a heart attack if he knew and lecture me for putting my reputation at risk. Maybe I should demand to be taken back to the houseboat. Or dropped off at a sandbar. Anything to avoid being an accessory to a bunch of outlaws. I have no idea what the penalty is for this kind of behavior, but I do know one thing. I wouldn't do very well in prison.

I clear my throat and mentally prepare my best 'it's not you, it's me' speech to get out of this ridiculous predicament when a splashing sound catches my attention. My eyes fly to the big catfish fluttering along the top of the water beside me. When it disappears back into the murky depths, another surfaces on the opposite side of the boat, and soon the water is teeming with life.

"Are we doing that?" I shout as Li'l Bit points out a huge blue catfish a few yards away.

"Grab the dip net, woman!" Eli yells.

Irene hammers down on the motor as I hold onto Li'l Bit's arm with one hand and the dip net with the other.

"I gotcha, honey. Now dip that big some'a bitch," he bellows into my ear.

I lean over and stick my net into the water, scooping up

the fish. It's heavier than I expect, so Li'l Bit helps me heave it into the boat. Before we have time to untangle it from the net, Irene spots more prey and shouts for us to hurry.

With the next two or three, I do fairly well, but we can't make it to most of them before they disappear beneath the water.

Irene waves to get Eli's attention. "Got too much weight in the boat."

Li'l Bit trades places with Eli and I offer him the net.

He shakes his head. "Keep at it. You're doing a fine job."

"I feel like I'm going to fall out every time."

"Here, this'll work better." Eli's arms circle my waist, steadying me. "Now your hands are free and you can balance."

My job is much easier, but his strong, callused hands occupy most of my thoughts. I've never been so distracted by a person's touch, and the result is me missing more fish than ever before. Laughing and flustered, I decide to take a break and let Eli take over.

But as he dumps a couple of fish onto the boat floor, I can't help worrying about the fate of the ones that sink after surfacing.

"They ain't dead. Just a little stunned," Irene assures, explaining how the electricity isn't strong enough to do any harm, and how the method is commonly used by government agencies to check fish populations. "Some of that 'it's fine for me, but not for thee' bullshit," she says with contempt. "That don't fly out here."

CHAPTER 18

When the sun reaches the top of the distant pines, our time on the water comes to an end. I help Eli drag in the long cord and put everything in its proper place while Irene and Li'l Bit head back with the fish.

Willow trees bend low over the shallows, creating mysterious shadows as the sky darkens. Eli hands me a beer and cranks the motor up high. I sit at the front, using the spotlight to scan the water for deadheads—stumps and trees hiding near the water's surface—and point to each circle of churning water in silent warning.

As we pass near a sandbar, the boat jumps and a loud *thump* sounds.

"Shit." Eli slows the engine and turns around.

"What'd we hit?"

"I dunno. Shine right back there."

I grip the edge of the boat and scan the water with the light. When the beam lands on the white underbelly of an alligator close to the boat, I freeze.

"Grab him. I'm comin'," Eli shouts, standing up.

My skin prickles with dread as one lone, scaly foot rises from the water like a scene from Jurassic Park. I hesitate, not liking my new role in this latest edition of the Eli LeBlanc swamp reality show.

"Do it!" he yells, barreling toward me.

Summoning all my courage, I grab the horrifying appendage. But as my hand closes around the monster's leathery foot, the claw curls around my fingers in what can only be described as a handshake.

I panic and scream, dropping the foot as Eli leaps onto the deck behind me. We watch in silence as the gator sinks back into the black depths from which it came. Though I'm relieved to be spared the adventure of wrestling the creature into the boat, I'm mostly upset with myself for dropping the ball. "He's gone! You shouldn't have made me do it!"

Eli shrugs. "It ain't nobody's fault, pasquale."

"What?"

"I said don't worry 'bout it," he says in a calm tone.

Eyes burning with disappointed tears, I cross my arms and look away. I know he's mad I failed, but he doesn't have to be passive aggressive about it. It'd be better if he just yelled and got it over with.

"What's the matter with you?" he says after I plop down beside him.

"What do you mean?"

"Why're you all worked up? You gave it your best shot. Don't be so hard on yourself."

It dawns on me that he's being sincere.

"So ... you're not mad?"

"Should I be? I mean, I can't say I like losin' all that meat, but it's not like you let it get away on purpose."

"Guess I'm just mad at myself."

"Well I'm mad at myself for runnin' over it in the first place. But accidents happen." Eli bumps my knee with his own. "You did your best and that's good enough for me."

By the time we get back to the houseboat, Irene is busy dropping seasoned filets into a brown paper bag filled with yellow corn meal. With focused eyes and a steady hand, Li'l Bit seems to have sobered up quite a bit as he stirs a black iron pot of melting lard positioned on top of a homemade fish fryer.

Eli takes the opportunity to entertain everyone with the story of our alligator encounter, which he embellishes a little for the sake of the tale. This prompts Li'l Bit to contribute a few stories of his own.

"How old was you, boy?" he says to Eli. "'Bout nine or ten when we shot that deer them rabbit dogs was runnin'?"

"Nine."

Li'l Bit nods. "Remember when your uncle Wyatt brought you up to the house that evenin'. We was goin' rabbit huntin', and Mama had her grease ready to fry 'em up when we got back. Brought my two best rabbit dogs, Sadie and June, and Wyatt hauled up a new dog he called Rowdy. Said he wanted to try him out.

"So we put 'em on a trail and they took off. Well, ol' Rowdy started yappin'. He was on somethin'. But I knew shit weren't right when Sadie and June didn't join the race. I told Wyatt that Rowdy had prob'ly jumped a damn deer. He told me there was no way in hell 'cause the man he bought that dog from assured him he'd never run a deer. I still weren't convinced that dog wouldn't trash on a track, but I give him the benefit of the doubt until ol' Rowdy started stretchin' out, 'stead of turnin' circles.

"They was headed down toward the railroad tracks, so we broke and run through Myrtle Prairie and straight for the tree line to head 'em off. We could tell they was runnin' a deer, and we had to put a stop to it. By now, we could hear 'em crashin' through the underbrush, comin' straight for us. Wyatt told me not to shoot that deer ahead of his new dog, sure it would ruin him for good.

"Well, li'l Eli was leadin' the group, right out in front, and weren't paying no attention. And 'bout that time, that big ol' six point came straight for us. Didn't even see us, he was runnin' so fast. And I'll be damned if li'l Eli, calm as a cucumber, didn't raise his 20 gauge, not eight feet from that some'a bitch, and downed him with one shot. Wyatt was sick 'bout it. Just knew ol' Rowdy was ruined. But we had to get that deer on outta there quick. So, Wyatt run for the truck leavin' me and the boy there behind."

Eli sits down on the edge of the porch, smiling as he leans back against a post.

"It was damn heavy work draggin' that big some'a bitch all the way to them railroad tracks, just me and the boy," Li'l Bit brags. "But we made it and loaded him up before anybody seen us, didn't we, son?"

Eli takes a chew of tobacco. "Remember hangin' him from the chicken coop rafters so nobody would see us skin him."

"That's how you cut your teeth, ain't it, boy? Got to keep your shirt tail that day," Li'l Bit says with a laugh. "Yes, sir, them was some good times."

Eli's eyes light up at the memory, and I can see why he wants me to experience his culture firsthand. Their stories. Their traditions. Their very identity. It's all tied to the land.

"Shirt tail?" I say, curious about Li'l Bit's choice of words.

Irene frowns. "Ain't you ever heard of somebody gettin' their shirt tail cut?"

I shake my head.

"Ha, well it's what they do to you when you miss a deer. Kinda like to shame you and let everybody know."

"Well, if I ever go deer hunting with any of you, I'll be sure to borrow a shirt from him," I say, pointing to Eli.

Everyone laughs and Eli's eyes sparkle. "It wouldn't be the first time you ruined one of my shirts."

BESIDES THE EVER PRESENT RUMBLE OF THE AC UNIT, THE houseboat is dark and quiet. Irene and Li'l Bit left hours ago, but I can't sleep.

I hang my head over the edge of my bed. "Are you awake?" I whisper.

"Whatcha doin' now, pasquale?" Eli says, reaching up to gently touch the ends of my hair dangling in the moonlight.

"Waiting."

He clears his throat. "For what?"

"A story."

The bed creaks as he shifts position. "How 'bout you tell me one, then I'll tell you one?"

"What do you mean? I don't have any stories."

"Sure you do."

I shake my head. "No, I really don't. Not like yours."

"They don't need to be like mine. Tell 'bout when you were a kid. What'd you used to do for fun?"

"Read, I guess."

"I already know that. Come on, there's gotta be somethin' else."

"I don't know ... We had a lot of fun playing in Mama Pearl's beauty shop," I say, giving him a quick recap of our often ill-fated beauty experiments. "Other than that, I liked fiddling around in my herb garden and going to flea markets with Mama Pearl."

"Like me a good junk sale myself."

I rest my chin on my hands. "Every Saturday morning we'd all load up in that old gold Cadillac Mama Pearl refuses to get rid of and we'd scan the newspaper and roadsides for a sale.

When we'd find one, Mr. Lavergne would pull over and park, and us girls would run inside to see if they had anything good. That much walking was too hard for Mama Pearl, so if we found something she might like, we'd bring it out to the car for her to see." I smile at the happy memory. "Truth is we probably brought her a little too much," I say, thinking of Belle Terre's rooms bursting at the seams. "But it was fun and it made her happy, you know? It was our thing. Something we could all do together."

"You don't go anymore?"

"Not as often."

"That's too bad."

I clap my hands together. "Okay, I've held up my end of the bargain. Now it's your turn."

"Alright. Whatcha wanna hear?"

"I don't know," I muse, like a child selecting a favorite bedtime story. "Tell me a scary one."

"A scary one, eh? Let me think, well there's plenty 'bout The Cult."

"I've heard all those."

"Even the one where the lady in the fancy evenin' gown was cryin' at the gate, but wouldn't let nobody help her?"

"Uh huh."

"Well, how 'bout the little girl by the side of the road?"

"No, I haven't heard that one." I inch my elbows under me.

"Well, let's see. Guess 'bout ten or twelve years ago, a buddy of mine and his wife was headed home from a game of 42 over at the Masonic Lodge late one night. They had to pass right by The Cult's front gate, and all of a sudden, they saw a li'l girl, 'bout four or five years old, walkin' real close to the road. Said she had long blond hair and had on a thin old-fashioned style white dress. And both her hair and her dress were blowin' in the wind. They didn't notice her there until they were almost past her, so they slammed on the brakes. But, when they turned 'round and jumped out to find her, she was gone. Just disappeared. And the weirdest part was, the air was completely still with no wind at all."

I shudder at the delicious thought, fully aware of how stupid Jeffrey would find our conversation. He's a man of facts and science, with no patience for anything spiritual. It's a topic we've mutually agreed not to discuss, making Eli's willingness to indulge my whimsical request feel like a guilty pleasure.

"Do you believe in ghosts?" I say, not wanting it to end.

"I've done some thinkin' on it, and I guess I do."

"Why?"

"Well, in the book of Luke, when Jesus appeared to His disciples after the crucifixion, they were real scared because they thought He was a ghost. But He assured 'em He wasn't, saying, 'Why do you doubt who I am? Look at my hands. Look at my feet. You can see that it's really me. Touch me and make sure that I am not a ghost, because ghosts don't have bodies, as you see that I do!' Now, if ghosts don't exist, don't you think Jesus would've clarified that?"

I'm impressed by his argument. When it comes to labeling people, my first instincts are usually correct, but with Eli, I find myself faltering. I desperately want to hate him, but every fiber of my being says otherwise. "Have you ever seen a ghost?"

"No, not yet and I hope I never do. But I have family who has. Used to tell stories 'bout Clarence all the time.

"Clarence? He's seen a lot of ghosts?"

"No, Clarence *was* the ghost." I can barely make out the corners of Eli's eyes crinkling in the gloom. "Over close to Orange, right off Highway 62 before you get to the rice dryers, used to be an ol' shotgun house. It was set back off the road a ways, right in the middle of a big circle of live oak trees. Beautiful place. My great uncle Bravo and his wife, Aunt Dolly, lived there. Raised twelve kids in that li'l house. But man, they had some unnatural tales 'bout ol' Clarence.

"Uncle Bravo said the first time he saw him was late one night comin' across the yard under the security light. Said Clarence walked straight for him then vanished into thin air. See, Uncle Bravo never slept in the house. Had him a bed there on the screened-in porch. Anyhow, he said Clarence was wearin' faded green overalls that were too small and too short for him, and he had left one gallus hangin' so they wouldn't cut him in two. Said he was a li'l fellow and always barefooted."

"That's really creepy."

"They said one night he grabbed Uncle Bravo by the foot and flipped him outta bed. And if you ever saw my uncle, you'd know what a claim that is. He had to be at least four hundred pounds on the hoof. Said all the kids come runnin' to see what happened when they heard him hit the porch floor."

"Did the kids see Clarence too?"

"Not that night. But a few years later, the whole family was havin' a get-together, laughin' and talkin' and bein' loud, when all of a sudden they heard what sounded like timbers fallin' in the attic and the sound of babies screamin' and cryin'. Then the dishes in the kitchen started flyin' off the shelves. Scared everybody to death and ran the whole party outside. Guess ol' Clarence didn't like all the hoopla." Eli's laugh is low and warm. "'Course there were li'l things over the years too. Like the time one of the grown girls was bakin' a cake and got out a carton of eggs. She laid the carton on the counter and grabbed a mixin' bowl. Well, when she reached for an egg from the carton, she found one was already sittin' on a folded dishrag right beside her. So, she picked up the egg, cracked it into the bowl and reached for another one, but when she looked, lo and behold there was another egg sittin' on the dishrag just like before. Like somebody was helpin' her."

The hair stands up on the back of my neck and a chill trickles down my spine. "I don't know if my nerves can take much more of this creepiness or I might just end up down there with you."

"Hey now, don't threaten me with a good time."

"I'm serious."

"I am too."

His frank words cause chills of a different kind, but I pull the blanket up to my chin and turn the conversation in a safer direction. "Come on. Tell me something happy, so I can sleep."

"Something happy, eh?"

"Tell me about your rodeo days. Do you miss it?"

"Yeah, guess I do sometimes. The travelin' and freedom of it ... and the women."

"Well, *that* I can believe," I say with a snort.

"But there ain't much else to tell. Didn't last too long out on the circuit."

"How did you get started in it?"

"When I was 'bout twelve or thirteen, I wanted to be a roper, but we didn't have the money for no fancy ropin' horse. Mama said if I wanted one, I'd have to buy it myself. So, I wished and hoped and wished some more and I'll be damned if Li'l Bit didn't show up one day askin' if I could take a horse off his hands. Lookin' back, I guess he heard I'd been askin' for one, but I didn't know it then. Gave me a black Spanish saddle, too. Hard as a brick with little silver brads all over it. Horse's name was Black Eagle. He was a broom tail. One of the last of the wild horses caught 'round here."

"I never knew there were wild horses in this area."

"Oh yeah, used to be quite a few, but they're all gone now. Black Eagle sure weren't much to look at, but damn he was smooth to ride. Just like sittin' in a rockin' chair. He had a real narrow chest and weren't nothin' like a quarter horse, but I loved him all the same. Broke him out in front of the house. We had a real deep ditch out there, so I waited until a hard rain and led him into the water where it was harder to put up a fight. When he got used to me bein' on his back, I brought him out and ran him in the woods behind the house. That's how I got this," Eli says, touching the scar on his cheek. "Damn limb caught me, but I got to where I could turn that horse just by leanin' left or right, dependin' on which way I wanted him to go. He sure didn't want to run into no tree, so he learned pretty quick to pay attention. But even with all that trainin', he was proud cut and never really got past green broke. If even a few days went by that I didn't ride him, I'd have to break him all over again."

"I've heard of a horse being proud cut, but I'm not really sure what it means," I admit.

"Means Black Eagle thought he was still a stud horse. Whoever gelded him didn't do it right, so he'd act crazy. 'Specially 'round a mare."

"Did you ever learn to rope off him, like you'd planned?"

"No, never could get that far with him. But I sure did hunt off him a lot. And he weren't scared of nothin'. I could shoot a gun off his back, throw a live hog across him, and ride him through any creek in this country, just about."

"Where's he now?"

"Died a few years ago of old age. Don't really know how old he was when I got him, so he probably lived longer than most horses."

"Do you miss him?"

"Yeah, I do. We understood each other."

CHAPTER 19

As promised, we arrive at the Point bright and early to meet Irene. Devoid of its usual crowd, the sandbar sits lonesome, like an abandoned carnival, waiting for the weekend to arrive.

We find Irene squatting in her garden with a huge sombrero shielding her face. Seeing us, she stands and wipes her hands on worn overalls cut off right above the knee.

"Hey, goodlookin'," Eli calls.

She shoves her hand trowel into her back pocket with unnecessary force. "Been waitin' on y'all for hours."

I look at Eli in confusion. It's only 8:15.

She nods toward the house. "Made some coffee ... it's prob'ly cold now."

Eli laughs loudly and catches her in a rough embrace. "Aw, you know you can't stay mad at me."

She gives in to the attention, grabbing Eli's face with one

hand. "Quit tryin' to charm me. You know you're already my favorite." She gives him a quick peck and shoves him away. "Come on, I'll show you my papayas."

Past a fence overgrown with fragrant wisteria, several raised beds hold an impressive harvest.

As I pick up a ripe fruit and hold it to my nose, the banana-candy fragrance makes my mouth water. "Your plants look very healthy, Irene. Have you ever used any sort of chemical fertilizer or insect repellant on them?"

She sputters and snorts. "Don't b'lieve in that cancer-causin' shit."

"That's wonderful!" I clap my hands together. "Would you be interested in becoming a supplier to the clinic?"

"Really?"

"Of course. I'll have to check with Doc on the specifics, but I'm sure we can work out a deal where you'll be very well-compensated."

Her eyes widen. "Y'all don't need to do that. I got plenty. Tell Doc he can have all he wants. Eli, go on in the kitchen and get us some of them Walmart bags. You know where they are."

When we've filled the last bag to capacity, we follow Irene into the house where I'm assaulted by the strong scent of yeast. It takes a moment for my eyes to adjust to the dim interior, but I can't make out the origin as we step up to Irene's avocado green kitchen sink and take turns washing our hands.

When we finish, she claps hers together. "Alright. Since we got that job outta the way, now it's your turn to help *me* some."

Eli lifts an eyebrow. "Whatcha got, Aunt Irene?"

She walks over to the cabinet and pulls the lid off a five-gallon bucket. "Gonna make up a batch of muscadine wine."

Mystery solved, I peer into the bucket of yeasty juice, intrigued. "How'd you learn to make wine?"

"My grandma Gertie. Now, don't get me wrong, she was a God fearin' woman 'til the day she died, bein' Pennycost and all. But Grandma always did march to the beat of her own drum. Used to quote 1 Timothy 5:23. 'No longer drink only water, but use a little wine for your stomach's sake and your frequent infirmities.' Guess it worked too, 'cause she lived to be a hundred and five." Irene laughs and hands me a handwritten notecard stained with age. "That's her recipe, right there."

"Muscadine Wine" is scrawled in shaky cursive across the top, with "Mrs. D.W. Bergeron" underneath. I touch the name with the tip of my finger and consider how odd it would be to use the old custom and sign my name as Mrs. Jeffrey Frost. But I guess it's better than Sunday Frost. I never expected to end up as a weather condition.

I point to the bucket of fermenting juice. "Is it hard to make?"

"That's what I'm 'bout to show you," Irene says with a twinkle in her eye. "Eli, grab that other bucket over there and put this cheesecloth inside a colander. Should be one in the cabinet up there."

I've had muscadine jelly many times, but never muscadine wine. I breathe in the deliciously familiar scent as we strain the pulp from the mixture of berries, water, and yeast.

"Eli, dump them bags of sugar into that clean bucket. And here..." Irene hands me a long spoon "...you stir it up as he dumps 'em in. Stir it up real good 'til all that sugar melts."

I squat next to the bucket as Eli pours in pound after pound of sugar. When he's done, his body lingers close behind, his arm grazing mine as he holds the bucket steady. I stir harder, fighting the urge to close the gap. To lean in and feel the heat of his chest pressed tight against my back. It only lasts a moment. A wisp of time that shouldn't leave a print. But when he moves away, I feel the loss.

"Now, this next part is important, you hear?" Irene says, holding up a large white balloon. "We gonna put one of these on the top of the jugs and store 'em in a cool, dark place. As the wine ferments, it'll blow the balloon up real big and after a while it'll finally deflate. That's how you know it's ready to drink. But listen." She gives us a stern look. "Don't be usin' them cheap-ass dollar store balloons. What you need are some quality party balloons. That's real important. Otherwise, this shit'll turn to vinegar and be just plain awful."

Eli and I both swear to never use "cheap-ass" dollar store balloons when making wine, and though Irene still glares suspiciously, the oath seems to satisfy her for the moment.

She wipes her hands on her stained apron with determination. "Now, we better get a move-on to the clinic."

"What?" Eli and I say in unison.

She looks surprised. "You said Doc needs them papayas."

"Oh, yeah. But not right away," I say. "I can bring them to him once I'm finished with everything else."

"No tellin' how long it'll be 'fore you're done traipsin'

'round these woods and by then they could all be ruined. We'll bring 'em on over there today," she says with a tone of finality. "Come on, I'll drive."

"We better mind her or she's likely to call the whole thing off," Eli whispers, ushering me outside toward Irene's worn-out Toyota. Coated in dirt and dull gray primer, the truck has at least an inch of sand in the floorboard and a bed full of trash.

Irene places the bags of papayas in the passenger seat with care and gestures to the bed. "You kids load up."

"You mean ... in the back?" I say, not fully comprehending.

"Ain't no room left in the front," Eli states, unfazed by the suggestion.

One glance at the trash-filled truck bed has me whirling in protest, but Eli's solid form stands in the way. My face only inches from his chest, I attempt to dart around. But he's faster, grabbing me up and hauling me into the truck with ease.

Before I can get my bearings, he braces himself with one hand and leaps over the side, claiming a seat on the only clean fender well. I frantically search for somewhere else to sit, but he's already banging his fist on the roof of the cab signaling for Irene to drive.

When the truck lurches forward, I panic and make a blind grab for Eli, who pulls me onto his lap.

I keep scanning for a place that isn't covered with fish guts or rotting garbage, but Eli reads my thoughts and tightens his hold. "You're fine right here. Ain't botherin' me a bit."

CHAPTER 20

Of course Eli isn't bothered, the brute. But even as I heave an irritated sigh, I'm keenly aware of his muscular thighs shifting beneath my own and the strength of his arms circling my waist.

"Relax," he croons. "You're stiff as a board."

It seems like the more I try to ignore him, the more my body betrays me.

At last, I take a deep breath and give myself permission to lean back. Rest my arms on top of his and try to forget how good it feels to be in such a precarious position.

When his chest rumbles with silent laughter a moment later, my eyes dart around, searching. "What's funny?"

He clamps a warm hand on top of mine. "I'm ticklish."

I stare at the spot, mortified to realize I've been absently stroking the soft hairs of his forearm. With stilled hands and a scarlet face, I close my eyes and will Irene to drive faster as we wind our way along the backroads, each mile bringing us closer to my neck of the woods.

Before we can cross over the Sabine, the sight of an old man on a red three-wheeler causes Irene to slow and roll down her window. "Hey there, Tobe. Why don't you back up a bit, so we can pull in?"

The man smiles without making eye contact and kicks his three-wheeler into reverse. When he backs up without turning his head, I realize he's blind.

I turn to Eli. "What's he doing, sitting out by the road like that?"

"Listenin'."

"For what?"

"Cars."

"You mean, he was planning to drive down the highway?"

"No, just cross it." Eli jerks his head toward the tiny dirt road across the street. "Goes over to Ol' Man Havard's to drink coffee with him a couple times a day."

I study the small wood frame house in the distance. "He lives here alone?"

"Yeah, Tobe's a tough ol' bird, that's for sure." Eli motions to a garden where rows of vegetables sit neatly spaced and immaculate. "See that garden? Does it all himself. He'll make a row, then turn 'round and set one of the tractor tires down in the rut to go down it the opposite way. That way he has big, wide rows that are easy for him to find."

We spend a few minutes chatting with Tobe about every-thing from the weather to who might have shot his barn cat before Irene grabs his arm for a handshake. "Guess we better get on now."

"Wait just a minute," Tobe says. "Got somethin' for you." He steps into the house and returns with a gallon size Ziploc bag full of Skittles. "There now, let that girl have 'em," he says, handing over the bag and rubbing his face with one hand. "They sore up my jaws, and the dog won't eat 'em."

Irene plops the bag of Skittles in my lap and gives me a wink.

"Do I really sound that young?" I say as Tobe zooms away.

"Yeah, but at least you look full growed," Eli says, making a blatant show of staring down my shirt.

"Stop being a creep," I say, unable to keep a straight face at his antics.

"Y'all hang on," Irene yells, shifting into gear. But before she can pull back onto the road, we pause for a moment to let Zeb Prince pass.

"He's still alive?" I whisper as Zeb kicks his dappled gray Paso Fino stud into a faster gait. The nervous horse jigs sideways for a moment, flashing the whites of his eyes, but Zeb takes it in stride, keeping his focus straight ahead. Long hair hangs in stringy clumps under a short-brimmed leather Stetson, and his thin western shirt is left unbuttoned, revealing a chest gleaming with sweat. The butt of his infamous sawed off shotgun sticks out of a leather scabbard at his knee, and he touches it as his mouth moves in a constant mumble. I wait for him to look our way, but he never does, like always.

I only remember seeing him two or three times as a kid,

but a crazy man riding a crazy horse is not something easily forgotten.

"Heard he got outta Rusk just the other day," Eli says, absently.

Rusk State Hospital for the mentally insane is a place with a notorious history made even more real by the stretch of morbid-looking brick buildings with eerie billows of steam rising from the rooftop. I've always pitied the people imprisoned there and shudder to think of the barbaric "treatments" they are made to endure. It's rumored that Zeb has been admitted by his family at least a dozen times but always returns home after a few months. It's said he could power up a light bulb with all the electric currents that have passed through his brain.

My heart goes out to Zeb as he clops into the distance with no real destination in mind. "Poor man."

Eli follows my gaze. "Sad part is, he'd prob'ly be alright if everybody'd just leave him the hell alone."

I meditate on his words as we cross over the river and the familiar landscape of Old Salem takes shape, tidy and tame and acceptable. Sandwiched between the Baptist Church and the public library, the Navarre Medical Clinic sits right in the heart of town, and I cringe at the thought of being identified bouncing along on Eli's lap in the back of Irene's dilapidated Toyota.

"We're gonna get a ticket riding around like this."

"Nah. Ain't nobody gonna see us," Eli says, waving at two old men sitting on a bench outside the feed store.

"*They* just saw us! Do they not count as people?"

"I mean the law. They're all over at Dorothy's this time of day."

As we pass the church, Emma honks and waves as she pulls out of the parking lot.

When Eli waves back, I jerk his arm down. "Would you please stop acting like we're in a parade?"

His lips form a straight line, but I can tell he's trying not to laugh. "Never got to be in a parade myself. Kinda like it," he says, waving at a stranger walking into the library.

When Irene screeches to a halt in front of the clinic, I jump to my feet.

Eli offers to help me down, but I smack his hand away. "I don't need any more of your assistance, Mr. LeBlanc," I say, trying to ease over the tailgate without actually touching it.

"Oh!" Georgia squeals, bursting out of the office and running toward us. "I told Doc I thought that was you!" she says, wobbling a bit when her hot pink stilettos hit a rock. "What're y'all doing back so early? I thought you had another day or two left."

I pull out a bag of papayas. "Irene let us harvest these from her house and didn't want them to ruin out in the heat."

Eli layers all the heavy bags on his forearms and hoists them into the air.

Georgia tears her eyes away from his muscles to study the fruit. "Oh, aren't they just gorgeous! Doc is gonna be so pleased. He's with a patient right now, but I'm sure glad y'all stopped by." Her eyes track Eli as he heads for the door. "Just set them down right there at my desk, honey, and I'll take care of the rest."

When he and Irene disappear inside, Georgia grabs my arm. "Tell me everything," she whispers in a rush.

I pull away. "Um, well, we got most of the things on Doc's list except the snake root. Now, that's a story all by itself ..."

She lights a cigarette and bats the smoke away with a manicured hand. "No. I don't give a damn about the list. I wanna know about *Eli*. How's it working out with you two?" She elbows me in the ribs. "How's it been *living* together?"

"Goodness gracious. Don't say it so loud."

"*Please*," she begs, fluttering black falsies that are coming unglued at the edges.

"If you must know, it's cramped. And the houseboat is like fifty years old. It doesn't even have a bathroom. We have to bathe in the river. Like animals."

Georgia's eyes round. "How exciting!"

"It most certainly is *not* exciting. It's ... *inconvenient*. Especially when he decides to walk around stark—"

"*Naked?*" She squeals, jumping up and down at the juicy tidbit.

"What's all this about?" Eli says from a few feet away.

I stiffen and Georgia looks like she just swallowed a bird.

"Nothing. Are y'all about ready?" I say, irritated by his eavesdropping.

He nods toward the building. "Just waitin' on Aunt Irene. She's in there yackin' with somebody. Shouldn't be too long."

Georgia drops her cigarette and grinds it into the pavement with the toe of her high heel. "I better get back to work." She looks at Eli with regret. "Don't be a stranger, you hear?"

His smile reveals a dimple meant to charm. "Always a pleasure, ma'am."

She heads back inside, giggling and patting her hair into place.

"I got a surprise for you kids," Irene calls, striding toward us. "What you say I treat y'all to an ice cream?"

With heat shimmering like waves across the pavement, an ice cream sounds divine. But before I can answer, I notice Eli slipping into the now-empty passenger seat. "Hey, that's not fair!"

He pats his lap and grins. "There's room for two."

I bite my tongue and climb into the truck bed without giving him the pleasure of a response.

Just as I settle onto the fender well, Georgia runs back outside holding a large vase of yellow roses. "I can't believe I almost forgot! Looks like you have an admirer, Miss Sunday."

I take the flowers and open the tiny attached envelope.

Dearest Sunday,

I know I've been a little stubborn, but I want you to know I've had a change of heart. When you walk down the aisle to become my wife, it should be in the dress of your choosing. The color doesn't matter. Nothing matters except your happiness.

All My Love,
Jeffrey

Heat radiates through my chest at Jeffrey's words, and I

shake my head in disbelief as I slip the card inside the envelope. He really is the man of my dreams.

Irene slides open the window in the back glass and gives me an expectant look. "Everything alright?"

"Absolutely perfect."

"Good. Now for those ice creams I promised."

I grip the vase to my chest as we ease down Main Street, but blink in confusion when Irene puts her blinker on too soon.

"What are you doing?" I say, leaning down to shout through the back window.

"Gotta run through the bank. Didn't bring my purse," Irene says.

Dread courses through my veins as we enter the business lane of the drive-thru and I cringe at the thought of seeing someone I know. When it comes to the likelihood of running into old acquaintances, a hometown bank is worse than the grocery store and post office combined.

When Irene slams the truck into park in front of the window, I briefly consider lying in the bed and covering myself with trash. Instead, I duck my head behind the vase of flowers and squeeze my eyes shut, pretending to be a two-year-old. If I can't see them, they can't see me, right?

"What're you doin'?" Eli says in an amused voice.

I crack open one eye. "Trying to disappear."

"Now why would you wanna do a thing like that? Shouldn't you be catchin' up with old friends right 'bout now?" He winks and nods to the teller behind the glass.

I stare at the woman and Baylee Brown stares back.

Baylee was everything I wasn't in school—blond and tan and perfect. Or at least her mama thought so. I can still hear Mrs. Brown's shrill voice detailing Baylee's accomplishments to anyone who would listen.

"You just have to see her new dress. It's drop-dead gorgeous. Drove all the way to Dallas to buy it from the reigning Miss Teen Texas. Baylee just had to have it, and her daddy won't tell her 'no' about nothing. He's gonna be working overtime the rest of the year to pay for it. But mark my words, if she don't win the title of Miss Old Salem, I'm sure gonna have something to say about it. If another one of them Hamilton girls gets it this year, this mama's gonna come unglued on that pageant director."

Baylee's still blond and tan—leathery if I'm being honest—but her pageant days are clearly over, and the realization gives me a vindictive sense of satisfaction that some might call mean-spirited. But when I think of what a bitch she was, especially that night at The Flame, I really don't care.

"Well, Sunday Frederick. Just look at you," she says, blinking rapidly as her gaze sweeps over the truck. "They said you were back in town. I assume life's treating you well?"

I sit up straight and lift my chin as if I'm not in the back of a landfill on wheels. "Very well. Thanks for asking. And you?"

Her smile falters. "Oh, you know. Same old, same old." Her attention snaps back to Irene. "Will that be all, Miss Bergeron?"

Irene lifts her hand to wave and pulls onto the road.

I bend down and look at Eli. "Remind me to move my account somewhere else."

"You could try, but seein' as there ain't no other banks in Old Salem, looks like you're stuck with Baylee."

I groan.

"If it makes you feel better, did you hear Zack left her?"

The news that he and Baylee ended up together wasn't much of a shock. They were made for each other. But the idea that *he* left *her*, instead of the other way around, makes me sit up and pay attention.

"What happened?"

"Ol' Zack got caught runnin' around with Baylee's first cousin. Oh, it was a big to-do. Heard it all went down right there in the bank when that girl came in showin' off one of them ultrasound pictures, braggin' that it was Zack's. Wish I could've been a fly on the wall that day, I tell you."

"I had no idea."

Eli's head dips forward. "Heard Baylee flipped out and climbed through the damn teller's window holdin' that girl by the neck. Prob'ly woulda killed her if the law hadn't showed up when they did."

My mouth falls open and I burst out laughing at the idea of little miss perfect Baylee having her dirty laundry aired for all to see. But after a moment of reveling in her misfortune, I regret wishing her ill. She may be a hateful, spoiled peacock, but she still has feelings. At least, I hope she has feelings. Everyone has feelings, right?

I shake my head. "I just can't believe it."

Eli snorts. "I can't b'lieve it didn't happen sooner."

When we reach Irene's, the sky has dimmed, and the air holds the damp smell of rain.

"Careful," Eli says, throwing his arm in front of me as we hurry across the lawn.

Startled, I look down and scream at the sight of a huge black snake with yellow markings. "Kill it!"

"Well look at that," Irene says, bending to pluck the snake from the ground.

I bite my lip and calculate the distance to the nearest hospital.

"Just a king snake," Eli says in a calm voice. "Ain't poisonous."

"I don't care. I hate snakes," I say, gripping my vase of roses as if they'll protect me from harm.

"Aw, there ain't no reason to be scared of this one." Irene studies the creature. "He's just what I been needin' to get rid of that damn chicken snake that's been stealin' all my eggs. Come on, let's see what happens when we set him loose."

Poisonous or not, I follow at a safe distance as she and Eli stride toward the shed beside the chicken coop.

Irene hands Eli the snake. "Set him up in them rafters. I can't reach 'em."

He stretches to place the snake on the nearest rafter of the shed, and we all watch in anticipation as the agile hunter goes to work, weaving its way in and out, back and forth, in search of his prey.

"Look at him go," Irene says with pride. "He can smell that some'a bitch, sure can."

Seconds later, just as Irene predicted, a terrified chicken

snake shoots out of one of the eaves, straight as an arrow, landing on the ground with a thump. The king snake follows, hot on its trail, and the pair slide across the yard in a frantic race for the wood line.

When the king snake puts an end to the gluttonous adventures of the chicken snake, Irene slaps her leg and gives a loud whoop. "That'll teach that egg-suckin' varmint." But her triumph is short-lived as the sky darkens and the wind picks up, whipping her thin hair across her forehead. "Guess I better go get my plants in. Y'all be careful out there."

Thunder rumbles in the distance and a drop of rain hits my arm. The air vibrates with energy as we run across the sand, the water bucking and rolling beneath the waiting boat.

"Sit down back here with me and hang on." Eli cranks the motor and hands me a faded beach towel from under the front compartment. "Here. Cover up. We're gonna go fast."

I'm not sure Eli's version of "fast" is something I care to experience, but with the river getting choppier by the second, we'll have to be quick.

Water sloshes from the vase cradled in my lap to join the fat drops pouring from the sky and stinging my face like needles as we accelerate. Using the towel as a shield, I squeeze my eyes shut and clench my teeth to keep them from rattling with each jarring bump.

"Can't keep goin'," Eli shouts after a few more tense moments. "Too dangerous."

The boat makes a sharp right, and I lift the towel long enough to catch a glimpse of light burning across the sky, its wicked fingers illuminating a strange, dilapidated houseboat.

Eli pulls alongside the structure and grabs a post. "Go on," he yells into the storm, dragging me to my feet.

Safely deposited on the spongy porch floor, I stand dripping and feeling useless as Eli ties off the boat and struggles to open the warped front door.

"Whose place is this?" I say, looping the soaked beach towel over a porch rafter.

"Belongs to Rat Reynolds, but he ain't used it in years," he says, motioning to the debris-filled porch where remnants of old trot lines lie in a heap next to a yellowed ice chest.

After a hard few shoves, we burst into a one-room dump littered with trash and broken furniture. A vinyl card table, one metal folding chair, a kerosene lantern, and a single cot seem to be the only remaining useable items.

Eli lifts the tiny aluminum window overlooking the porch, but it doesn't do much to freshen the stale air. "Hope this thing lets up soon," he says, squinting at the sheets of wind and water.

My eyes settle on the lone cot in the corner. "And if it doesn't?"

"We'll have to stay here."

With reluctance, I place my pummeled and drooping roses on the table and help him rummage through the collection of dusty cabinets lining the back wall. My ice cream is long gone and I could use some real food, but the hunt only yields one tiny can of Vienna sausage and two cans of pork and beans. After a long and fruitless search for a can opener, Eli haggles at the beans with his pocketknife while I gingerly pop open the can of Vienna sausage. There are no bowls or flatware, so we divide our spoils between a chipped glass pie pan and a metal pot lid flipped upside down as a makeshift plate.

I study the pie pan in my lap. "This must be how it feels to be homeless."

"Homeless? With roses?" Eli says, nodding to the vase.

I glance at the wilted flowers and roll my eyes. "You know what I mean. It's not like we can eat them or anything."

"Now you're usin' your noggin'," he says, shaking a finger in my direction. "But I'm sure bein' homeless is a whole lot worse than this, pasquale."

I take a bite of a tepid Vienna sausage and feel slightly unconvinced. "You got anything to drink?"

"Just some beer out there in the ice chest." He points to the boat. "Get me one too while you're up."

I glance at the storm raging outside and remain seated. "Tell you what, I'll flip you for it. For who gets the beer."

He lifts an eyebrow and reaches into his pocket. "Don't have any change. How 'bout rock, paper, scissors?"

"Alright."

"Best two outta three."

After round one, I accuse him of cheating. After round two, I'm sure of it. After round three and a lot of arguing, he agrees to a fourth where I fare no better.

Sighing in defeat, I slink to the door and study the rain blowing sideways. As much as I despise getting soaked a second time, there's no way around it. I lost, fair and square.

I step out and crouch low, gripping a post as the boat pitches violently, bumping the side of the porch. Before I can get my leg onto the front deck, Eli bails past me into the boat, grabs the cooler, and returns in a flash.

"Just wanted to see if you'd do it," he says with a grin.

"Well, aren't you just the perfect gentleman."

He drops the cooler inside with a thump. "Never said I was a gentleman. Least, not the kind you're used to."

"What's that supposed to mean?"

He plunges a hand into the icy water and fishes around. "Just that the gentlemen I know don't go 'round puttin' on airs and takin' advantage of people. Ol' Jeffrey might clean up nice, but a hog in a silk waistcoat is still a hog."

And just like that, my gratitude for Eli's selfless act is replaced by a burning desire to slap the stupid grin right off his chiseled face.

"Stop being an asshole."

"Just tellin' the truth."

I narrow my eyes and fold my arms over my chest. "Oh, because you're *such* an expert on relationships?"

"I ain't gotta be an expert in poker to call a spade a spade. And I always know a losin' hand when I see one." He pops the top on a beer and takes out his soggy tobacco pouch. "Damn it, if I couldn't use a chew right now," he says, tossing it on a pile of yellowed newspaper in the corner of the room.

"Sounds to me like it's a good time to quit that disgusting habit," I say, not even trying to hide my contempt.

For many people in the South, tobacco—especially smoke-less tobacco—is just a way of life. To this day, the ledge over the speedometer in Mama Pearl's gold Cadillac is lined with dried tobacco wads Mr. Lavergne considers too good to throw away. One time, I asked him how long he thought he could go without a chew. He said he reckoned a man could live for an hour or so. Of course, as a doctor, I don't endorse this behavior. But if I'm being truthful, Eli's habit isn't really the issue. The issue is how freely he throws insults and accusations Jeffrey's way. My fiancé may not be perfect, but neither is Eli and it feels good to have something to needle him about in return.

We sip our beer in silence as the storm rages outside until boredom results in the discovery of a chess set in the top of a forgotten cabinet.

"Who taught you to play?" I say after a few rounds.

"Uncle Wyatt."

"I'd like to meet him."

"He died when I was ten."

"Oh … sorry. I didn't realize."

Eli shrugs but the nonchalance doesn't reach his eyes. "It's okay. I have lots of good memories, mostly of him takin' me huntin' and fishin' … stuff like that."

"He was the one who named you Wampus Cat, right?"

"That's him."

"It must've been hard to lose him," I hedge, a bit uncomfortable about approaching the subject. This is farther than I've ever gone when prying into Eli's emotions. No matter how irritated he makes me, I can't help wanting to know more. To dig deeper into what makes him tick.

He clears his throat, his eyes growing distant. "My uncle weren't really what most people would call a good man. Got in trouble a lot with the law. Mostly for stealin' and stuff like that, but nothin' that ever really hurt nobody ... Except the time we burnt down the woods."

I'm taken aback by his matter-of-fact tone, but try not to show it. "Is that when Texas outlawed hunting with deer dogs?"

"Yep."

"What do you mean when you say 'we burned down the woods'?"

"Just that. All the hunters 'round here knew the timber companies were behind the ban, so they got 'em back the best way they knew how. Right in their pocket. Remember sittin' in the middle of Uncle Wyatt's old red Ford with a box of cotton rope in my lap when I was just a li'l fellow. I'd hand him a piece, 'bout yay long." Eli holds up both hands, about eight inches apart. "He'd light it on fire, give it a second to catch, and throw it out the window."

"Is that the kind of thing you think'll happen when we open the ranch?" I venture, unsure I want the answer.

He studies the floor. "Prob'ly worse, if you wanna know the truth. These people ... the ones who've hunted and fished this land all their lives ... they're never gonna understand. Never."

I twist my hands in my lap, out of reasons to disagree. "So, your uncle never got caught setting the woods on fire?"

He crosses his arms and leans back in his chair. "Not in the act. But believe it or not, Texas Monthly came out and did a whole report on it ... with pictures and all. Still have one of Uncle Wyatt standin' there with all his best deer dogs."

"Oh yeah, I remember that. Was it the one that basically called everybody out here a bunch of inbred idiots?"

"That's the one."

"So, how'd your uncle manage to stay out of jail if everybody knew he did it?"

"You know, I've thought a lot 'bout that over the years and I don't rightly know. Guess them are things a li'l boy don't remember too good. He was a good uncle and he loved me. That's what I remember most."

A pang of understanding shoots through me at the sentiment. I know what it is to love like that. Mama Pearl isn't someone many people understand. She isn't perfect, but she loves me unconditionally and that's all that matters.

My chest tightens at the thought of Eli left all alone in the world when his uncle died. Ten seems too young to be abandoned in such an unstable environment.

He clears his throat and walks to the window where the storm grows worse by the minute. "Looks like we're spendin' the night here."

When he turns to study my face, the electricity in the room rivals the bolts streaking across the sky.

Eli takes a seat in the chair. "You can have the cot. This is plenty fine for me."

It's a generous offer, but hardly seems fair. "What if we slept head to foot?" I blurt in an effort to compromise.

He frowns and walks over to the bed, bending low to inspect the filthy linens. "Damn, if this don't look like somethin' a gyp had a litter of puppies on."

I cover my eyes. "Please don't say anymore. I don't want to know."

"Well, pasquale, I've survived worse." He rolls his neck to the side until it cracks. "Go on and get situated. I'll blow out the lamp."

Fully clothed, I lie down with clenched teeth, not giving myself permission to look at the bedding up close. Then the light is gone, the room illuminated only by flashes of light through the window.

I scoot close to the wall when Eli settles in, but it's hard to get comfortable. Turning my head to the side, I flinch when my nose collides with his large, damp feet.

"Eli?"

"Uh huh?"

"I think I've changed my mind."

He chuckles and starts to get up.

"No, you don't have to sleep in the chair," I amend. "It's just the head to toe thing isn't really working for me."

He lies back down in the opposite direction, settling an arm behind my head as a makeshift pillow. "This okay?"

"Uh, yeah," I say, hating how good his body feels next to mine. "It's not like I've never slept on a cot before."

"Exactly when have *you* had to sleep on a cot?"

"Plenty of times. My sisters and I used to have campouts in the yard when we were kids." I smile at the memory of our safe little tent positioned not six feet from the front porch steps. "Or at least, camping's what we called it. It was more like glamping, really."

"Well, I ain't never been glamping, but I have a feelin' this ain't it." Eli rolls to face me and my skin prickles. "Goodnight, then," he whispers, his heart beating fast against my shoulder.

"Goodnight." I try to shut my eyes and go to sleep, but the feel of him so close makes it impossible.

"You wanna roll over?" he suggests when my fidgeting becomes obvious. "We might fit better that way."

My head knows spooning isn't a good idea, but my body has other ideas. Before I know it, my backside is cradled against Eli's hips, and my eyes round at the hardness pressing into me.

"Sorry 'bout that," he says, stating the obvious.

Not knowing how else to handle the situation, I wave off his concerns with a shaky laugh. "It's fine. We're both adults. I'm sure it's just a product of our circumstances."

He just laughs and pulls me closer. "If you say so, pasquale ..."

CHAPTER 21

Morning rays streak across the battered houseboat, warming my legs as I step onto the porch. A breeze comes across the water, sweet and new and welcome after our rather interesting night in the rundown haven.

I find Eli crouched low by the boat, his head bent over a tangled rope. I stop and stare at the glistening gold strands of sandy hair and jump a little when he catches me.

The corners of his mouth twitch as he stands to stretch his back. "Damn it, if I don't feel like I been rode hard and put up wet."

I know he's only talking about the storm and our cramped quarters, but my face burns at the memory of more intimate things. Between the storm, the tiny cot, and Eli's virile body wrapped around mine, I barely rested at all.

But ... I can't quite bring myself to complain.

Eli was a perfect gentleman, after all. Sure, he got a little aroused, but who can blame him? My butt *was* pressed up against him. It's a natural reaction. Nothing more.

I run my fingers through my knotted hair and grab my phone from my back pocket. It's dead. I hope I haven't missed anything from Jeffrey. The thought of him sends a pang of guilt through my chest. I need to go home. Sooner rather than later.

Just one more night and my life will be back to normal ... I hope.

❧

As Eli's houseboat comes into view, the sound of barking dogs echoes over the water.

Irene steps onto the porch with a worried expression. "Where y'all been?" she says, catching the side of the boat.

Eli jumps onto the porch and ties us off. "Got caught up in that storm last night. Had to ride it out at Rat's place."

"You tellin' me that shit-hole's still standin' after that gully washer? Wish I could'a been a fly on the wall for that rodeo."

"Aw, it weren't too bad," Eli says with a shrug that doesn't fool Irene.

Her eyes shift between us. "Hmm ... Well, guess y'all better go on and get a change of clothes so we can get goin'."

"Where?" I say.

Irene looks at me like I have two heads. "Get that hog thyroid."

I laugh and try to play it off as a joke, but the truth is I completely forgot. About all of it, actually. Eli is proving to be just the distraction I don't need.

After we change clothes, I peek through the window as Eli heads out to meet Irene and two other men, all wearing dog leads made of plastic-coated wire cable with brass snaps strapped across their chests. I plug my phone in to charge as they carefully set about loading dogs into large aluminum boxes positioned on the back of their four-wheelers, with three or four in each box and others tied and placed on top. Most are yellow with black mouths, but a few are red brindle or colored like Bleu, with black, white, and gray markings. They all wear unusual collars, each a different color, with black antennas jutting from the sides.

I start to turn away when a ferocious-looking dog catches my attention. A large pit bull with a neon yellow vest encasing his chest. He's loaded into a box separate from the others, and I make a mental note to find out why.

Everyone has on rubber boots, so I slip into mine and hurry outside.

As I near the group, Eli introduces two men who couldn't be more different. With a curly mullet of auburn hair and a lean, rawboned build, Gator greets me with a crimson face and split-second eye contact. But Coleman doffs his cowboy hat and holds my gaze with confidence. "It's a true pleasure to meet you, ma'am," he says, taking the hand I offer and holding it reverently. Tall and clean-shaven, Coleman seems bent on making a good impression. A ladies' man, through and through.

"It's a pleasure to meet you, as well," I say, a little embarrassed by the intensity of his attention.

At Irene's nod, we load into the trucks and drive single file toward the main road with four-wheelers, dog boxes, hog hobbles, dog collars, chains, and sheets of metal balancing on the lowboy trailer behind Eli's truck.

"All we need now is Irene sitting back there in a rocking chair," I mumble, looking out the back glass as we enter the business district of Devil's Pocket.

"You ain't seen nothin' yet," Eli says, pulling into the Get 'N Go.

Mildew stains and faded advertisements cover a tattered storefront where customers come and go, none giving our convoy a second thought—aside from looks of longing from a few men clearly headed to work.

We step inside—Christmas bells jingling as the screen door slams—and my eyes water as the putrid combination of burnt grease, roaches, and cigarette smoke wafts over me in a hot wave. By the temperature, I assume the air conditioning is broken or the owner is cheap, one being as likely as the other.

I hurry to grab a Dr. Pepper and am last in line when I spot a small woman working behind the grill in the back. Permed bangs cling to a forehead beaded with sweat as she positions sausage patties on the grill. I watch in horrified fascination as she retrieves two pieces of light bread—one in each hand—and buries her face in the slices with a long sigh of relief.

Unable to tear my eyes away, I hold my breath in anticipation of her next move. I half-expect her to just slap the bread right on the grill beside the patties. But with her face sufficiently blotted, she turns and dumps the saturated slices in a nearby garbage can.

"It's really the wrong time of year to hog hunt," Eli says when we return outside. "Too damn hot."

By the way my shirt clings to my body like a second skin, I have to agree.

He points to the tree line. "Gonna head right over there. We'll leave the trucks here."

I step back as he jumps over the lowboy and backs the four-wheeler down the aluminum ramps attached to the back.

"That buggy seems a bit full," Coleman says with a sly grin, observing Eli's four-wheeler and overstuffed dog box. Coleman gives me a wink and indicates his sparkling blue side-by-side. "May I extend the invitation for you to ride with me instead?"

"Come on. Let's go," Eli interrupts, waving me over.

I arch a brow. "What makes you so certain I'm riding with *you*?"

Eli jerks his head toward Coleman in disbelief. "Were you thinkin' of ridin' with him, then?"

"What if I am?" I say, enjoying Eli's irritation.

He steps close, the air crackling between us as his breath tickles my ear. "When that two hundred and fifty-pound some'a bitch comes rushin' outta them woods, we'll see who it is you wanna be close to, pasquale."

The thought of being attacked by a wild boar is enough to make me forget my stubbornness and squeeze between Eli and his cumbersome dog box full of barking canines. I don't mind being pressed against him, but the foul odor of hunting dogs coming from the box makes me gag.

Luckily, Eli surges forward, shifting up to fourth with his foot while I wrap my arms around his waist and pray we won't wreck. Trees flash by in a blur as we take the lead down a narrow trail leading into thick woods. We crest a hill and slow to a stop, the others following suit, and all the dogs except the vested beast are unloaded.

They go to work, frantically sniffing the ground with Bleu leading the pack, bounding in and out of the large pines, nervously searching for a track.

Coleman sidles up beside me. "Is this your first time?"

"It is. And you?"

"Oh, I've been a thousand times. Can get pretty dangerous out here. I've seen a hog cut a dog to pieces, but I've never lost one," he brags. "Got a hog the other day that weighed in at three twenty-five. Wrestled him to the ground all by myself." He juts his chin in the air and cuts his eyes to see my reaction. "Didn't wanna get my catch dog hurt, you know."

At Eli's loud snort, Gator chuckles, ducking his head and flushing bright red.

"Oh my, well that's very, uh ... interesting," I say, unsure what to say to the exaggerated tale.

"They on one," Eli says, studying a handheld GPS device.

"What's that for?" I say.

"Tracks the dogs. It'll take us right to 'em. Listen."

The faint sound of constant barking floats through the air as Eli studies the screen.

"Think they bayed?" Irene says.

"Yep." Eli slides in front of me and cranks the engine. "They're over in that club over yonder."

"Are you a member?"

He reaches into his pocket and pulls out the largest set of keys I've ever seen. "Does it matter?"

I let out a short laugh and snatch them from his hand as we accelerate. "You must have one to every club in Texas."

"Pretty much," he yells over the engine.

"Won't we get in trouble?"

"Have to get caught first."

I'd like to say his statement gives me pause, but being immersed in this way of life is having an effect. Relaxing my judgement. For better or worse, I can't decide.

We stop to unlock a gate and follow a red clay trail banked high on each side. The air turns cool, limbs brushing our legs until we surface into an open clear-cut where the tall pines have been stripped away, leaving behind fresh-smelling jumbles of earth and stumps. Rolling terrain stretches for miles, rising and falling in wild disarray with new life emerging from the soil in the form of young pines.

At the edge of the cut, we dip into a deep ravine where shadows from the tall timber and thick underbrush give the illusion of dusk. I cling to Eli as we maneuver through skidder ruts and over fallen logs. Throughout the dim valley, the ground is moist and muddy and the air holds a sickly sweet perfume.

I wrinkle my nose as we cross a deep hole. "What's that smell?"

"Hog."

"No, I don't think so. It's sweet. Like molasses. Or fenugreek."

"All I know is when you smell that, a hog's close by."

"Maybe the hogs eat fenugreek roots and the smell lingers in the air."

"Could be."

As we come to the end of an overgrown trail, the dogs' barking grows louder and the terrain more difficult. Eli releases the vested dog from his solitary confinement, and we abandon the four-wheelers to continue on foot.

I nod to the dog that seems to take all Eli's strength to contain. "What's he for?"

Irene adjusts the knife in her belt. "That's Bear. Damn good catch dog." At my confused look, she elaborates. "Them other dogs' job is to bay-up the hog. Bark at it and keep it from runnin' away. They're trained never to bite, just bark. But, Bear's only job is to catch the hog and hang on. Never let go 'till we get it tied or shot. That's why he wears a vest to protect him from the hog's tushes."

"You don't shoot all of them?"

"Naw. We ain't like them stupid sons-a-bitches from Houston or where ever. Them kind ain't got the balls to get in there and catch a hog, so they just shoot 'em. Even if it's a boar. But you can't eat a boar hog. Meat's no good. We always change 'em to a bar, that's a meat hog, and let 'em go. Then, when we catch 'em again later, the meat's good for eatin'. And we dock their tail, too, to make 'em easier to spot."

"Don't you mean a barrow?" I say, using the proper terminology for a castrated hog.

"That's what I said. A bar," she reinforces as if I'm losing my hearing.

"What if you catch a sow?"

"Well, this time of year they usually got some baby pigs, so we always let 'er go."

"I see. But I'm still confused about why it's legal to hunt hogs with dogs, but not deer."

Eli speaks up. "Hogs are bad 'bout rootin' up young pine saplin's, so the timber companies want to get rid of 'em any way they can. Ain't any difference in deer huntin' with dogs or hog huntin' with dogs, 'cept what the timber companies want. At the end of the day, it's all 'bout money."

I look down at Bear, who is pulling on his lead. "He seems anxious to get going."

Eli grins. "Then let's go!"

Bear bolts forward and the pair crash through the forest with the rest of us close behind. As the underbrush closes in and the mud thickens, the thought of being chased up a tree by a vicious hog with "cutters" jutting from its jaw makes me shake with adrenaline. Mr. Lavergne loved to tell about his hog hunting escapades when I was a kid. From what I recall, Piney Wood rooters are far from average swine. Found in a variety of colors and sizes, they're a breed specific to East Texas and can outwit even the most seasoned hunting dog.

I struggle to keep up with the group's unrelenting pace, but my legs burn and my breath comes in shallow gasps. When I pause to maneuver over a fallen log, my foot slips and

I fall to my knees just as the group makes a sharp right turn. Branches and vines pull at my clothing as I scramble to follow, but the trees thicken overhead, blocking out most of the light. In the gloom, it occurs to me that I carry no weapon. Not even a knife. If the hog escapes the dogs, I'm completely defenseless.

I keep walking, fast, scanning for a tree large enough to climb. Having lost sight of the others, a slow chill descends as I become more and more disoriented. My hair stands on end as I stumble through the thicket at a mad pace, fighting to contain the fear clouding my mind. Turning to retrace my steps back to safety seems like a good idea, but every direction looks the same. I force myself to slow down and listen for the dogs.

Time crawls as I close my eyes and wait for the pulsing in my ears to subside. Then I hear it. Up ahead. To the left.

The barking grows louder and choppier until a faint glimpse of Bear's bright yellow vest streaks through the trees.

A hog squealing. Loud shouts. A shot fired.

I break into a run, but it seems like forever before I make it to the clearing where the group huddles around a huge black hog. By the looks of it, getting lost may have been for the best. Eli's clothes are soaked, Irene has mud in her hair and a nice-sized rip in her shirt, and Gator has blood on his jeans and scrapes and cuts all over his arms. The only exception is Coleman. Aside from the tiny bit of mud on his boots, he looks as fresh and put together as ever.

Irene motions to the hog on the ground. "Got us a good size bar!"

"Sorry to leave you behind, pasquale," Eli says. "But Bear wasn't lettin' up. Drug me through the same damn creek twice!" He gives me a wink. "But I knew you could take care of yourself."

I square my shoulders with pride. I had taken care of myself, and it felt good.

Gator eases forward and Irene slaps him on the back. "Look at you, boy. Skunt up like a tongue ox."

The cuts on Gator's arms don't look deep, but I can't help asking if he's okay. Embarrassed, he looks down and mumbles something too low for me to hear.

Eli leans against a tree and takes a chew of tobacco. "I tell you, it's a wonder nothin' worse happened. The way them dogs was cuttin' up, we could tell they had a big 'un bayed. But the way that sucker was backed up in that myrtle bush, we couldn't see no nuts or nothin'."

I inch closer to the carcass. "How'd you get him out?"

"Cast Bear in there and when he caught, Aunt Irene and Gator scooped his back legs and flipped him. Then, I got him hobbled so we could start checkin' the dogs. Make sure they was alright."

"What about you, Coleman?" I venture. "What did you do?"

Coleman eyes widen. "Oh ... well, I um ..." he stutters.

"Useless as tits on a boar hog," Irene mumbles. "When it gets down to the nut cuttin', them purty ones ain't never got the grit."

"Y'ALL GO ON AHEAD," ELI SAYS TO THE OTHERS WHEN WE get back to the trucks. "Gonna stop off at Joe's for a minute." Without warning, he kicks off his boots and gives me a crooked smile as he strips out of his muddy clothes. Left wearing only his boxer briefs, he climbs into the cab. "Don't want that shit all over my seats."

My breath catches at the sight, but I try not to stare as we make our way over to Joe's Carwash. Located across the road from the Get 'N Go, it completes the business district of Devil's Pocket and seems especially busy for a weekday.

As we sit in line for a stall, Eli points to a slouchy brown and tan single-wide planted in the thin space of grass separating the carwash from the highway. "That's the house I grew up in," he says matter-of-factly.

"You grew up ... here? At the carwash?"

"No, not here. Used to be down close to Irene's 'fore Mama sold it to Joe. Looks like he's done some work on it. What I wouldn't have given for one of those when I was a kid," he says, motioning to the AC unit hanging out of one of the windows. "We'd sweat in the summer and freeze in the winter. Sometimes when it'd get real cold, Mama would light the oven and leave it runnin' all night to knock the chill off."

"She left a gas oven running? All night?" I say, unable to keep the shock and pity from my voice as I stare at the rundown dwelling.

Eli shrugs. "When I left, I swore I'd never live like that again." At my frown, he shakes his head. "Oh, I know what you're thinkin'. My place ain't much to look at either. But it's comfortable and it suits me ... for now."

Before I have time to process the statement, the truck in front of us leaves and we pull up. Eli jumps out and shoves quarters in the machine as if wearing only underwear and rubber boots in public is a common occurrence. Mortified, I glance around and slouch low in my seat as he stands with one leg propped on the side of the lowboy, spraying mud off the four-wheeler.

When he climbs back inside, I shake my head. "Are you asking to go to jail?"

"What you talkin' 'bout?"

"Public indecency! What do you think?"

Eli glances down in astonishment. "But I'm all covered up."

I press my lips together to keep from smiling. Damn him for making even the most embarrassing situation fun. I've never been so uncomfortable and comfortable around another human being in all my life. But one thing's for sure, no matter how hard I try, I can't stay mad.

CHAPTER 22

Thankfully, Eli slips on a pair of shorts as we prepare to scald and scrape the hog back at the houseboat. I can't blame him for remaining shirtless in the heat, but the sight of sweat beading on his tan skin only makes mine burn.

Irene builds a hot fire under a cast iron pot that reminds me of an old-fashioned syrup kettle, and Eli stands beside it, pushing the embers around with the toe of his boot as he waits for the water to heat. The temperature is tested periodically, using fingers or the quick dip of an elbow. For the hog to be properly scalded, it has to be just right. If too hot, it'll burn the skin and "set" the hair, never releasing it from the hide according to Irene.

I take a step back as Gator and Irene hoist the carcass onto the makeshift table made of rough plywood stretching across two saw horses. Eli covers the hog with a burlap sack to help retain heat as he pours hot water over the hog using a galvanized five-gallon bucket. He's adamant about working quickly in the hot sun to avoid the meat spoiling on the bone. After a few minutes, the burlap is removed, and Irene sets to work. Using long, even strokes, she scrapes the hair from the hide with a sharp butcher knife held with both hands, one on the handle and the other on the blade. I always assumed the process would be difficult, but the hair seems to melt off with each stroke.

"Can I try?" I say.

"Sure, baby doll," Irene says, handing me the knife.

"You could just dunk him in that creosote dip and save yourself a lot of trouble," Gator jokes, eyeing a dark barrel used to rid the hunting dogs of fleas.

Eli chuckles. "Been known to slip hair on a few, ain't it?"

Gator's face turns its usual shade of red as he bobs his head up and down in silent laughter.

When I mention skinning the hog to save the trouble of scraping the hide, Irene looks mortified. "Well, it may be legal to do it that way nowadays, but I don't like wastin' the best part. Cracklin's are my favorite."

"Skinning a hog used to be illegal?"

"Well, back in the old days every man had their own mark registered up at the courthouse to show which hogs belonged to 'em. Some cropped their ears and others docked their tails. I remember goin' hog huntin' with my granddaddy on horses when I was real li'l. I'd sit behind him and when we came up on a sow with a bunch of pigs, he'd use a string to catch up each pig. Them dogs would keep that sow busy while he'd pull 'em up on the horse, hold 'em across his lap, crop their ears, then let 'em down again. Never had to get off the horse that-a-way."

"What kind of markings did you use?"

"Let's see. There's the swallow fork, notch, crop, half-crop, hole, and about a thousand other ones I can't rightly remember."

"But, I still don't understand why that'd make skinning a hog illegal."

Irene frowns. "Guess it was seen as a sign you was tryin' to get rid of the evidence. Skin it and throw away everything except the meat so there's no proof you're stealin' another man's hog."

Gator nods to Eli with a glint in his eye. "Did you tell Sunday 'bout the one you got drunk that time?"

"What's this?" I say.

"Aw, he's talkin' 'bout a big ol' boar we chased all through this country one year. Tried traps and dogs and everything we could think of to catch him, but weren't nothin' workin'. Got all our shit cut down so many times, we was scared to send a dog in there after him. So, finally somebody come up with the idea to just get him drunk. Mixed up a bunch of cheap vodka with some soured mash and left it out for him. By the time he ate his fill of that shit, he didn't make it fifty yards 'fore he bedded up."

"You ready to find that thyroid?" Irene says, diverting our attention back to the task at hand.

The brownish-purple gland is supposed to be in the neck

between the lobes of the thymus, but it takes longer than I expect to locate.

"What you need it for, anyway?" Irene says, holding the knife while I probe around.

"Well, right now, a common method of treating thyroid disorders is natural medication made using thyroid glands from farm-raised pigs. By testing the gland of one raised in the wild, Doc will get to see how it compares in potency to the kind harvested from pigs raised in captivity."

After quite a bit of searching, Irene helps me retrieve and pack the slippery gland in a small cooler of ice. It's the last thing on my list. A signal it's time to leave. Go home. Back to real life.

But as I sit on the porch swing, hugging my knees to my chest sometime later, the faint smell of burning wood lingers over the slow-moving water, and I wish I could linger too. Stop time and stay in this place, invisible as smoke, until I have the answers.

"Well, that's done. Let them boys split up the meat with Irene," Eli says, rounding the corner of the porch. When his eyes meet mine, he stops short. "What's wrong?"

I plaster a smile on my face. "Nothing. I mean ... I was just thinking about leaving tomorrow."

His brows come together. "We get everything you need?"

"That's all of it."

"Oh. Well then ..." He swallows and looks away then walks into the house.

I sit on the porch a little while longer, watching the sun

dip below the trees on the horizon as the dried mud that covers most of my body flakes onto the porch floor. When the light fades, I go inside to gather my things for a bath.

Eli sits at the table with a beer in his hand as I head back outside.

But as soon as I strip and jump into the water, his tall form emerges.

"What're you doing?" I call out, hoping he'll get the hint to leave.

He walks to the edge of the porch and tugs at the top button of his shorts. "Takin' a bath. I smell like shit."

"Oh, no you don't. I was here first."

His continues undressing, his mouth lifting in a grin as he strips down to his underwear for the second time today.

"I'm not leaving. I mean it, Eli LeBlanc!"

"Never said you had to." The challenge in his eyes sends a shiver down my spine, and before I know it he's out of his shorts and into the water.

"Calm down. This river's big enough for the both of us," he calls, paddling toward me out of the gloom. "Toss me the soap, would ya?"

I want to tell him to find it himself, but the idea of him coming any closer is out of the question.

"Fine. But you just stay right there," I warn, feeling along the rough plywood. Peeking over the edge, I spot the elusive bar of Ivory a bit farther away than usual. No matter how I stretch, the soap remains just out of reach.

Then Eli's there, his chest lightly brushing against my

back as he reaches over, retrieving the soap. The idea of his naked body so close to mine makes me itch to be bold. To lean back and feel his skin sliding against mine. But I shrink away, sinking into the water like a coward.

Oblivious to my thoughts, Eli sets about scrubbing his hair, soap suds splattering my face in the process. I flinch and inch farther away.

He notices and paddles closer. "You're jumpy as a cat. What's the matter? I make you nervous?" he jokes.

My mouth goes dry.

"I do, don't I?"

I scramble for an excuse. "It's not you. I'd feel uncomfortable around any man ... this way."

He lets out a whistle. "Thought you was engaged."

"What does that have to do with anything?"

He's silent a moment. "Ah, I see ... Don't you like ol' Jeffrey?"

"Don't be rude," I quip.

"It's an honest question."

"Has anyone ever told you what an ass you can be?"

"Nobody as pretty as you."

"I'm serious."

"Listen, I'm not tryin' to upset you, I swear."

"I'm not upset," I lie.

"Then why won't you answer the question?"

"Because it's none of your business... But if you must know, Jeffrey and I are saving ... *that* for after we're married." Eli's soft laugh makes me bristle. "You're making fun of me."

"No. I promise I'm not."

"Then what? Tell me what's so funny about two people exhibiting a little self-control."

"Nothin'." His brows pinch together in genuine confusion. "You just make it sound so easy."

I lift my chin, proud of my restraint. "It *is* easy."

"Well ... it shouldn't be."

CHAPTER 23

Eli pulls himself onto the porch and takes his sweet time drying off as I fiddle with the shampoo bottle. Even though I'm technically mad at him, I fight the urge to peek. Just once. But my self-imposed standards get in the way, preventing any further dips in self-control. I've already gone too far. But as I imagine his bare skin glowing in the moonlight, my restraint seems more of a killjoy than anything else.

When I climb out of the water a little while later, Robert Earl Keen's "Feelin' Good Again" wafts from the kitchen radio, and I can't help tapping my toe to the lively tune.

"Put on somethin' pretty," Eli calls as I dart into the dressing area. "We're goin' out."

I peek around the corner. "What? Where?"

He smiles and pulls on his cowboy boots. "You'll see. Get dressed."

A few minutes later, I emerge from the houseboat to find him in a starched white western shirt and Wranglers. Standing in the glow of the fire with his hair combed neatly in place, he is quite striking ... in his own rugged sort of way.

My light floral dress is feminine and comfortable, but the way Eli's gaze sweeps over me makes me fidget.

"Where're we going?" I say, trying to cover my embarrassment.

"Rodair Club's got a band tonight. There's a 42 tournament goin' on too."

When I brush past, he sniffs the air. "You wearin' perfume?"

"Does tropical-scented bug spray count?"

"Good ol' Cajun cologne." He gives me a playful nudge and throws open the truck door. "Step up," he encourages, putting his boot on the running board in an obvious act of gallantry.

"You want me to *step* on your foot?"

"Well, I ain't gonna make you."

My eyes alternate between the muddy running board and my expensive Tony Lamas. The choice is clear, but the chivalrous display makes me uncomfortable.

"What's the matter with you?" I accuse, taking his hand.

"What'cha mean?"

"All that ..." I wave my hand toward the door as he slides in beside me.

"Quit actin' like you never had a man hold the door open for you."

"Of course I have, but ..."

"But what?"

"You know what I mean."

"I do?"

"It's not like you're my boyfriend or anything," I venture, cutting my eyes to see his reaction.

A muscle in his jaw flinches. "No, I sure as hell ain't."

By his clipped words and thunderous expression, I know he's pissed. But I have to stop our slow descent into unknown territory. Dangerous territory.

When he skids sideways into the parking lot of the Rodair Club and kills the engine, we sit in awkward silence, staring at the aged cypress exterior of the club as people come and go. Positioned against a sandbar for those arriving by boat or pirogue, the Rodair is famous for its live music and even livelier crowd. But the faint strains of happy accordion music floating from the giant screened windows are a direct contrast to Eli's current mood.

My eyes shift to the haphazard Christmas lights draped above the mildewed sign, and I try to think of something to say. Some way to take away the hurt etched into his features. This is a side of Eli I've never seen and feel totally unprepared to handle.

I turn slowly and clear my throat. "Listen, I didn't mean anything by what I said back there. I hope I didn't—"

His hand comes up. "No. I prob'ly overreacted."

"You sure?"

His features relax and he nods. "Yeah. You ready to go in?"

"Absolutely."

Music, laughter, and neon lights beckon as we approach the front steps, but the excitement is cut short when I spot

Romance's old Chevy pulling in ahead of us. I can't see his face, but the way he's slouched over the steering wheel stops me dead in my tracks.

"Is he okay?" I say to Eli.

"Yeah, why?"

"Look how he's bent over."

"Just a habit left over from years of night huntin'."

"How so?"

"Sits like that so the other guy can rest his gun on the driver's side windowsill if he needs to make a shot in that direction."

I breathe a sigh of relief when Romance kills the truck and jumps out, spry as ever.

"Hey, how's your leg?" Eli calls.

"Fine as frog hair," he calls back, bounding up the honky tonk stairs with a light step. "That gal's voodoo potion sure did the trick."

Eli's eyebrows shoot up. "Hear that? Looks like you're a regular miracle worker."

My chest expands with pride as I follow Eli up the steps. "Tell me something I don't know."

When we reach the top, he yanks me out of the way just as a drunk man crashes through the window, ripping the screen in the process. The man lies motionless on the porch a moment, then curses and rolls onto his side with a low moan. I scan his body for injuries. But, aside from a bleeding lip and a bruised ego, he seems to be fine.

Unperturbed by the event, Eli chuckles and lock eyes with a redheaded man standing by the busted out screen.

Eli nods toward the drunk sprawled on the porch. "Helped him find his truck, I see."

"Some'a bitch didn't know when to quit," the man replies, wiping blood from his knuckles with a greasy-looking rag. When they're sufficiently clean, he gives Eli a sly grin. "How the hell you been, son?"

"Oh, up to no good, as usual. Good to see you, Frog."

We walk inside where they chat for a moment, but when a buxom blonde saunters by, the man called Frog excuses himself with a wink. "Think I see my next ex-wife."

"Ain't no big-tittied gal safe 'round Frog," Irene declares, appearing from the shadows.

Eli laughs and shakes his head. "They don't call him the pot-bellied stallion for nothin'."

Irene hands each of us a beer and leads the way to a small table near the dance floor. A Cajun band is set up against the back wall, and the floor in front is packed with dancers.

When the song ends, the echo of voices and clack of pool balls mingle with the low buzz of attic fans pulling damp air in through dusty window screens. The draft causes low hanging lights to sway over green felt as players chalk cues and calculate shots.

I absently wonder how I'd fare in a game. But it's been years since I've played, and my opponents in the billiard room at Belle Terre are a far cry from a regular honky tonk crowd. I remember begging Mr. Lavergne to bring me to the Rodair, just once, to see what is was like. To my everlasting disappointment, he always shook his head and mumbled something about how Mama Pearl would tan his hide.

Saturday nights were his time off to enjoy as he pleased, which usually meant a trip to the honky tonk. Dressed in a tidy black suit with a crisp white shirt that glowed against his tanned skin, he'd head out the door with a spring in his step. I used to worry the habit would encourage a lapse in his sobriety, but true to his word, he never slipped. In his usual blunt manner, he admitted to being an alcoholic as long as he could remember. Spending every dime on the habit, he had wandered from place to place, doing odd jobs and drinking away his profits by morning. But when he came to Belle Terre, his transformation was miraculous. I think his need to be needed was what saved him. And needing is an area in which Mama Pearl excels.

I turn to Irene. "Do you come here often?"

"I'm here when he is, baby doll." Clearly smitten, she nods toward the man on stage with an accordion strapped to his chest. I recognize him as the legendary Wayne Toups. "He sure can tear up that squeeze box," she says, patting her chest.

Eli nudges her with his elbow. "Well, what you waitin' for? Band's 'bout to take a break. Now's your chance at him, Aunt Irene."

"You rascal! You know me better than that!"

When the band steps off the stage, couples sway to a Vern Gosdin recording while others prop against the wooden railings surrounding the dance floor. I like how the crowd is a mix of all shapes, sizes, ages, and ethnicities. The river bottom is certainly not bland. It's a place where eccentricities are celebrated and odd quirks create legends, not outsiders.

I spot Romance pushing a petite older woman across the floor in a two-step to "Set 'em Up Joe."

"Look," I say, poking Eli. "He's a really good dancer."

"How do you think he got his name?" a gruff voice says from behind us.

We turn to see Li'l Bit's huge form hovering close to Irene. His head dips as he touches her on the shoulder. "This seat taken?"

She looks surprised and a little flustered. Dressed in starched Wranglers and a pearl snap western shirt, Li'l Bit cuts a nicer figure than I would've thought after our first meeting. And if the blush on Irene's cheeks is any indication, she seems to agree.

"Well, you sure clean up nice," she says, admiring his attire.

He puffs out his chest, enjoying the attention.

"Want a beer?" she says.

He takes a breath and shakes his head. "Naw. Need to cut back."

"Well, that's real good to hear. Real good."

At Irene's warm smile, his shoulders relax and he takes a seat. "Might be out your way tomorrow. Got any plans?"

"Naw, just be piddlin' 'round the house."

"You wanna help me run some trot lines?"

Irene gives him a curious look then grins. "Thought you'd never ask."

Eli moves away from the pair to stand beside my chair. "It's good to see Li'l Bit get out."

"I think I know the reason."

He nods and offers his hand. "Come on. Let's give 'em some space."

We skirt our way around the dance floor to find a better vantage point of the 42 tournament on the opposite side of the room.

"Is this like regular dominos?" I say.

"No, not really. It's played in teams."

Eli attempts to explain the complicated game, but as the fourth trick is distributed to the players, they simultaneously push their dominos into the middle without a word, signaling the game is over.

After spotting Coleman over at the pool tables, we weave our way through a crowd that's equal parts Urban Cowboy, Swamp People, and a nineties Garth Brooks concert. The blonde Frog pursues is particularly interesting. With a banana clip adorning her brassy, permed hair and skin tight Rocky Mountain jeans with triangle cutouts down each leg, she's a sight. Batting lashes rimmed with electric blue eyeliner, she shamelessly flirts with Frog, but her gaze rarely strays from Coleman's lanky form at the pool table.

Clad in all-black with a wad of keys jingling at his hip, Coleman's snakeskin boots catch the light as he struts around the table, inspecting his next shot.

His opponent leans against the wall with a confident smile underneath a handlebar moustache the color of dirty dishwater. His faded orange Nomex look like they've seen better days, but something in his eyes tells me he's more than he seems.

Eli nudges me with his elbow. "Ten bucks says Cigar is 'bout to shit in the middle of ol' Coleman's trail."

"That so?"

Eli sniffs and rubs the back of his neck with one hand. "Coleman thinks he chawed rozzun, so Cigar'll let him win just enough to get the stakes up. Then he'll show him who's boss." When Cigar proceeds to make a game-changing shot, Eli wiggles his eyebrows. "Told you."

"Hey, there's Jess," I say, spotting her blond head darting through the crowd with Colorado close behind.

"Look!" she says, thrusting her left hand in my face.

It takes a moment to register the diamond ring and the meaning behind it. "So you're ... engaged?"

"No, we got married, silly," she beams, looking at her new husband. "Went to the JP this mornin'. Didn't see no sense in waitin'."

Eli slaps Colorado's back. "Look at you grinnin' like a 'possum eatin' peach seeds. Congratulations, man. Sure didn't know you was plannin' to jump the broom."

"Aw, it was kinda spur of the moment. But we're gonna have a big ol' crawfish boil in a week or two to celebrate."

As Eli orders us all a shot of whiskey, I study the couple with an unexpected pang of envy. They didn't have a real wedding ceremony. Or reception. Or big plans for the future. Yet there's beauty in the simplicity of their love. The world may see them as poor, and up until recently, I might've agreed. But it seems wealth only serves to muddle the certainty of a lover's convictions. Money can't be ignored or devalued. It's always there, adding sparkle to the overall package. It's always there, making people doubt the notion of true love.

When the band kicks off a lively Cajun jitterbug, Eli saves me from my grim musings by nudging me with his elbow. "Wanna dance?"

I'm sure he's only offering to be polite, so I hesitate.

"Come on," he says, pulling me to the floor. "You know you want to."

His feet move in time with the vibrant beat as he urges me into the familiar steps. With music pulsing around us, my movements become surer and more fluid.

"This ain't your first rodeo, I see," Eli says. And he's right.

Thanks to Mr. Lavergne, dancing became a tradition at the Frederick house growing up. We'd clear the kitchen after supper and take turns dancing in our socks to D.L. Menard, Nathan Abshire, Wayne Toups, Jo-EL Sonnier, and so many others. Excellent at the waltz, Mr. Lavergne would float across the floor twirling us as Mama Pearl clapped along. It's been a long time since we've had a family dance, and I didn't realize until this moment just how much I've missed it.

All too soon, the music fades, but Eli holds me close, waiting for the next song. As we sway to a slow, easy version of "Blues Man," he joins in and his deep baritone sends pleasant shivers through my body. Eli is clearly only singing about the haphazard life of Hank Williams Jr. But my heart hears something else.

Wait. No. I've got to stop doing this. A juvenile infatuation is one thing. But this is something else. I bite my lip, angry with myself for letting Eli get too close. Too intimate.

Even if his intentions are innocent, mine are increasingly not. And moments like this make it so much worse. Moments where I could lose myself in the feel of his body pressed to mine, muscles shifting under crisp cotton.

I close my eyes and breathe in his scent, all whiskey and water and woodsmoke. It speaks to something primal I've worked hard to suppress. Something I want to bury and be done with forever. But just like the river, it keeps flowing, pulling, bend after bend. A force of nature I'm helpless to fight.

I step on his toe and stumble. Maybe I'm just drunk.

"Here ..." He shifts his body to the right so our legs intertwine like puzzle pieces.

"I'm sorry," I say, looking away and praying the song will end.

He pulls back, studying my expression. "Come on, let's get you some fresh air."

Being alone with him is the last thing I need. But as I stare into his clear blue eyes, I can't say no.

CHAPTER 24

On the back patio of the club, I lean on the railing overlooking the river. Eli hands me a beer, and I sip in silence, enjoying the stillness as the moon reflects in a thousand glittering accents across the inky water.

"You okay?" he says after a while.

"Yeah. Maybe I'm just hungry or something," I say, grappling for an excuse that's sort of true.

He gives me a wink and disappears inside the club, reemerging a few minutes later with a funnel cake on a paper plate.

"Where'd you get that?" I say, surprised at the offering.

"Beer ain't all they serve in there, you know."

I take the plate and dig in, licking the heavenly white dust from the tips of my fingers. "There's nothing I love more than powdered sugar. Especially when you're cooking and it gets in the air so you can taste it." Eli frowns and I shove him lightly. "Come on. Makes me happy. What makes you happy?"

"Not powdered sugar. Battered a whole batch of pork chops in that shit one time. Thought I grabbed the flour."

"You're lying."

"Give you my word," he says with a straight face. "Them sons-a-bitches wouldn't brown-up, no matter what I did. Worst pork chops I ever tried to eat."

I burst into a fit of laughter. "But I'm serious," I say, grabbing the railing to catch my breath. "I really want to know what makes you happy."

Eli stares at me but doesn't respond.

I slap him on the shoulder. "What's the matter? There's gotta be something."

He looks away and clears his throat. "Guess the smell of gunpowder." He seems uncomfortable by the admission, so I nod in silent encouragement. "Right after you fire, that li'l bit of powder you smell. Reminds me of my uncle and the first time he took me huntin'." Something passes across his face as he takes my hands and pulls me close. His head dips, his face inches from mine. "You wanna know something?"

I gulp and try to nod, but remain rooted in place.

His fingers thread through my hair as he lingers at my ear. "You're the first person ever asked me that."

"Asked you what?" I say, unable to think clearly.

"What makes me happy." He inches closer, his lips grazing my neck like the brush of a butterfly's wing. "What if I said *you* make me happy too? What if I said I don't want you to leave tomorrow?"

Something in me shifts when his lips meet mine in a brief touch. But he pulls back, looking for my reaction. Asking permission.

I know we should stop. I know it's wrong. I know I'm engaged to someone else. But from the moment Eli touched me ...

My lips crash into his, hard and hungry. Remaining upright becomes a struggle until Eli's arms circle my waist, pulling me even closer as I lose myself in the moment. I cling to him, reveling in the feel of his body even as I push the guilt to the back of my mind.

A door slams. People from the club coming outside. It's the wakeup call I desperately need to stop and walk away. But when Eli pulls me toward the parking lot with determined steps, I don't resist. Excitement beats like a drum as I follow him through the darkness. And then he's lifting me up and settling me inside his truck.

He takes a breath, closing his eyes. "What are you doing to me?"

Not wanting the spell to be broken, I grab his shirt and tug him forward, our bodies colliding in a frenzy of need that feels surreal. I'm ashamed to admit, even to myself, that I've dreamed about this moment since I was sixteen years old—but never expected it to materialize.

I wrap my legs around his waist, urging him on as he trails hot kisses down to my collarbone. When his mouth finds the swell of my breast, my back arches as I push against him.

"Please," I say, needing something, anything, to quench the fire.

He slides my dress up around my hips, his hand settling between my legs. I know I should pull away. Tell him to stop. But denying myself now is out of the question. Oxygen would be easier to give up.

Eli coaxes until my vision blurs and I cry out, tingling with pleasure as he feathers kisses across my neck. Gasping for air, I sag against his shoulders wondering how a person can feel so good and so bad, all at the same time.

My rational side begs me to stop. To take a huge step back and think about the consequences. But I don't want to think. I want to feel. To throw caution to the wind and live fully in the moment. I nuzzle Eli's neck and fumble with the button at the top of his fly, anxious for everything he has to offer.

The action causes him to stiffen and pull back, the atmosphere shifting in a way I can't explain. "Listen. There's somethin' I want to tell you. Somethin' you should know. And if I don't say it now, I may never get up the nerve again."

"The Eli I know doesn't have a shy bone in his body," I say, amused by his tone.

"I'm serious, Sunday. Just hear me out."

I sit up straight, not knowing what to expect. "Okay?"

His head dips as he clears his throat. "I used to think I had everything I'd ever need. Ever want. But being with you made me realize that's not true. Waking up and seeing you every mornin'—I don't want to go back to the way it was before. This. Us. It feels like somethin' that's always been. Somethin' that should go on bein'." He raises a hand to my cheek. "I love you, Sunday. And I meant what I said. I don't want you to leave. Stay. Stay with me forever."

His confession is like a match striking in the dark, burning hot and beautiful and deadly. I stare at the flame, too scared to touch, too enamored to turn away. I open my mouth to say something. Anything. But the words are lodged in my throat.

Eli just proclaimed his love for me, and all I can do is blink.

"But you said it yourself. You don't need anybody," I sputter.

"Not anybody. Just you."

My mind works to make sense of the situation. How could I have let this happen? I'm not sixteen anymore. I'm an adult. And I'm *engaged*.

My time on the river may have been magical, expanding my horizons and my heart, but ... I can't put it off any longer. I have to go back to the real world and the commitments I've made there. Doing the right thing sucks sometimes. But it's still the right thing.

Tears fill my eyes as I will myself to speak the words. Words that will forever put an end to whatever this is between us. "I'm so sorry, Eli. I can't do this."

His expression cuts me like a knife. "I don't understand."

I pull away, needing space to articulate my reasoning. "I made a promise to Jeffrey, and I can't just—"

"You don't love Jeffrey." Eli spits the name like it's poison.

I bite my lip until it hurts and force myself to deliver the final blow. "Yes ... I do."

Eli shakes his head, taking a step back.

I want to reach for him, but I can't. Not now. Not ever again.

Squatting down, he stares at his boots and rubs a hand over his face. Moonlight filters through the trees, forming dangerous shadows across his sharp features.

"This isn't real," I say, trying my best to be rational no matter how much it hurts. "You and me ... I mean, the way we've been together twenty-four seven, it's natural to think you feel something. To think we feel something for each other. But we don't. It's just not real."

I wrap my arms around myself and wait for him to speak.

He stands slowly and lifts his chin. "You just keep tellin' yourself that, pasquale."

His words are soft, but they feel like a slap in the face as I watch him walk away. I want to call out. To beg him to stay and talk and come to some sort of mutual agreement. But all I can do is run to the edge of the parking lot and empty the contents of my stomach into the nearest bush. I tell myself it's from drinking too much, but my heart knows better.

When I finally stand up and look around, Irene is waiting with her hands on her hips. "Got a bone to pick with you," she says in a low voice.

I wipe my mouth with the back of my arm and take a steadying breath. "What's the matter?"

"What's the matter is you're a damn fool! Eli's mighty upset. Ain't seen him like this in a long time. Told me to bring you back to my house for the night." Her lips press into a tight line as she shakes her head. "You can drive home in the mornin', I guess."

The ride to Irene's is long and awkward as I drown in a pool of embarrassment and guilt. I know she's mad at me. Eli is too. But I have no way to fix it. Nothing to say that will make things right.

When Irene shows me to the spare bedroom, she tells me to make myself at home, but the usual warmth is gone from her words. This whole night has become a terrible jumble of emotion, and I'm desperate to sort it out. I know Eli is hurt and confused. I am too. But that doesn't give him the right to drag Irene into it. It's simply unfair and if I don't stand up for myself, no one will.

When she turns to leave the room, I stop her. "Listen, I understand Eli's upset, but you have to admit his behavior is a little bit childish. Who does he think he is just throwing me out like that?"

Irene waits a moment before responding. "I'll tell you exactly who Eli is. He's a man grew up mistreated. Been thrown away plenty of times by the people supposed to care about him the most. But he's done his best to put that behind him and make a new life for himself. So, when he says he cares for somebody, you can bet it's the real deal. That's who he is." She crosses her arms over her chest. "Now, Sunday, you know I've always thought the world of you too, but I ain't gonna stand by and watch you string him along."

My eyes well at her blunt words. "I never meant to do any such thing."

She holds up a hand. "All I'm sayin' is you need to either shit or get off the pot."

I nod and stare at the floor, letting her words sink in. "What'd you mean when you said you haven't seen Eli like this in a long time?"

Her eyes narrow. "Night of your graduation, while all you kids was off celebratin', Eli was gettin' shown the door by his mama."

"You mean ... she kicked him out?"

"Claudette had his suitcase waitin' out on the porch when he got home from the ceremony. Told him if he weren't gonna join the Marines like she wanted, then he could hit the road. Thought she'd force his hand. Make him do and then she'd get to brag that her boy was a United States Marine and all that. But Eli bucked her on it and struck out on his own." My throat tightens as Irene's face contorts at the memory. "When Claudette called me squallin' 'bout what happened a little while later, I went out lookin' for him, straight away. Found him camped out in an old half-burned-down trailer house behind the Get 'N Go. Brought him back here and watched him drink a whole damn fifth of whiskey, sittin' on my porch steps. I tried to get him to stay here that night. Sleep it off. But he wouldn't. Said he had to get away. I tried to stop him ..." She shakes her head, looking into the distance with hollow eyes.

"What happened?" I whisper, not sure I want to know.

"He lit out in his uncle's old boat fast as he could go. Didn't have no light or nothin'. Watched him run plumb up the trashy side of the river like he didn't care if he lived or died. Way he was drivin', I just told myself that was the last time I'd prob'ly ever see that boy. Think it's the hardest I ever prayed for another livin' soul." She wipes her eyes with the back of her hand and clears her throat. "When I got the call later on that night to come get him outta jail, you'd of thought I'd won the lottery 'stead of postin' bail."

"Jail? How'd that happen?"

"You know, I was so proud to see he weren't dead, I didn't even think to ask," she says with a laugh. "He lived with me after that for a spell. Just 'til he got his feet under him. We'd go out on the water almost every day, fishin' and talkin'. It's amazin' what a little attention can do for a kid. Sometimes it's all they need to get back on track." Irene sighs, her eyes softening as she pats my arm. "I know you didn't mean for nothin' to happen between y'all, but it happened all the same. And it ain't nobody's fault. Life's full of surprises. You just ain't lived long enough to realize you can't control who you love. Or who loves you."

Love? I shake my head. No, Irene is mistaken. Infatuation, maybe, but not love. Love takes time to develop. More than just a few days. Eli is confusing love with lust, plain and simple.

I stand up straight and lift my chin. "You're wrong, Irene. About all of it."

"Maybe I am ... But what if I ain't?"

CHAPTER 25

Irene's words haunt me on the drive back to Doc's office the next morning. I drum my fingers on the steering wheel and turn them over in my mind. She said life is full of surprises. But I don't like surprises. I like plans. And Jeffrey always has a plan. Sure, Eli helped me see a different side of life, but that's where it ends. What was I thinking letting him get so close? Letting him … No, I refuse to let my mind wander to what might have been. Last night was a mistake. The worst one I've ever made. Shame churns in my gut until hot tears spill over. How could I have let this happen?

I wipe my eyes and dial Jeffrey's number, needing to hear his voice. Needing forgiveness for something I can't even admit.

"Hello?" he says after one ring.

"Hey, it's me."

"Did you get the roses?" he says in a rush.

"They're beautiful."

"As are you, my dear. I can't wait to see you."

We talk a little more, but I can't bring myself to say what's really on my mind. I want to confess. To come clean about everything. But how?

I hang up and park at the clinic's back entrance.

"Sunday! Back already?" Doc says, eyeing the cooler with interest as I walk into his office.

I found it, along with my clothes and other supplies, sitting on Irene's porch this morning. A grim reminder of the hurt I've caused.

Doc waves me inside and leans on the desk with his hands clasped together. "So, tell me all about your trip."

I hesitate, not knowing where to begin. "We found everything except the snakeroot," I say, sticking to the basics.

Doc nods. "I thought you might have trouble with that one."

"Charlie Shankle sells it, but he refused to tell us where to find it. We even followed him one night to try to see, but we ended up at the The Cult, instead. Which is a whole other story ..."

Doc frowns. "Cult? You mean Eli's place?"

I shake my head. "No. The Cult. You know, that big creepy compound down the road from Belle Terre?"

"Yeah, I know the place. Used to belong to a friend of mine. Plastic surgeon out of Houston. Very private man. It's a nice piece of property. Beautiful gardens. Big house in the back. When he died last year, his estate put the place up for auction. Eli got a pretty good deal on it. You didn't hear?"

The idea of Eli LeBlanc as the new owner of The Cult is the most preposterous thing I've ever heard. "But that can't be right. I mean, where did he get the money?" I say, thinking out loud.

Doc snorts. "Don't let that boy fool you. He makes damn good money and has more of it squirreled away than most men twice his age."

I open my mouth to question Doc further when Georgia walks into the office with a worried look. "Sunday, you have a phone call."

"Oh ... thanks. Be right there," I say, realizing I've left my cellphone in the Jeep.

"You can take it in here," Doc says, motioning to the phone on his desk.

I pick up the receiver. "Hello?"

"Sunday?" It's Emma. "Sunday, I ..." Her voice cracks.

"What's wrong?"

"It's Mama Pearl," she chokes out between sobs. "She's gone ... You need to come home."

CHAPTER 26

"What do you mean, she's gone? What happened?"

"I think maybe a heart attack. She went to lay down for a nap, but when I checked on her a while ago, she ... she wasn't breathing."

Grief threatens to choke me, but I push it aside to focus on the logistics. "Does Dani know?"

"Yeah, she came in last week."

"I'm on my way."

I knew this was coming, but it doesn't soften the blow. Mama Pearl's death is the haunting inevitable that's followed me all my life. Like a silent wave building, it crashes to shore with a mixture of pain and guilty relief tinging the waters gray. I don't know what to think. How to feel.

I jump in my Jeep and dial Jeffrey's number, barely able to choke out what has happened.

"Oh, Sunday. I'm so sorry." His voice is full of pity as he promises to come first thing in the morning. "I'd come now, but I have an important meeting with the investors later this afternoon. Can you forgive me?"

The idea that he isn't coming right away hurts, but I'm too distraught to argue. I just want to get home.

When I pull up to Belle Terre, Emma is standing on the porch beside Mama Pearl's empty hammock.

"Where is she?" I say, hurrying up the front steps.

Emma massages her temples, her eyes red and puffy. "In the house. The JP just left. I guess the visitation will have to be here. You remember how much Mama Pearl hated funeral homes." She grabs my hand. "Mr. Lavergne's working on the casket now. He wants to make it himself. Insists he's the only one who'll do it right."

Mama Pearl was very particular—or peculiar, rather—about every aspect of her life, and this attitude follows her in death. She always made it clear she wanted a homemade, pine box-style, closed casket, a graveside service, and no involvement with a funeral home. She detested the thought of being embalmed and left on display in a casket lined with "tacky satin fluff." Her wishes may not be the norm, but we will all make sure they are honored. With all she's done for us, it's the least we can do for her.

Tears blur my vision as we enter Mama Pearl's bedroom where her abundant candle collection casts a warm glow outlining her body draped in a favorite quilt. I know it's her, but it's like looking at a stranger. I touch her hand, hard and cold and still, so unlike the Mama Pearl I know.

Irene and Dani stand at the head of the bed, arranging her hair now more white than blond. "Already got her washed up," Irene says. "Now we just need to get her dressed."

The idea fills me with dread, but it has to be done. I turn to Emma. "Can you get her lace shawl and that linen nightgown she always liked?"

She retrieves them from the chifforobe beside the bed and stands still as a statue, just like me.

"Hand that gown here," Irene says, impatient with our hesitation. She takes out her pocket knife and opens the blade. Emma's eyes widen as the fabric makes a ripping sound, the knife slicing a long, vertical line down the back.

"Stop! You're ruining it!" Emma screams.

"Aw, I ain't ruined nothin." Irene drapes the gown over Mama Pearl. "See, I had to do it like that. Now, come help me get it up her arms."

I should've guessed Irene would know what to do. With Mama Pearl's gown arranged, we sit at the foot of the bed listening to the clock's *tick, tick, tick* from the hall. No one speaks. There's nothing to say.

When Mr. Lavergne taps on the door, I jump at the sound.

He peeks inside, shuffling his feet and motioning to the wooden casket sitting in the hall behind him. "It's ready. Tried to hurry it up. Hope it's good enough."

"Oh, it's beautiful," I say, studying the fine craftsmanship.

He looks at the floor. "You know I'm just a jake-leg carpenter."

I walk to the foot of the bed. "Why don't we position it down here?"

He nods and slides it into place, but I have no idea how we're supposed to lift Mama Pearl and place her inside. As the ominous task looms, even Irene seems at a loss. But a knock at the front door interrupts.

Emma answers and Eli's low voice rumbles down the hallway. When I stick my head out and our eyes lock, I don't know what to feel. How to act. I know he was close to Mama Pearl, but after the way we parted, I'm amazed he bothered to come at all.

He motions me into the hall where we stand, each struggling to find the right words.

"Listen," he says, clearing his throat. "I'm real sorry about Mama Pearl. And for last night. I just needed to come and ... What I mean to say is I'd like to help, if there's anything needs doin'."

His offer is gracious and more than I deserve, so I try to respond in kind.

I glance into the bedroom and my shoulders slump. "There is one thing."

He follows my gaze and nods in understanding.

"But you don't have to if ... if you're uncomfortable," I whisper.

He frowns and brushes past me into the room where everyone is gathered around the bed.

Eli rubs his chin. "This ain't gonna be easy, but I think we can do it if we work as a team."

Following his directions, we each grab a handful of the

bottom bed sheet. Rolling the sheet in our fists, it takes all of us, lifting in unison, to place Mama Pearl inside the casket. I help Emma lay the quilt over her lap and take a step back. Neatly arranged, wearing her linen and lace, Mama Pearl looks like an angel. Our angel.

The rest of the day is a blur of visitors. A few, like Doc, Charlie Shankle, and Sister Faye, truly care about our loss. Most are merely curious about the mysterious Belle Terre and the oddities therein. They filter through the house like ants, one in front of the other, whispering wide-eyed as they navigate the trails through the clutter. It's stressful and embarrassing and irritating all at once. And by the end of it, I'm completely drained. Numb, really. All I want is sleep. To drift off and wake up to realize this was all just a horrible nightmare. I need time, not a social event, to come to grips with what's happened. But reality is rude and unyielding. It doesn't wait until you're ready.

When the crowd filters away, Irene pats my shoulder. "You should go on and get some sleep now. Got a lot to do tomorrow."

I try to take a deep breath, but grief rises in my throat like hot lava at the thought of saying goodbye.

Her expression turns worried. "You want me to stay with Mama Pearl tonight, baby doll?"

Eli shakes his head. "No need, Aunt Irene. I'll sit up with her."

Sitting up with the dead is a time-honored tradition in our part of the world, usually performed by older, retired friends of the family who use the time to show their respect for the one who's passed and reminisce about the good old days in their long, exaggerated manner.

Mr. Lavergne steps forward and shakes Eli's hand. "I was gonna do it myself, but I'm mighty obliged to you, young man."

I want to thank Eli too, but can't find the words to express the gratitude in my heart. Nothing does it justice.

Irene leaves and the others go to bed. But I stay, hovering near the casket and wishing for something to say.

"Why didn't you tell me? That night at The Cult. Why didn't you tell me it's yours?" I say for lack of anything better.

"I was going to ... Guess I just wanted to have a li'l fun with you first."

He settles into a rocking chair and waves a hand toward the staircase. "Go on to bed, now. Get some rest."

"Okay," I whisper, feeling like a coward as I slink out of the room. After a few steps, I turn back around. "I want you to know I appreciate what you're doing, truly. But I just... I mean, after everything that's happened, you could've left like everybody else. Why are you doing this? Why are you still here?"

His blue eyes pierce straight through me. "I think you know exactly why I'm here, pasquale."

CHAPTER 27

The sound of knocking jolts me upright. "Come in," I say, trying to get my bearings.

Jeffrey steps into the room, resplendent in a light blue dress shirt, navy blazer, form-fitting camel-colored chinos, and Italian leather oxfords.

"Time to get up, sweetheart," he says in a gentle voice.

I blink and catch my breath as the memory of our loss washes over me, the pain just as sharp and raw as the day before.

Jeffrey strides forward and sits on the bed, gathering me in his arms and kissing my hair. Any animosity I felt during our phone conversation melts at his touch.

"What do I do now?" I sob. "She was all I had. She was my family." I bury my face in his chest, inhaling his cologne.

He rocks me gently. "That's not true. You still have Dani and Emma and Mr. Lavergne. And you'll always have me and

Mom and Dad. We'll make our own family. We can have twenty kids, if that's what you want."

I laugh through my tears. "I'm not looking to be on reality TV."

"There's my girl. Everything's going to be fine." He pulls back a little, eyeing my wild hair and puffy face. "Listen, the funeral's in two hours, so why don't we get you put together?"

All I want to do is curl into a ball, pull the quilt over my head, and never come out. But I know he's right.

"Thank you for being here," I say, reluctantly standing up.

"Where else would I be?" He squeezes my hand and glances down at himself. "I hate to ask, but do I look okay? You said to dress casual, but I brought a suit, just in case."

"No, you look great," I say, thinking how out of place he still seems despite his effort to appear otherwise. "What you're wearing is fine. No one else will have on a suit, except maybe the preacher."

He nods, but his eyes dart to the window. "There's one other thing we need to talk about."

I stiffen, not sure I can handle any more surprises. "What's wrong?"

He hesitates, searching for the right words. "They said the funeral will be a graveside service, but nothing's ready. I sent Mom to find out what's going on."

"What do you mean?" I race to my window for a view of the family cemetery not far from the house—the beautiful fenced-in nook with wild roses, wisteria, and gardenia adorning the generations of loved ones at rest.

Jeffrey comes to stand behind me. "Well, for starters,

there's no tent, no chairs, and no AstroTurf. The casket's just sitting on a stand right on the open grass beside the plot. It's covered in some sort of evergreen arrangement. I think we should call the funeral home right now and get this all straightened out."

I close my eyes and breathe a sigh of relief. "No, it's alright. Everything's just as Mama Pearl wanted it."

"You mean ... it was *planned* this way?"

Jeffrey's forlorn expression makes me smile in spite of myself. "Yeah. I promise it's not a big deal. She hated all the conventional things associated with funerals, so she did away with it all when planning her own."

"Oh, okay. I guess I'll just go downstairs and wait then."

He shuts the door with a quiet click and before I know it, we're all gathered around freshly-tilled dirt, listening to Will Jackson play "Amazing Grace" on his fiddle. Jeffrey is by my side with his hands clasped together, and Gwendolyn keeps glancing my way.

After the song, Brother Sayer's deep voice opens the service with 1 Corinthians 15: 54-55. "When the perishable has been clothed with the imperishable, and the mortal with immortality, then the saying that is written will come true: Death has been swallowed up in victory. Where, O death, is your victory? Where, O death, is your sting?"

Clamping the Bible shut, he tucks it under his arm and stares intently at the casket, measuring his next words. "Mama Pearl was a mystery to most people. She rarely left Belle Terre and was content to keep to herself. But her spirit stretched well beyond the confines of her home. She had a servant's heart. A heart that saw a need and did something about it. She didn't have to give generously to charity and mission work, or fund the soup kitchen in town. She didn't have to allow her neighbors access to her property." He nods to Dani, Emma, and myself. "And she didn't have to do such a fine job raising these three young women as her own. But she did it anyway. Because it was right. Because it was good."

Jeffrey moves behind me and begins massaging my shoulders. In the heat, the attention is irritating. I wriggle out of his grasp and glance up to catch Eli watching us with a curious expression.

When it's time to lower Mama Pearl into the ground, Eli, Mr. Lavergne, Charlie Shankle, Doctor Navarre, and Zeb Prince step forward in silent reverence. Mama Pearl never mentioned knowing Zeb personally, so I'm surprised to see him among the pallbearers. I appreciate his gesture, but the rumors of his unpredictable nature make my palms sweat as he takes his place beside the casket.

Jeffrey remains rooted by my side as the men bend to grab the ropes, so I nudge him with my elbow and incline my head as a signal to take his place with the other men. He blushes crimson at the gaffe and stumbles a bit as he jumps to join the group of volunteers.

Side by side, Jeffrey and Eli help lower the casket. Dressed in his crisp, white western shirt, Wranglers, and cowboy boots, Eli is Jeffrey's opposite in every possible way.

Jeffrey's hair is black as pitch and as polished as a raven's wing. Eli's is sandy-blond and always disheveled. Jeffrey has pale, smooth features and large, amber eyes rimmed with dark lashes that beam with the freshness and vitality of youth. Eli's tanned face and clear blue eyes hold the scars and stories of men twice his age. Jeffrey's expensive attire is brand-new and of the latest fashion. Eli has on the only nice clothes he cares to own in a western style that hasn't changed much since the 1800s. Jeffrey has dreams and plans for the things he wants to accomplish. Eli has accomplishments but no real plans.

Will takes out his fiddle to signal it's time for the final farewell. As he plays "It is Well with My Soul," our family steps forward to drop light pink roses in unison. Mr. Laverne kneels on one knee, his eyes closed and head bowed. Dani, Emma, and I hold hands, tears flowing freely down our faces.

After the song, Zeb Prince steps forward and assumes a dominant stance. I know Zeb is supposed to be crazy, but in this moment, I hope he doesn't *do* anything crazy.

The crowd stiffens in anticipation of Zeb's next move and when his voice booms out, Gwendolyn gasps and my stomach drops. Eli takes a step toward him, but stops as the unexpected clarity of Zeb's words register.

"Hark! from the tombs a doleful sound,

Mine ears attend the cry;

Ye living men, come view the ground

Where you must shortly lie.

Princes, this clay must be your bed,

In spite of all your towers;

The tall, the wise, the reverend head,

Must lie as low as ours.

Great God, is this our certain doom?

And are we still secure?

Still walking downward to the tomb,
And yet prepare no more?
Grant us the power of quick'ning grace
To fit our souls to fly,
That when we drop this dying flesh,
We'll rise above the sky."

My nose burns, prompting a wave of fresh tears so raw I can barely catch my breath. Zeb clearly understands the pain of isolation from which Mama Pearl is finally free. His honest gesture isn't much, but the impromptu performance means more to me than anything before it.

"You ready to go inside, sweetheart?" Jeffrey says, taking my arm.

I hesitate and glance at Eli. He locks eyes with Jeffrey, but turns away.

The rest of the afternoon, I hide in the kitchen, busying myself with the food in an attempt to avoid pitying looks and halfhearted sentiments from people I barely know.

Sister Faye catches me and narrows her eyes. "You sure you don't wanna go out and rest a spell? You look plumb wore out. I'll finish up these dishes."

I give the door a wary glance. "No ... I'd rather stay in here with you."

She frowns and walks over to place her warm hands on my head. I don't have to hear the words to know she's praying. After a moment, she speaks with the authority of a prophet. "I know you feel lost right now, but the Lord still has work for you. Important work that only you can do. And He'll give you the strength to do it when the time is right."

I shake my head as her words wrap around themselves, a confusing knot I can't muster the energy to untangle.

"Now go get out of this kitchen. I mean it," she says, shooing me toward the door.

Realizing I've lost, I weigh my options and head for the last place anyone will think to look. Tucked away at the back of the house, Mama Pearl's beauty shop is the same as always —a haven of nostalgia that now feels more like a shrine. I plop down in the dryer chair, turn it on, and drop the hood. I don't know why, but the warm air works like a soothing balm, drowning my quiet sobs and drying my tears almost as fast as they stream down my face. Head down, I tuck my feet beneath me and squeeze my eyes shut. When they reopen, a familiar pair of cowboy boots stand before me.

I wipe my eyes and click off the dryer, lifting the hood to lock eyes with Eli. But I can't hold his gaze more than half a second as expectation radiates from him like waves lapping the shore. One more second and I'll be gone. Washed away forever.

"I just wanted to check on you before I leave. Make sure you have everything you need."

I focus back on his boots and nod. "Jeffrey's staying a few days to help."

Straightening to his full height, I feel him pull away. "So you don't need me ... for anything?"

I shake my head, wishing things were different. Wishing I could go back to the time when my world wasn't falling down around my ears.

The door squeaks as Jeffrey walks into the room. For a

tense moment, his eyes dart between Eli and myself, knowing he's interrupted something but unwilling to leave.

"Right," Eli says with a curt nod. Then, with deliberate steps, he turns and strides out of the room.

He doesn't look back.

◈

"NONE OF THESE ARE FULL SETS OF TWELVE," JEFFREY SAYS, flipping a plate over to see if the piece is marked. "Why don't you pick your favorite set and we can sell the rest?"

I look at Mama Pearl's china cabinet and know Jeffrey is right. But my past will forever be a part of me, and as crazy as it seems, the junk littering every room of Belle Terre is a part of me too. A part of all of us. I know most of it will have to go, eventually. But it should be my decision. And Emma's. And Dani's. And Mr. Lavergne's. Not Jeffrey's.

I wring my hands together and try to think of an excuse. "It's only been a few days. Can't we wait a little longer?"

Jeffrey's phone rings. "Hello? Yeah, just a minute. Let me step outside."

I join Emma at the sink to watch Jeffrey pace back and forth through the garden with his phone to his ear.

She hands me a glass of lemonade and frowns as I gulp it down. "What's his deal?"

"He's just stressed out. He's not trying to be rude, I swear."

"Could've fooled me."

I want to argue but can't summon the energy, especially when his attitude irks me just as much.

Jeffrey snaps his phone shut and comes back inside. Taking a seat at the table, he scans the room. "We should really have an estate sale as soon as possible. How did this place get so bad to begin with?"

Emma shrugs. "We used to go to a lot of flea markets."

"So, you're saying *all* of this came from flea markets?"

"Yeah, and garage sales and antique shops."

He frowns and shakes his head, at a loss. "Well, it's time for it to go. No person on the planet needs this much junk."

Tears pool in my eyes. Jeffrey may not understand it, but I miss our days spent scouring flea markets as a family. I miss Mama Pearl. And everywhere I look are memories I'm not ready to part with so callously.

I shake my head. "You make it sound so cut and dry. But it's not that simple. It's a process that'll take time."

He rubs the back of his neck. "That's just it. We don't have time. The investors are ready to fund our project right now. We need to start construction on the lodge as soon as possible."

Emma and I exchange a look.

"But what does that have to do with getting the house cleaned out?" I say.

Jeffrey clears his throat and ushers me toward the living room. "Emma, would you excuse us a moment?"

When the door clicks shut, he shoves his hands deep in his pockets and the action fills me with dread. It's unlike him to be nervous.

"What?" I snap, irritated by the suspense.

He releases a long breath. "I really hate to be the one to say this, but the reason we need to clean out Belle Terre is because ... it's been condemned."

My mouth opens, but nothing comes out. I replay his words again in my head, hoping to make sense of the declaration. Hoping that by some miracle he's joking.

"I ... I don't understand."

He takes a step forward, reaching. But I pull away. "Listen Sunday, this is not what any of us want, I know. But there's light at the end of the tunnel if you'll just keep an open mind. Come on, let's sit down. Yes, that's it. Deep breaths."

If what he says is true, I want to know why. And how I can fix it. "Explain. Now," I demand.

"Alright. Just calm down. Good girl. Okay, so yesterday I had an inspector come take a look at the house while you were gone. He looked at every inch and it's not good. The roof is bad, there's water damage upstairs, the foundation is rotten, and don't even get me started on the termite problem."

I shake my head. "But that can't be right. Mr. Lavergne has always kept everything in such good repair. Are you sure that—"

"Mr. Lavergne is old," Jeffrey states. "I'm not trying to be harsh, but it's the truth. I'm sure he does his best, but the damage is done. I have the report if you want to see it. The house will have to be torn down. That's all there is too it."

I try to internalize what he's saying, but the pain is too

much. Salt in the wound. The ripping away of the very last thing connecting me to Mama Pearl.

"I know you're upset," he continues. "But this may be a blessing in disguise. We still haven't settled on a location for the lodge." His arm sweeps the room. "This could be it. A beautiful and practical way to preserve the Belle Terre home place. Standing at the end of these oaks, the lodge would be exceptional."

I jump to my feet, unable to listen to his musings any longer. "I need some time to think."

"Of course, dear."

I walk to the fireplace, resting my forehead on the carved mantle. Who will I be without this house? Without Mama Pearl? Who would I have been without both of them, shaping and molding me over the years. My childhood may've been odd, but I've always been happy, and loved, and encouraged. Right here in this house. The very place I wanted to share with my own children and grandchildren.

I lift my chin to study the portrait of Mama Pearl's late husband hanging over the fireplace. Dressed in his Masonic finery, Hob's knowing brown eyes are comforting as I read the familiar inscription under the painting.

"Then, when at last your weary feet shall have come to the end of life's toilsome journey, and from your nerveless grasp shall drop, forever, the working tools of life, may the record of your life and actions be as pure and spotless as this Apron now is; and when your soul, freed from earth, shall stand naked and alone before the Great White Throne, may it be your portion to hear from Him Who sits

thereon, the welcome plaudit: Well done, thou good and faithful servant! Enter thou into the joy of thy Lord!"

I take Uncle Hob's gold Masonic ring from the keepsake box on the mantle and slip it on my thumb. I only know him through Mama Pearl's stories, but the picture she painted was every bit as vibrant as the portrait overhead. He was funny and kind. A great man in every way. But his death left her alone and full of remorse for how she let the grief take over. She often mused about the things she might have accomplished had she been stronger. But in my opinion, taking in three girls to raise and love *is* a great accomplishment. No amount of public recognition can possibly compete with the gratitude I feel. With the gratitude we all feel. Mama Pearl and Mr. Lavergne proved that love and attention are gifts anyone can give, no matter their circumstance or personal limitations.

Jeffrey clears his throat, easing up behind me. "Ah, the Grand Lodge of Texas," he observes, looking up at the painting. "I've done quite a bit of research about it lately and actually plan on petitioning soon, myself."

I'm surprised by Jeffrey's announcement. "Really? What made you want to join?"

"One of our investors gave me the idea. Being a member of such a prestigious organization would open the door to all kinds of business connections."

My mouth falls open. "*That's* the reason you want to join?"

"Don't look at me like that. I'm just being realistic." He takes my hand, squeezing my fingers. His eyes widen. "Where's your engagement ring?"

I stare at my bare fingers and my mind shifts to the last night at Eli's houseboat when I removed the ring to scrub off the mud from the hunt.

"Oh ... I must've left it at Eli's," I confess without thinking.

"What do you mean you left it at *Eli's*? I thought you stayed with Irene."

"We ... uh ... stopped by his houseboat to cool off," I say, scrambling for an excuse. "I took it off to wash my hands and I guess I forgot to put it back on."

Jeffrey purses his lips. "Well, it's probably down at the pawn shop by now."

"Why would you say a thing like that?"

His eyebrows shoot up. "We *are* talking about that redneck that tried to talk to you at the funeral, right?"

My fingernails cut into my palms, but I know defending Eli now will come with a price. And the last thing I want is for Jeffrey to start speculating.

I glance at the door. "I'm going for a walk."

"Wait up. I'll come with you."

"No. I need some air. Alone."

I rush outside and find Mr. Lavergne weeding the flower bed. He stands up and smiles, wiping dirt from his hands. "What's on your mind, sha?"

I shrug and look away, not sure how to explain. Not sure I can vocalize the fate of our home without crying. "Everything just seems to be changing so fast."

He pulls me in for a hug, his eyes growing misty. "I won't change. You can be sure of that, sha."

I try to smile, but the action causes a tear to roll down my cheek. Mr. Lavergne isn't just hired help—he's family. He has cooked meals, done housework, ran errands, and gladly chauffeured us girls everywhere we needed to go. He may not be my biological parent, but he certainly is my father.

He pats my back. "Need any help with the wedding?"

The wedding. With everything that's happened, it's been pushed to a place in my mind that feels almost frivolous. I shake my head and make a mental note to check in with Dean at some point.

The corners of Mr. Lavergne's mouth turn down. "I know Mama Pearl was sure lookin' forward to it."

"I loved making her proud," I say, unable to keep my lip from trembling as I replay the many times she told me Jeffrey was a good catch.

Mr. Lavergne rests his hand on my shoulder. "Mama Pearl was proud of you from the day you was born. No matter what you do or who you marry. Never forget that."

He returns to his weeding, but I'm not ready to go back inside. Not ready to face the questions I know Emma and Dani will have when they hear the horrible news.

I plop down under a live oak and close my eyes, digging my fingers deep into the lush grass until I hit dirt. Part of me wishes I was back on the river, where life was simple and slow and my only worries revolved around the meaning of the blasted nickname Eli gave me.

But that's all gone. I'll never go back. I made a choice and that's that. This is where I belong. With Jeffrey, for better or worse. No matter what obstacles lie ahead, he is my home.

CHAPTER 28

TWO WEEKS LATER

I sit staring out the window of Jeffrey's Land Rover as he gushes over the plans for the new lodge. The architect is driving in from Austin to meet us in fifteen minutes, a special concession due to the circumstances, and I can tell Jeffrey is anxious to put the final touches on the blueprints.

I try to focus on what he's saying, but my mind is far away. Trees blur into a solid mass of green until we come to the bridge spanning the Sabine River. The glimpse of muddy water is gone in a flash, but the sight feels like a kick in the stomach. I squeeze my eyes shut and try to block the memories that seem to find me wherever I am, every minute of the day. I've made peace with losing Mama Pearl, and I've come to terms with Belle Terre's looming fate. But no matter how hard

I try, I can't forget the look on Eli's face after the funeral. Can't shake the feeling that I'm making a horrible mistake.

I don't know. Perhaps it's simply my inexperience that's confused the excitement of an affair with true passion. Maybe all I need is one night with Jeffrey and the traitorous memory of Eli's kisses will fade until the spark he kindled is snuffed out forever.

Jeffrey swirls a lock of my hair around his finger and tugs gently. "What's the matter, dear?"

"Nothing. Why?"

"You just seem ... distracted or something."

I shrug. Distracted is an accurate description, but the inner turmoil I battle isn't something I want to discuss.

"Well, I have a surprise that should make it all better," he says with emphasis. "I've scheduled us a few sessions with Anthony Barre."

"Who?"

"Anthony Barre," he repeats slowly. "Surely you've seen him on Instagram. He's the most sought after choreographer in the South."

"What do we need a choreographer for?"

"Our first dance."

"But, I don't really like that kind of thing."

Jeffrey waves away my concerns. "You just aren't used to the idea yet."

"No. I said I don't want to do it."

"I'm just asking you to think about it." He shakes his head. "You always do this, you know."

"Do what?"

"Shoot down my ideas. Then you come around. Just like the ranch. You didn't want to do that at first, either."

"Well, maybe I should've said no to that, too."

His eyes narrow. "What's that supposed to mean?"

"Nothing." I turn back to the window.

"Are you trying to say you don't want to do the ranch now?" he says in exasperation.

"I don't know anymore."

"But ... we've been planning it forever."

"I don't think a couple of months counts as *forever*."

"You know what I mean."

"I just feel like we're rushing into it. Rushing into everything, maybe."

He blinks at the confession. "You said you wanted to get married right away. You said—"

"I know what I said, Jeffrey." I close my eyes, trying to gather my composure.

"You're just stressed. But I am too. And I'm doing everything in my power to make you happy, but you just keep snapping at me over every little thing."

I can tell he's at his boiling point, but something in me just doesn't care anymore.

As he shifts into park, his phone rings to the tune of the wedding march. "It's Dean," he says, putting it on speaker.

As usual, Dean gets straight to the point. "Okay, I realize there've been extenuating circumstances, but we need to discuss the gifts for the bridesmaids and groomsmen. I'm thinking they need to coordinate, yet be individualized."

Jeffrey turns to me with lifted brows, irritation seeping out of his pores.

"Whatever. I don't care," I say, shoving the car door open.

Jeffrey holds up a hand for me to wait. "Listen, Dean, we're at an appointment with our architect. We'll talk more later."

After an hour of studying blueprints and samples of wood, stone, and granite, I check my watch, counting the minutes until my fitting at the bridal shop. Our argument in the car put me in a mood and I need some time away from Jeffrey to regroup.

Luckily it's not long until Emma's car horn gives me a reason to grab my purse. "I better run."

Jeffrey looks up from the blueprint. "We haven't made a decision about the guest rooms."

"Just do whatever you want. I don't see why each one needs its own private library, wet bar, and hot tub, but I'm tired of arguing about it," I say, frustrated with his inability to compromise.

"It's all about opulence. To be the best, you have to go above and beyond on every detail." Jeffrey takes my hand, gazing into my eyes with determination. "I know the plans seem extravagant now, but when it's over, you'll see I'm right."

Emma blows the horn a second time and I snatch my hand away, glad for the excuse to make a beeline for the door.

"I'll meet you there when I'm done," Jeffrey calls after me.

The bridal shop is located in the same complex as Doc's office, and I've known Heather, the owner, for years.

She greets us at the door, her hands flying up in excitement. "Oh, Sunday, I have your dress all ready for you. It's simply gorgeous! I'm so jealous ... I wish I was getting married."

"You're already married!"

She laughs and leads the way into a lush, champagne-colored dressing room, and my mood lightens at the sight of my vintage-style gown. With its twenties' flapper vibe, the soft lace and delicate beading is even more breathtaking than I remember.

"Heather, will you help me into it?" I say, sliding Hob's ring from my thumb and slipping it into my jeans pocket.

She zips me up, and I stare at my reflection. With understated elegance in a timeless silhouette, the dress is captivating. I spin around and look at the back. Dipping low, the cut of the gown accentuates my delicate frame and long curls. Jeffrey wants my hair up for the ceremony, but I prefer it down.

When I step into the mirrored sitting room, Emma squeals in delight. "You look perfect!"

I touch the blush-colored silk. "You're sure the color's okay?"

"Are you kidding? It's beautiful!"

I imagine myself walking down the aisle on Mr. Lavergne's arm as the wedding march plays. Dani and Emma are beautiful in their dove gray gowns and all the guests murmur their approval as I pass. And then I see him ... standing tall beside Brother Sayer, his blond hair contrasting with dark golden skin. He looks up and holds my gaze, his blue eyes gleaming with pleasure.

"Eli's gonna love it," I say, gazing into the mirror.

"What?" Emma barks.

"I said Jeffrey's gonna love it."

Her head pivots side to side. "That's not what I heard. You said *Eli's* gonna love it."

I laugh at the absurd notion. "You're crazy."

Heather raises a brow. "I have to agree with Emma. You said Eli."

Emma reaches for my hand, her large hazel eyes brimming with honesty. "Listen, Sunday. Something's not right and you know it. Something happened while you were gone and I think I know what it is."

Her intuition sucks the air from my lungs.

"It's okay to change your mind, you know," she says gently. "We all just want you to be happy."

"I *am* happy." But as soon as the words leave my mouth, Eli's voice echoes in my mind. *"You just keep tellin' yourself that, pasquale."*

Emma's piercing gaze reads my guilt and indecision as I pick at a thread on the bodice of my gown. "Are you sure Jeffrey's right for you?"

"Of course he is. He's perfect."

"He's not perfect and you know it. He's safe." She sighs and shakes her head. "I just want you to make this decision for yourself. Not for me. Or Mama Pearl. Or Jeffrey. For *you*."

My breath comes out in a whoosh. It's hard to admit, but I know she's right. I need to find out who I am and what I want ... on my own.

"Your phone's ringing!" Heather says, running toward the

dressing room to retrieve it. She returns a moment later with sly grin. "Speak of the devil."

I frown. "No, I don't feel like talking to Jeffrey right now."

She thrusts the phone my way. Eli's name is on the screen.

"Well, what're you waiting for? Call him back," Emma demands, pacing back and forth. "Here, I'll do it." She yanks the phone out of my hand and hits redial. "Hello? Yeah, Sunday's right here, hang on."

I glare at her as my throat constricts. "Hello?" I choke out, feeling foolish as Emma presses her ear to the other side of the phone, making me sweat.

"Just thought you should know I'm headed your way. Got somethin' you might want," Eli says in an even voice.

I grip the phone tighter. "Oh?"

"You busy?"

I look at the fabric surrounding me and try to ignore Emma's expectant smile. "Not at all," I lie.

"You at work?"

In a bit of a daze, I give him directions to the bridal boutique.

"Okay ... be there in a few minutes."

I put the phone down and sit staring into space for a moment.

"Go get out of that dress! Hurry!" Emma squeals, shoving me out of my chair.

I come to my senses and jump to my feet. My heart pounds in my ears as I'm pushed into the dressing room and wrestled back into my normal clothes.

"Damn it," Emma says, checking her watch. "I have to be

at the church in five minutes." She points at Heather. "You better tell me everything!"

Rushing to the door of the boutique, I force myself to slow down and scan the parking lot for Eli's truck. It only takes an instant to recognize Lucille, but the big RV attached to her sparkles like it's brand new.

By the looks of it, Eli is moving on with his life. What if his feelings have changed? What if ... I freeze, suddenly unsure.

I glance at Heather's expectant face, shining through the boutique window and the sight gives me the courage to put one foot in front of the other. To see this thing through.

Eli's door is open, his left leg propped on the running board as I approach. When he doesn't turn, my stomach drops. I remind myself that he called me, not the other way around, but it doesn't do much to ease my fears. He's thinner than the last time I saw him, with scruffy whiskers and dark circles under eyes that refuse to meet mine.

"You headed somewhere?" I say after a beat of awkward silence.

He nods, keeping his focus straight ahead. "Got some work out in West Texas. Should last a couple of months."

"Oh ... good."

He clears his throat and thrusts my engagement ring toward me, still avoiding eye contact. "Found this sitting in a coffee cup by the window a couple days ago."

I hold the ring in my palm a moment, studying the intricate design. "I've been meaning to come by and get it, but ..."

I don't need to explain how awkward that would've been. We both know.

"Got this too," he says, taking the mysterious necklace from his rearview mirror and holding it out.

Shocked, I reach forward to accept the unusual gift.

"Wanted to give you somethin' to remember me by." Eli turns to me for the first time, his eyes boring into mine, searching. "If I was a gentleman, I'd tell you I'm sorry for everything that happened out there ... But the truth is, the only thing I'm sorry for is how it all turned out."

My heart squeezes inside my chest as I examine the small green bottle dangling from the leather cord. "What is it?"

"Open it."

I pull the cork and empty the contents in my palm. A small, iridescent bead glimmers in the sunlight, its unusual shape smooth and cool to the touch.

"It's a freshwater pearl. Found it in the river when I was a boy. Thought you might like it."

"It's beautiful," I say, a bit stunned. "But I can't accept something so special ..."

"No, I want you to have it." He looks away, seeming to struggle for the right words. "Unless you don't want it. It ain't perfect. Prob'ly ain't even worth nothin'."

"I've always believed true beauty is found in imperfection."

He tilts his head to the side. "You sure that's what you b'lieve?"

My gaze moves between the misshapen pearl in my right hand and Jeffrey's perfect three-carat diamond in my left.

Eli clears his throat and nods to the bottle. "If you'll look, there's also—"

"Wait!" I hold up a hand. "I have something for you, too."

I reach into my pocket and pull out Hob's Masonic ring. "Here," I say, placing it in Eli's hand. "It belonged to Mama Pearl's husband. I think she would've wanted you to have it."

Eli's mouth slackens and he blinks. "You sure?"

"Absolutely. I can't think of a more perfect home for it. Listen, I—"

A faint voice saying my name interrupts my train of thought. I take a step back and crane my neck to listen. "I could swear I hear Jeffrey."

Eli jumps down and follows me to the edge of the building where Jeffrey is visible at the far end of the alley. He's turned away, his phone pressed to his ear. I almost step forward, but something tells me to stop. To wait. The air prickles with tension. Something's wrong.

I can feel Eli close behind, touching my arm in question. But I motion for him to be quiet. Jeffrey doesn't see us and I want to keep it that way.

"Oh, yeah. Sunday misses her, but it's probably for the best, you know. I mean she was basically immobile. No quality of life," Jeffrey says, his voice echoing down the corridor.

I stiffen and Eli takes a step forward, but I put my hand on his chest.

"For sure," Jeffrey continues. "I picked up the plans for the lodge today. We'll break ground as soon as the old house is out of the way. No, of course she won't find out. She never even asked to see the report. But I know how that shit works.

They may say all it needs is a new roof, but as soon as that's done, there'll be something else. Historical is just another word for money-pit. And you know how Sunday is, so sentimental about every damn thing."

Jeffrey's words hit my heart like a sledgehammer, making it hard to breathe. Part of me suspected he felt this way, but to hear that he blatantly lied is more than I can take. My engagement ring cuts into my palm, but the pain hits deeper. In a flash, everything I thought I knew about Jeffrey is gone. His kindness has been calculated, his charisma cunning. Bile rises in my throat as the pieces from the past weeks fall into place. All the warning signs I've missed. Or ignored. My body quivers with rage. But I can't decide if I want to claw Jeffrey's eyes out or melt into a sobbing heap right here on the sidewalk.

Before I can do either, Eli pushes past me with firm strides.

"Wait!" I run after him, but it's too late.

Jeffrey's phone clatters to the ground as Eli grabs him by the collar.

"Why you sneaky li'l some'a bitch!" Eli bellows, giving him a hard shake. "When I got wind of what you wanted to do to Belle Terre, I knew it was a crock of shit the minute I heard it. You ain't nothin' but a money-hungry weasel and I'm fixin' to teach you a lesson you ain't never gonna forget."

When Eli pulls his arm back, I grab it. "Don't," I say, shaking my head.

A muscle in his jaw flinches as his eyes bore into Jeffrey's sweating face.

"Sunday, please I can explain," he begs as his eyes dart from me back to Eli.

I take a step forward, prepared to do battle. But it occurs to me that at this point, no amount of arguing in the world is going to change who Jeffrey is or the kind of deceit he's capable of. My thoughts scatter to the wind alongside what's left of my feelings for him.

I give Eli the signal to release his hold. As much as I'd love to let him beat the shit out of Jeffrey, I have plans to hit him where it'll really hurt.

I stand up straight, glaring into Jeffrey's round eyes. "Ever since we met, I've given you the benefit of the doubt. Constantly overlooking things trying to see the good. Trying to believe in you. Encourage you. But that wasn't enough. You needed more and more and more. But you know what? I've had enough of your shit. I'm done."

"Sunday, be reasonable," Jeffrey says as if he's talking to a child. "You're upset. You don't want to do this."

I throw my ring to the ground at his feet. "I can do anything I damn well please."

"I never meant to hurt you." He reaches for me even as I jerk away. "You weren't meant to hear any of that."

"*Obviously.*"

He licks his lips. "I'm sorry. That came out wrong ..."

Eli gives a cool laugh and spits on the ground. The action causes Jeffrey's face to turn red.

He snarls and points at Eli. "What's he even doing here?" His eyes dart between us. "Or is this how it was planned?

Sneaking around, eavesdropping on my private conversations just to make me look like the bad guy."

I narrow my eyes at his sorry attempt to turn the tables. "No, Jeffrey. We didn't plan anything. In fact, that sounds like something only *you* would do."

His nostrils flare. "Well if you're so high and mighty, then why'd you lie about staying with Irene?" When I don't respond, his feverish eyes glow with smug satisfaction. "Didn't think I'd find out about your little rendezvous with that River Rat, did you? So, I guess that means we both have things to be sorry for."

I scoff at Jeffrey's pitiful attempt to make me feel guilty. Just another manipulation.

He takes a tentative step forward, his palms held out in exaggerated supplication. "Listen, we've both made mistakes. But we can't just throw away all our dreams over a few hurt feelings."

I shake my head. "I'm not throwing away *our* dreams, Jeffrey. I'm throwing away *your* dreams."

CHAPTER 29

Eli bends to look through the window of my Jeep. "You sure you don't want me to drive you home?"

My hand shakes as I crank the ignition. "No. I've got it."

"Is there anything I can do?"

"Haven't you done enough already?"

His head jerks back at the insult. "What the hell is that supposed to mean?"

"Don't pretend you're not happy about what just happened. You always said Jeffrey was just after my money. Well, congratulations. You're right. Now you can go pat yourself on the back and laugh with all your buddies about how fucking stupid I was not to see it all along."

"You got it all wrong. The last thing on Earth I want is to see you hurt." He shakes his head, his expression pained. "But

I ain't gonna lie and say I'm not glad that jackass showed his true colors before it was too late. You're worth more than that. A lot more."

"Well, I'm glad you're happy," I say, revving my engine.

He calls out for me to wait as I speed away. But I don't look back.

❦

I BARREL UP THE BACK STEPS OF BELLE TERRE AND THROW open the door. My life is falling apart, bit by bit, and I'm powerless to stop it. With a pounding head, I pop the top on a beer and sag against the kitchen wall, chugging half the bottle in one gulp.

"Sunday? That you?" Emma's soft voice floats from the sitting room a few feet away. She's seated across from two young boys who sit fidgeting on the sofa. They look nine, maybe ten, with hair that needs to be cut and jeans that are too short.

At Emma's disapproving look, I jump up and tuck the beer behind my back. "Oh, sorry. Didn't know we had company," I say, wiping my mouth with the back of my hand.

She gives the boys an encouraging smile. "Why don't you go have a look around outside while Sunday and I talk."

When the boys head for the porch, she turns to me. "Aren't they precious?"

"Who are they?"

Her eyes light up. "Two of the kids who wanted to go to

the wilderness camp. But the program filled up before they could get in."

I take another long drink. "And?"

She bites the nail of her index finger, her eyes wide and questioning. She doesn't have to say a thing. I know what she wants and half-expect her to drop to her knees and beg.

"No." I shake my head, backing away. "Absolutely not. They can't stay here."

She grabs my arms. "But why? We have plenty of room. It'll just be a few weeks and I'll take full responsibility. I promise it won't interfere with your job or the wedding or anything."

I set my beer on the counter and put my head in my hands. My life has become a series of overwhelming changes, questions, and decisions I never saw coming. I want time to freeze so I can catch my breath. But that's not how life works. Bad things happen and people slip away, whether we are ready or not. I try to close my eyes before the tears fall, but one slips out and rolls down my cheek.

"Sunday! Tell me what's wrong," Emma demands, her worry shifting from the boys to me.

"I don't want to talk about it."

"Yes you do. Come sit down at the table."

"I don't even know where to start," I say, pouring myself into a chair.

"You were talking to Eli when I left. What happened?"

I shake my head, cringing at the memory as I give her a quick recap. "I just feel so stupid. So blind. Jeffrey was just after my money all along. And I feel like everybody knew but me."

"That bastard," Emma whispers, shaking her head.

"So the wedding's off," I say, hating how real and final those particular words sound.

She takes a deep breath, but doesn't look very surprised. "You know, I've prayed an awful lot about this very thing since we talked the other day. I just had a bad feeling about him in the pit of my stomach. But I didn't have anything to go on."

"I guess you got your evidence," I say, feeling like the dumbest person on the face of the planet.

"I know you're upset right now, but one day you'll look back on this and see it for what it is. A blessing."

"That's just it. I'm so mad at him, but ... I'm not as *sad* as I feel like I should be." I run my hands over my face in frustration. "And of course, only *I* would manage to feel guilty about something like that."

Emma drums her fingers on the table. "What did Eli say?"

"Before or after he tried to punch Jeffrey?"

"Oh, I wish he would have!"

"I should've let him." I try to laugh, but my smile wavers. "This whole time, Eli's been right about Jeffrey. About everything. I feel like he almost wanted this to happen. And that makes me mad too."

Emma leans back in her chair. "Are you really mad at him? Or yourself?"

"I don't know. Both, I guess ..." I shake my head. "I mean, I knew Jeffrey had a selfish streak. His parents spoiled him rotten. But I wanted us to work so badly that I was willing to overlook it. Kept telling myself that, with time, he'd change. Grow out of it. But people don't change. In the end, they always go back to what they are. What they really are." I stare at the tablecloth, feeling completely lost. "And now everything's gone. Mama Pearl. Jeffrey. All our plans."

"Then maybe it's time for a new plan." Emma gives my hand a squeeze then rises slowly, letting her words sink in. "I better go check on the boys."

I look out the window to see Mr. Lavergne showing them how to feed our cow, Elsie. When her calf runs around the pen, jumping and kicking, one of the boys laughs and Emma laughs too. She ruffles the other boy's blond hair, but his face remains serious. He reminds me a little of Eli. The same coloring, the same guarded expression. Like he's afraid to be too happy. Too comfortable. Too hopeful. Emma plays with the calf in an attempt to make the boy smile, and his reluctance to indulge in such a basic emotion breaks my heart.

But I know Emma. Despite her age, she's a fighter. She'll find a way to break down the walls of pain that surround his heart and set him on a new path. Just like she wants for me.

Part of me wants a fresh start more than anything in the world. But the other part wants to shut myself in my room and drown my sorrows in a half gallon of Blue Bell. To indulge in a steady diet of sugar and self-pity until I'm too far gone to care anymore.

But I can't hide forever. I've seen what that can do to a person. I've got to keep going. Keep moving. One foot in front of the other, no matter how much it hurts. I need a new plan. A new goal. A new future. And I need to start now.

I study the boys through the window and an idea forms. I have no clue how to accomplish it, but I know I have to try.

Eli is right. When it comes to Belle Terre, it's time to do something good.

CHAPTER 30

TWO MONTHS LATER

I pick up the invitation, reading over it one last time.

Announcing the Grand Opening of
Belle Terre Wilderness Haven

Join Us For

INTRODUCTION TO OUR MISSION
PROGRAM DEMONSTRATIONS
CHARITY AUCTION FOR A SEAT ON THE BOARD OF DIRECTORS
BEER, WINE, AND REFRESHMENTS

Proceeds from this event will help support the Belle Terre Wilderness Haven's goal of helping troubled children, free of charge.

Saturday, October 24th - 6 PM
1638 Fire Tower Rd. - Old Salem, TX

"Where Hospitality to Children is a Way of Life"

I consider adding a personal note, but can't think of anything to say that doesn't sound pathetic. So, I slip the card in the envelope and scrawl Eli's name on the front.

"I know it's short notice, but you'll make sure he gets it?" I say, handing it to Irene.

"You bet, baby doll. Heard he got back in town last night."

I remind myself to take a breath. "Do you think he'll come?"

Her forehead wrinkles. "Cain't guarantee nothin', but I'll do my best to get him here."

We haven't spoken since the day I left him standing in the parking lot, and I've felt terrible about it ever since. It was foolish of me to treat him so badly, and I wouldn't hold it against him if he never spoke to me again. But I'm desperate to make it up to him. To show him I've grown and changed. If only he'll come.

Swallowing hard, I try to focus on the task at hand as Irene motions toward the stacks of white chairs on a trailer attached to her truck. "Where do you want all these set up?"

"Out under the trees where it's shady will be just fine."

She turns to the group of volunteers gathered in the yard and starts barking orders.

"This kind of work suits her," Emma says, coming to stand beside me.

"Every kind of work suits Irene."

"Did I tell you she donated ten gallons of homemade wine for the event?"

"Well, that's sure to draw a crowd," I say, remembering Irene's special recipe.

"Have you thought about offering her a full-time position here?"

"Do you think she'd accept?"

"You know, she probably would."

A particularly muscular volunteer carrying a stack of chairs catches my eye. "Emma, are my eyes playing tricks on me or is that Mr. Pickens from across the street?"

She nods. "He looks great, doesn't he? I can't believe he's a personal trainer now. He even volunteered to teach a fitness class here at the haven."

I stare in fascination, trying to recognize the reclusive man who used to get winded walking to his car. "But ... how? I mean, he's just so ... different."

"People can change when they want to, you know." She grins and waves me forward. "Come on. I'll show you what everyone else has been working on." She leads the way through the row of booths situated between the oaks lining the driveway. Each one showcases a different type of program we plan to offer, but I've been so busy with the other aspects of the event, I haven't had time to see what the volunteers have prepared.

"When I mentioned the idea of a children's haven at church, the women's Sunday school class jumped all over it," Emma says, motioning to a table covered in homemade quilts. "Several of the ladies sew and most are retired, so they have lots of free time on their hands to volunteer and teach classes."

"Who makes soap?" I point to a booth where bars are arranged in baskets.

"That'd be Irene." Emma picks up a basket. "She also makes these. Handwoven. She really is good at everything."

"I told you."

Emma leads the way down the shady lane, stopping to explain each booth and volunteer. "Here we have woodworking by Mr. Lavergne, of course. He'll also offer information about raising livestock and gardening, with the help of Tobe Willy. And here we have home remedies and basic first aid by Doctor Navarre and wildcrafting by Charlie Shankle."

My mouth drops open. "How'd you talk him into it?"

"It wasn't easy. But after I promised we wouldn't ever ask him to reveal the location of his infamous snakeroot, he warmed up to the idea. And Sister Faye wants to teach classes about cooking, canning vegetables, and making jelly."

"That's wonderful!" I eye the targets lined up in the next booth. "Who practices archery?"

"You'll never guess."

"Romance?"

"Nope. He's doing sugar cane harvesting and syrup-making."

"Who, then?"

Emma gives me a playful shove. "Well, you should know. You work with her every day."

The idea of Georgia pulling back a bow with her polished pink nails throws me for a loop. "You're kidding."

"She's good too." Emma points to the line of first place trophies displayed along the back of the booth. "It just goes to show you can't judge a book by its cover."

I nod, considering my own misplaced opinions in the previous months. "Isn't that the truth."

"Watch out." Emma pulls me out of the way as Li'l Bit's Ford rumbles up the drive.

He kills the engine and jumps out, ignoring the whines of the hunting dogs whose heads are sticking out of the passenger window. "Hey there, gal. Sorry I'm late. Junior there slipped his collar. Like to never got him outta them woods behind the house."

I give him a hug. "That's perfectly fine. You can use the booth there at the end."

"I don't remember putting him on the list," Emma says, flipping the pages of her notebook. "What'll he be in charge of?"

Li'l Bit stands up straight and sticks out his chin. "Anything and everything that involves the great outdoors. Huntin', fishin', campin', you name it, I'm your man."

"Oh, okay. That's great ..." Emma looks to me for reassurance.

"Almost forgot," Li'l Bit says, lowering his voice. He jerks his head toward the bed of his truck. "Got somethin' else y'all might be interested in." He drops the tailgate and rocks back on heels with a big smile. "Brought along my double-thumper. Thought I might set it up and give a li'l demonstration."

I stare in astonishment at the small copper still sitting beside a roll of copper tubing and other equipment used to make moonshine.

Emma's eyes widen, her nails digging into my arm.

I want to laugh but catch myself. Clearing my throat, I try

to let him down easy. "Oh … that's really interesting. And it goes right along with the theme of rediscovering our area's roots. But I'm not sure the public would understand its usefulness as it pertains to educating children."

Li'l Bit jerks his head down. "Oh. Yeah. Guess I see what you mean."

"Why don't we save that demonstration for ourselves, that way I can take notes," I say with a wink.

His face breaks into a grin as he agrees to show me the finer points of moonshining whenever I'm ready.

"I hope we didn't hurt his feelings," Emma whispers as we walk away.

I glance back to see him turn blood red when Irene gives him a kiss on the cheek.

"Nah. He has better things to think about." I check my watch. "Shit. I better go get a shower."

Emma purses her lips. "Fixing up fancy for anybody in particular?"

My pulse quickens at the thought. "Shut up," I say, swatting her arm.

"Let me know if you need help squeezing into that little black dress I saw hanging in your closet."

"It's supposed to be fitted."

"Last I checked, 'fitted' and 'second skin' aren't the same thing."

Despite my earlier bravado, my hands shake as I clasp the delicate gold chain behind my neck. I pause to run my finger across the pearl at my throat. Its smooth surface shimmers in the light of my dressing table like the moon reflecting off the river at night. The green bottle it came in hangs on the edge of the mirror, a constant reminder of what might've been.

I take it down and pull out the cork as if the action will release a genie to take me back in time. Do things over. But the bottle remains as hollow and empty as I feel. Or is it?

A glimpse of something catches my eye. Paper curled tightly inside. After a bit of struggle, I pull out the slip with two fingers—a note written in bold, even script.

Sunday,

As you know, Wampus Cat has been my nick-name for as long as I can remember. But my uncle used to call me by a different one when I was a kid. One I didn't know the meaning of and never thought to question, even after I passed it along to you. But after you left, I did a little digging and found this. As fate would have it, the definition is perfect. Just like you are to me.

Eli

Inside the note is a scrap torn from a dictionary reading:

Pasquale

Pronunciation: pah-skwa-lē

Word/name: Latin

Meaning: Born on Easter or associated
with Passover

"Sunday. Are you still up there?" Emma calls, making me jump.

"Be right down," I holler back, unable to tear my eyes away from the paper.

"You need to hurry up. Everybody's asking where you are."

As much as I'd like to beg for a little more time, I know she's right. I can't get caught up in a fit of nostalgia. I have obligations. I glance in the mirror one last time.

Half my hair is swept up, revealing the gold hoops dangling from my ears. The only thing left is a coat of ruby lipstick, but my hand shakes so badly, it takes three tries to get it right. Slipping on my heels, my eyes travel back to the piece of paper. Maybe it's a sign. Maybe Eli will accept my invitation, after all.

Feeling a bit better, I descend the staircase, my heels clicking down the now immaculate halls of Belle Terre. It took a lot of work to sort through everything and decide what to keep, but selling most of the hoard was the right decision. The first step in letting go and moving on. The money we earned will provide a good foundation for the haven. No matter how much Mama Pearl loved her things, she loved children more.

The beauty shop was the only room left untouched, right down to Mama Pearl's Virginia Slims in the crystal ashtrays. It was her happy place and deserving of not only respect, but new purpose. We agreed that Dani would use the space to keep the children's hair in shape while offering introductory classes for the older ones, just as Mama Pearl would have wanted.

As I open the front door, the magical beauty of Belle Terre takes my breath. Hundreds of tea lights line the walkways and hang from the trees, illuminating the grounds in a warm glow as people mill around the front yard. Dressed in their Sunday finest, their faces hold expectant curiosity as they wander from booth to booth, chatting with the volunteers. I only wish Mama Pearl could be here to see it. But, in a way, I guess she is.

My stomach does a flip when I think about the speech I have to make. Public speaking has never been my forte, but I have no choice. This was my idea. My mission. Asking someone to speak on my behalf would be cowardly, and I'm sick of being a coward. From now on, I want to be brave. Take chances. Live without regret. My life is no longer someone else's version of perfection. I want *imperfection* and all the freedom that comes with it.

As I step onto the porch, a familiar voice makes me freeze.

"Sunday? Can I talk to you a minute?"

I click the door shut and turn to see Baylee Brown sitting in a rocker.

"Uh, sure," I say, wishing I'd grabbed a beer from the kitchen before facing the public.

She stands up and twists her hands together. "I just want to start off by saying how much I admire what you're doing here. And ..." She licks her lips and looks down. "I'd like to help."

Her offer is so unexpected, it takes me a moment to fully comprehend. Can this be the same girl I grew up with? It certainly doesn't seem like it.

Baylee hurries to continue. "I realize I don't have much to offer. I've only ever worked at the bank." With a trembling hand, she takes a sip of wine and glances at the crowd.

She may have been a bitch in high school, but her offer seems sincere.

"Of course you can help," I say, finding my voice.

My response may not be as satisfying as telling her to piss off, but it's the right thing to do and that's an area where I need more practice.

"You know, I was just telling Emma we need someone to serve as Treasurer on our Board of Directors. Why don't you call me tomorrow and we'll talk about it?"

Baylee's eyebrows shoot up. "Oh! That sounds perfect."

"I really appreciate you taking the initiative to help." I pat her shoulder. "We need more people like you."

Baylee lifts her chin and a smile lights her face.

"There you are," Emma says, bouncing up the steps. "Everybody's settled. It's time for your speech."

I grab the glass of wine from her hand and down it in one gulp. "Okay. I'm ready."

With ankles that feel like cooked spaghetti, I walk to the podium situated at the edge of the porch and test the mic. Darkness has fallen, and the candles' warm glow provides an enchanted feeling of optimism that I hope will continue as the evening progresses.

Taking a deep breath, I welcome the crowd and grip the podium, praying my words will hit their mark.

"There's no such thing as private property in the shady river bottoms of deep East Texas. People come and go as freely as the muddy water flows, using the river and its resources as they see fit. It's a life of tradition, slow and easy, never veering too far from the familiar comfort of days gone by. The culture is easier to snub than to appreciate, and I'm ashamed to say I once took the simpler path. Not long ago, I had big plans for Belle Terre. But they were only plans to benefit myself."

I clear my throat and look at the row where Irene, Li'l Bit, Romance, and many others from Devil's Pocket sit watching.

"Over the summer, I had the privilege of spending some time with an amazing group of people who helped me understand Belle Terre's unique history and ongoing importance to our area."

I pause to search the crowd for Eli's face but can't find it. With disappointment tightening my chest, I plunge ahead, wishing he could hear my next words.

"One person in particular said something that stuck with me. He simply told me to do something good. So, it's with that thought in mind that my sisters and I came up with a plan to utilize Belle Terre's resources in a way that will benefit not only the locals, but new people as well. Each using our own unique talents, together we will merge the past with the present, the old with the young, the lonely with the hopeful."

I motion to the banner stretched above my head.

"Please join us as we celebrate this new chapter with the grand opening of the Belle Terre Wilderness Haven, where we will continue the tradition of hospitality to children that Mama Pearl modeled so well."

As the audience bursts into applause, my chest expands.

"It's our goal to provide a safe place for children and youth to connect with nature through adventure therapy, free of charge. We will also offer medical care, counseling by trained professionals, and classes to teach life skills that are all too often overlooked in a troubled environment." I motion to the two rows of booths. "As you've seen, we have several volunteers set up to demonstrate some of the programs. Feel free to explore each booth, and as you do so, please take time to ask yourself what unique gift you may have to offer a child in need. Thank you."

As the crowd applauds a second time, I make my way down the stairs, shaking hands along the way. Everyone talks at once, asking questions and offering up ideas of ways they can help. I'm overwhelmed and humbled by their support, but the one person I want to see most remains absent.

When the crowd eventually drifts toward the booths, I take the opportunity to grab a glass of wine and escape the limelight for a moment. As I lean back against the rough bark of an oak, the accomplishment feels bittersweet. I've never been more satisfied with my professional life, or more unsatisfied with my personal.

Have I hurt Eli so deeply that the damage is irreparable? Surely he knows I was speaking out of anger. Lashing out at whoever I could blame in the heat of the moment. But what if he doesn't? What if he thinks I truly blame him for everything with Jeffrey?

I gulp the rest of my wine and spot Emma heading my way.

Before I know it, she's squeezing me so tight I can hardly breathe. "I can't believe this is actually happening!"

"Me either. I just wish ..." I try to swallow the lump in my throat as my fingers touch the pearl at my neck.

Her smile is sad. "I know. I was hoping he'd be here too."

I bite my lip and stare into the distance. "Did I tell you I went out to the river yesterday?"

"No ... why?"

I look away, embarrassed by the confession. "I don't know ... I just needed to be there. Sit and watch the water and think."

"Are you sure it's not more than that?"

I shrug, unable to meet her gaze directly.

"When you broke it off with Jeffrey, you said people always go back to what they are." She tilts her head to the side, thinking. "Maybe that's why you went back to the river. Some part of you knows it's home."

I glance toward the house and shake my head. "This is my home."

"Home isn't always a place."

As her words sink in, Irene makes her way to the podium and picks up the mic. "Now after that speech Sunday just gave, I know each and every one of you is chompin' at the bit to help get this thing off the ground. Now you're prob'ly thinkin' we're gonna ask you for your time or your money, but you'd be wrong. We're gonna ask for *both*." She grins, making the audience laugh. "The good news is we have somethin' to offer in return. The highest bidder tonight will receive a trustee position on the Wilderness Haven's new Board of Directors." She slaps her hand on the podium. "So, let's get started!"

When Irene begins the auctioneer chant, I'm entranced. She sounds just like a professional.

"Is there anything Irene *can't* do?" Emma whispers, equally mesmerized.

"I'm bid a fifty, now fifty, now fifty, now fifty-dollar bidder, gotta fifty, now who'da gimme seventy-five, seventy-five, five, five, seventy-five, now you, sir ..." Irene points to a man in the back. "Now eighty, now eighty, now eighty dollar bidder, bid at it, bid at it, who'da want'a gimme eighty, thank you, ma'am, lady in the front."

As Irene chants, the bid climbs higher and higher until it reaches five hundred dollars.

"Who'da gimme six, six, six, can I get a bid, can I get a bid, give from your heart, give from your heart, who'da gimme six, six, six, all done at five, all done at five, five, fixin' to pull the trigger, whatcha gimme now ..."

"Ten thousand dollars," a deep voice calls from the back of the audience.

I crane my neck to get a glimpse of the bidder, but there are too many people in the way.

Irene slams her fist on the podium. "Sold! For ten thousand to Mr. Eli LeBlanc!"

The crowd parts like the Red Sea as Eli makes his way through. But he isn't headed for the podium. He's headed for me.

"I can't believe you did that," I breathe when he's close enough to touch.

He gives me a lopsided grin and nods to the podium. "You were great up there. Talked me into it."

"You heard my speech?"

"Every word."

My heart hammers in my chest. But I shake my head, leading him away from the crowd so we can talk privately. "I appreciate what you're trying to do, but I won't take your money. It's too much."

He comes closer, his blue eyes flashing with intensity as he takes my hand and presses it to his chest. "Why not? You already took the most important part of me."

I try to swallow, but my mouth feels like cotton. "Do you realize you just bought yourself a spot on our Board of Directors? Is that what you really want?"

His eyes fall to the pearl at my throat, prompting a slow smile to spread across his face. Flickers of heat lick through my veins as he bends his head to my ear. "What I *want* is to be close to you."

My skin burns with desire at his confession. I want to fall into his arms. To run my fingers through his hair and breathe in his scent, all whiskey and water and wood smoke. But first I need to apologize. To explain. "Listen, I'm sorry about the things I said that day … I was upset with Jeffrey, and I never meant to—"

Eli shakes his head. "You don't have to say anything. That's in the past. And I wanna focus on the future. Our future, if you'll have me." Unable to keep the smile from my face, I tap my chin in mock contemplation as his eyes sparkle with hope. "What do you say, pasquale?"

I throw my arms around his neck, savoring the feel of his lips as he pulls me close. With Eli's heart beating against mine, I know exactly where I want to be. Who I want to be. Who I am.

I close my eyes and I'm back on the river.

I'm home.

ACKNOWLEDGMENTS

Above all else, I'd like to thank God for giving me the desire to write this particular story, for sending friends, editors, and allies to help shape that yearning into a skill I'm proud of, and for the perseverance to keep going in the face of adversity. Your favor is all I need.

I'd also like to thank my wonderful family.

Randy, this book wouldn't be possible without your love, patience, and colorful tales. Thank you for repeating some of those stories over and over, just so I could capture the cadence of the dialect. And for encouraging me to hold true to my convictions, no matter what.

Guy, thank you for being so sweet and understanding as I've dedicated so much time to this book. Being your mama will always be my biggest joy and greatest achievement. I love you.

Sweetie and Pop, thank you for reading my awful first drafts, for the hours spent brainstorming everything from plot twists to character names, and for always being my biggest fans.

Without your prayers, wisdom, creativity, and old family stories this book would not exist.

Granny Jewel and Pawpaw Billy Ray, thank you for your eagerness to read everything I write. Your good opinion means the world.

Max, thank you for all the revisions, hand-holding, endurance, faith, and sacrifice you've made to help bring this book into the world. You are the sister I never had.

I'd also like to thank the following people for their feedback, encouragement, and prayers over the years. It truly takes a village.

Heather & Kenedi Fuller

Laurie Goodman

Meridith Haynes

Kristen Jordan

Jennifer Park

William Jensen

Dana Storino

Danielle Tannehill

Karen Brandimarto

Shane & LaJuana Shilling

Sharon Peterson

Joel Adamson

Rachel Skadal

Sarah Mcanally

Esther Fuller
Alyssa Harley
Sharon Brinkman
Stephanie Holt
Brittany Ellis
Jennifer Sattler
Pam Dougharty
Stephanie Plake
Jennifer Morgan
Debra Yarbrough
Tommy and Betsy Peevey
Vicki Hinson
Britney Miller
Donna Pettyjohn
Gin Sexsmith

ABOUT THE AUTHOR

Kate Boudreaux is a native Texan who specializes in authentic Southern storytelling across genres. Her work has been optioned for film and praised by some of the South's most exciting voices. *Backwater* is her first novel.

www.ingramcontent.com/pod-product-compliance
Lightning Source LLC
Chambersburg PA
CBHW021212310726
48971CB00006B/1544